A Breathless Hush in the Close

Ann Morgan

Published in 2008 by YouWriteOn.com

Copyright © Ann Morgan

First Edition

Published by YouWriteOn.com

For Mum and Dad

There's a breathless hush in the Close to-night –
Ten to make and the match to win –
A bumping pitch and a blinding light,
An hour to play and the last man in.
And it's not for the sake of a ribboned coat,
Or the selfish hope of a season's fame,
But his Captain's hand on his shoulder smote –
'Play up! play up! and play the game!'
(*Vitaï Lampada*, Henry Newbolt, 1897)

At what address did you start the journey you are
making **NOW**?
(*London Buses Passenger Survey*, 01/06)

1

The envelope was on the doormat, but George was ignoring it. He had ignored it when it rattled through the letterbox as he lay in the warm fug of his bed; had ignored it when he stumbled downstairs some time later to see about breakfast; had barely glanced at it when it tangled with his pyjama-leg on his way up to brush his teeth and blanked it when he rushed down to stop the toast from setting off the fire alarm. Now, sitting on the sofa eating minty toast and cursing himself for jumping the gun with the tooth-brushing once again, he wasn't even giving it a second thought.

Outside in Newbolt Close, the day was operating itself remarkable well: the bin-men had come and gone, the clouds were sweeping peacefully across the sky and three houses down Sue Cohen's cat, Toffee, was sitting on the windowsill, mewing faintly at the birds it would never be allowed out to catch. The world was orderly, calm, and tinged with a definite, midday feel. It would be at least 11.35am, George bet himself, eyes stealing to the mantelpiece. The clock, a dubious antique his father had brought back hopefully from a trip to Bognor Regis, read quarter to twelve. George grinned. If he switched the TV on now, he'd be able to catch the last half hour of *David & Trudy* before the lunchtime news. He rooted around for the remote control, casting a sheepish glance out of the window at the garden gate as he did so. It was a Tuesday, which meant his mother was unlikely to be back before two. However, this was no guarantee: in the last few weeks she had developed a nasty habit of carrying out surprise raids at odd hours, eager to catch him 'working'. It was unsettling and always put paid to any possibility of him even thinking about work for the rest of the day.

After a minute or so, he found the remote control next to the sherry decanter on the table by the Christmas tree. Doubtless it had been put there by some well-meaning guest at his parents' drinks and nibbles party; some administrator, trying to be helpful whilst the hors d'oeuvres were handed round. George shuddered. All his parents' friends seemed to be administrators; cautious people in grey suits with attaché cases and pension plans; most of them working in some capacity or other for local government and all seemingly saving for a holiday cottage in Walton-on-the-Nase. All, except, of course, for his godfather.

The letter flashed suddenly into George's mind, buzzing like a light sabre. He thought quickly to avoid it. Perhaps he should have some sherry, eke out the Christmas cheer a little longer? It was nearly lunchtime after all. He ran his tongue speculatively along his teeth. The taste of mint lingered. No; he would give the sherry a miss today. At least until after *Neighbours*.

He lifted his leg and pointed the remote control under it at the television, flourishing it audaciously for the benefit of the watching crowd. The screen flickered into life, a saxophone brayed and lights came up on a studio, where two freshly-coiffed hosts sat beaming on monstrous sofas, arranged in front of a window that looked out onto the Thames. Applause rippled somewhere out of shot.

David turned a fatherly face to the camera.

'Welcome back,' he said.

'Thanks, Dave,' sighed George, sinking gratefully onto the sofa.

The camera panned to Trudy who tilted her head and smiled.

'Still to come in the last half hour,' continued David, '*New Year: new wardrobe*, the millennium's changed, but have you? We ask three fashion experts about the year 2000's must-haves.'

'And *Game for a Laugh*,' said Trudy. 'Another mystery sportsman exchanges match points for marigolds and gets down to some extreme washing up.'

'But first,' said David, assuming a serious face as the camera zoomed in, 'The extraordinary story of the man who went to the ends of the earth to avoid the Millennium Bug. Quite literally. It's incredible, this; you'll be amazed.'

The camera moved to Trudy and three guests who had appeared beside her on the sofa: a Japanese man and woman and a leggy blonde in a tight, two-piece suit. George lowered his toast to his plate and stared more closely on the screen.

'Yes,' said Trudy. 'Now we all know how worried a lot of people were about the potential effects of the Millennium Bug before the year 2000 arrived –'

'Couldn't have avoided it,' said David, shaking his head.

'Yes,' said Trudy. 'It was the theory that computers wouldn't be able to cope with four digits of the year date changing and that all our electronic systems might crash –'

'Might stop working all together,' said David.

'Yes,' said Trudy. 'At the very worst it could have affected our supermarkets, our electricity –'

'Really everything we rely on to live a normal life. All of civilisation.'

Trudy pushed back her hair with a carefully manicured hand.

'Yes,' she said. 'But what you might not know is how seriously some people took the threat.'

'That's right,' said David, nodding sagely. 'Now I'm sure a lot of us were concerned. Some of you may even have taken a few precautions: filling up the car, stocking up on tinned food –'

'Taping up the windows with sellotape,' said Trudy.

'I didn't tape up the windows with sellotape. When did you see me do that?'

'He did,' said Trudy, looking straight at the camera.

'Anyway,' said David. 'Whatever, er, measures you took, I doubt that many of you would have considered loading up with survival gear and heading for the Australian outback. But that's just what our next guest did. Akio Tanaka was so worried about what might happen on the stroke of midnight that he bought up a supply of army survival gear, including a flak jacket and a gas mask, and got on a one-way flight from Japan to Australia. Incredible. He's here today with his interpreter, Sue, and with psychologist, Lucy Thinkwell, to tell us a bit more about what made him go, literally, to the ends of the earth. Good morning.'

'Good morning, Akio,' said Trudy, smiling and waving at the small man in the middle of the sofa, who nodded back. 'We'll come to you in a moment. But first Lucy –'

'Great name for a psychologist isn't it, Thinkwell?' said David, leaning forward. 'I don't expect it took you long to work out what you wanted to do.'

Lucy smiled, crossing her shapely legs beneath the fabric of her skirt and causing George to twitch his own.

'Actually,' she said, 'I wanted to be a dancer.'

'Oh really?' said David. 'My mother was a dancer. What kind of dancing?'

'So Lucy,' said Trudy, smile firmly in place, 'Can you tell us a bit more about what Akio might have been thinking? Was his fear typical of the way a lot of people were feeling before the New Year?'

Lucy shifted in her seat while she considered the question, causing her skirt to ride an inch up her thigh. The toast plate slid to the floor, scattering crumbs. George slid an exploratory hand down to his crotch.

'Well,' said Lucy. 'The fear of the Millennium Bug was a very interesting phenomenon. For many of us, it was the first serious potential threat to our way of lives for several decades and as a result –'

The phone in the hallway trilled into life. George stopped and looked down at himself, judging the state of play. He considered leaving the phone to ring off by itself, while he went back to Lucy and her interesting phenomenons... Then the image of his grandfather, holding the receiver with a trembling hand, listening to the unanswered rings, came crashing through his thoughts. He stood up with a last wistful glance at the television – Lucy was leaning across Trudy to make a particularly salient point – and went out to the hall, shuffling off crumbs on the way.

The letter leapt into view and he turned his head, picking up the receiver to block out its stare.

'Hello?'

'George?'

'Yeah.'

'It's Sue from down the road.'

Sue with her spare key, and her Matzos, and her grotesque, imprisoned cat. He'd been round to feed it a couple of times during Sue's last weekend visit to her mother's house in Leeds, and the thought of it, hunched on the windowsill in the front room with its litter tray and its premium rabbit chunks, twitching its luxuriant tail as it glowered out upon the world, was enough to make him consider joining the RSPCA.

'Oh, er, hi,' he said. His eyes stole back to the lounge door. If he was quick, he might still be able to catch the tail end of Lucy Thinkwell.

'Is Mum in?'

She always did that, said 'Mum' instead of 'your Mum', as though he were some snotty six year-old.

'No.'

'Oh, I forgot. She works today, doesn't she?'

'Er, yeah, she does. In the morning.'

'Oh well. I'll give her a call later.' He heard her move to put the receiver down and then check herself. 'So how are things with you?'

'Fine.'

'Working hard?'

'Yes.'

'What is it you're doing now?'

George sighed.

'It's complicated,' he said, scrunching up his toes, feeling the carpet catch in them. The letter hovered on the edge of his vision like a wasp.

'You're doing some kind of course, aren't you?'

'Yes.'

'What's the course?'

'It's a post-grad thing. Literature.'

'Where?'

'U-L-S-E-R.'

'What, as in one of those sore spots you get in your mouth?'

'Actually ulcer's spelt with a 'c'.'

'Oh right.'

George watched a minute tick by on the hall clock, precious time ebbing away until his mother returned at quarter past two and the day was officially over.

'So what does that stand for then?' continued Sue. 'I'm awful with abbreviations.'

'The University of Lewisham and the South East Region.'

'Oh. Is that a good one?'

'It's alright.'

'Still, I suppose it's the course and not the place, isn't it? That, and what you get out of it at the end.'

'Yes.'

'What do you get out of it at the end?'

'A diploma.'

A pause. He was sure he could hear the page of a magazine turn at the other end.

'Well at least you can live at home while you get on with doing your applications. How's that going, by the way?'

'Fine.'

'It's Law School, isn't it?'

'Yes,' said George, shifting the receiver to the other ear and staring balefully at a crack in the bottom of the banisters caused one dizzy, mad afternoon years ago when he had dared to ride his tricycle inside.

'And Mum was telling me you're writing a book?'

'Yes.'

'What's it about?'

'Lots of stuff,' he squirmed and the letter caught his eye. 'Look, I better go, I've got a… thing cooking.'

'Oh right. Yes, I must go too,' said Sue, quickly. 'Toffee's made a mess on the carpet. You tell Mum I called.'

'Ok.'

'Bye now.'

George caught the sound of Sue crooning at the cat as the receiver was replaced. He wondered if what she'd said about the carpet had also been a lie, a way of looking as though she had things to do. Perhaps they had both been lying to each other? According to his mother, Sue had done nothing but sit in her armchair reading her way through the works of Danielle Steele since her husband left her two years before. That, and come round for mournful coffees twice a week, sessions that until quite recently had usually ended in tears.

Probably he should feel sorry for her, should endeavour to answer her questions with wit and enthusiasm, try to be a pattern of the son she never had; but the thought of it bored him. Worse, the whole thing – the prodding questions about his future and his life – simply made him clam up and itch to run for the hills. He couldn't help it. It was an involuntary thing, utterly beyond his control.

He shuddered suddenly and snatched up the receiver, punching the numbers in without a thought. A pause, then the recorded message; bright, unchanged. His breathing slowed.

'George French,' he said. '27 Newbolt Close, London. 020 874 7589.'

He replaced the receiver and took a deep breath. There. Something achieved for this morning at any rate.

He went back into the living room. David and Trudy were discussing the pros and cons of skirt-trousers. Lucy Thinkwell was long gone and, besides, he was no longer in the mood. He felt like lying down and losing himself in something – one of those black and white films they showed in the dead hours of the afternoon – but it was only half-past twelve and there was lunch to get through before that. There was nothing for it: he would have to get dressed.

He went up to his room and started to throw on some clothes, deciding not to bother with a shower. He had discovered that it was possible to skip showers for several days without any noticeable ill-effects, as long as no-one got too close. And no-one did. Indeed, in the ten months since his last – and pretty much only – relationship ended there had been a distinct lack of feminine involvement in the intimate areas of his life. With the exception of the drunk girl at the house-party he went to in August, who, after staring at him squintily for ten minutes, had asked him if he might 'fancy a fuck', there'd been no interest from anyone at all. Had the girl not just thrown up on the only available bed, George might have been tempted to take her up on her offer. As it was, he ended up seeing her home in a taxi and then walking all the way home from Kensal Rise.

George frowned as he bent to tug on a holey sock, fighting back the sour after-taste of the morning's events. He disliked the person he became when faced with people like Sue: the cramped, pseudo-teenager backed into monosyllables by incessant, motherly nagging. For that was the truth of it: the way Sue treated him was very like his mother. It was like all of them: his father, frayed with years of squirreling away insignificant sums, now quietly anxious to see a return on all that effort, that investment; his godfather, smiling benignly at his mahogany desk (here the letter on the doormat almost shivered itself into pieces with excitement, its familiar stamped crest glowing neon green); his friends, themselves climbing the ladder of advancement, unable to conceive of anyone else not doing the same. For all that modern society was supposed to be fractured and disaffected, a seething mass of individuals who just happened to occupy the same patch of land, there was still amongst these people an unchallenged expectation that one should 'Play up! play up! and play the game!', and a quiet disdain for anyone who refused to step up to the crease.

Pressing 'play' on his tape recorder, he sashayed moodily over to the mirror to see about his hair. Mick Jagger's voice whined and droned behind him and he nodded along. This was what they didn't grasp, all these people, all these friends. This was the trouble: they didn't understand the way life really was, how difficult it could be. It had all worked out nicely for them, so they assumed it always would. His father had left school at sixteen and stepped straight into his dad's shoes at the paper firm. No messing about there, no painful indecision: the conveyor belt of life had swept seamlessly on, coasting him through youth and young-manhood into quiet middle-age. But things had changed. The game they wanted to see him playing did not have the same rules any more. Or at least, not for him. You couldn't always get what you wanted, but if you tried sometimes, well, there was an outside chance…

He tilted his head and tried to train a strand to cover a stubborn spot on his hair-line. What they didn't understand, these people, was that work was complicated. *His* work was complicated. There was more to it than any of them could have imagined because, along with all the things they knew about – the course and the book and all of that – what he was actually going to do, the main thing, was to make his name as something fabulous, a musical performer probably, maybe something in the manner of Bob Dylan, and then go on like that. True, he hadn't actually performed anywhere as yet – hadn't, in fact, written any songs – but he had gone so far as to buy some CDs and circle some gigs he might go to in *Time Out* and, clearly, these things took time. The other things, the book and the course, were merely a smoke-screen to keep everyone off his back; a cape waved to distract the charging bull of respectability, whilst he stood coolly by. He would dash off the piece for the course and churn out the book as deadlines demanded. After all, he was a promising boy, wasn't he? The first in his family to go to university, the first to win an assisted place at a private school. Tipped to do quite well by, ooh, at least two of his tutors. Good Lord, what could he not achieve? He wasn't worried. But the whole enterprise wasn't helped by people taking it all so seriously, apparently unable to see the joke. Why couldn't they just leave him alone for a while to go off and be brilliant, so that he could come back and wow them without all the boring bits in between? Why keep picking and prodding and enquiring away, so that he barely had time to think? George sighed as he ran a hand over the patchy stubble on his cheeks. People believing in you was all very well, as long as you were the you they believed in.

In the mirror George caught sight of his guitar propped patiently in the corner next to his trainers and his old school books. He smiled as he put the last touches to his hair. At least with his guitar, or something else creative, even stand-up comedy –

The sound of the telephone cut into his thoughts. With a jolt, George realised that he had been speaking out loud. He froze and listened intently to the noises in the house, hoping that his mother hadn't come home by surprise. There was nothing, no footsteps in the hall. George went out of his room and down to answer the extension in his parents' room. He sat on the flowery coverlet and put the receiver to his ear, averting his eyes from the yellowing bra draped over the dressing table stool.

'Hello?' he said.

'Oh hello. Could I speak to George French, please?'

His heart leapt: a woman's voice, young. So it had worked, then, all the messages.

'I'm here,' he stammered. 'I mean, it's, er, George French on the line. Speaking.'

'Oh hello,' said the woman again. 'It's Debbie here from administration at the University of Lewisham and the South East Region. How are you? Alright?'

'Oh,' said George. 'Hi.' And then belatedly: 'Yes thanks.'

'Good. Just phoning to let you know that Dr John Worthy is back from his, er, sabbatical, so we can fix up a date for your tutorial if you've got your diary to hand?'

'Ah,' said George, pulling a face. 'Mmn. Tricky. The thing is, I'm quite snowed under right now.' He glanced around busily at his mother's shoe rack, the dressing gown hanging on the back of the door. 'Is there any way I could call you back when I've had a chance to, er, look at some dates?'

'Well,' said Debbie. 'OK. Best to fix it up sooner rather than later. It's not always easy to tell when Dr Worthy is, er, going to go on sabbatical, so it's a good idea to grab him while you can.'

'Right,' said George. 'Will do. Thanks for the tip.'

'You will try and call back today, won't you? Only tomorrow's my day off and I'm on my own this week.'

'If I can. Thanks.'

'Alright then.'

'Bye.'

'Bye.'

George listened for the dial-tone, then slammed down the phone on the bedside table and stormed back to his room.

All these people phoning up, sending letters, interrupting! Bursting in upon his day! What if he'd been working? He wasn't working, but what if he had been? They would have completely destroyed the flow of his ideas! They could have diverted a current of genius that would have changed the course of mankind! As it was, between them, between Sue and that Debbie woman with her nasal twang, they had put him in completely the wrong frame of mind to attempt any sort of work today. Which he might have done.

He caught sight of his face in the mirror, flushed and breathing hard. Actually, his hair didn't look bad. He didn't look bad: well-chosen T-shirt, slim-fitting jeans, even allowing for the ripped belt hook. Once he'd put on his coat and chunky scarf, he'd look positively stylish. He'd look as though he could be anything: a poet; a designer; a young, eccentric millionaire. He'd go out and walk about a bit; stop by the Indian shop and pick up some fags; go and smoke them on the heath with all of London laid out below; look tormented. Perhaps someone would recognise him as an actor or musician and offer him a deal. It wasn't impossible.

He stomped down the staircase to the front door, taking particular delight in treading the envelope on the doormat viciously underfoot. Looking down on his way out, he saw the green crest of Farrell & Fortune, his godfather's firm, now scuffed with dried mud from the bottom of his shoe.

He went out of the front door and shut it with a bang. He would leave the envelope to the attentions of his mother; let her paw it and pat it and hold it up to the light. There was no point in opening it now. Besides, he already knew what the letter would say: the bastards were going to offer him a job.

2

George pushed open the gate and staggered in, walking on the balls of his feet to spare both the raw blisters around his ankles and his bladder, which was sloshing like a water bomb. His lateness was his own fault: the result of a mad whim at around four o'clock, when the thought of watching *Countdown* got too much. He had decided to walk to the party. It seemed liked the perfect end to a day of not much: a clearly defined task; a challenge; something that could be executed and completed all in the course of one winter afternoon. After all, how far could Clapham be from Golders Green? They were both on the same tube line; both in the same city. It couldn't be much further than Camden and he had walked there several times. With nearly three hours to get there, he was sure to arrive in ample time. He might even have time for a pint in a local pub to help oil the wheels. He strode boldly down the high street, smiling pityingly at the people he caught sight of in their cars, now and then waving his hand. Poor, dear parochial things. Why were they driving to Tesco's when they could, like him, be walking to Clapham?

An obliging rosebush stood to one side of the entrance and he decided to avail himself of it. He had stopped at several pubs on the way, a strategy which had helped take off the edge of the despair after Camden had taken an hour to reach, but had made the last leg of the journey, particularly the stretch down through Brixton, something of a challenge. He would be glad to be inside, tucked into a corner with a can and the excuse of loud music for not having anything brilliant to say. He was just finishing off, congratulating himself on having managed it all without being seen, when the sound of someone fumbling at the catch of the door caused him to freeze. Zipping up hurriedly – narrowly avoiding a nasty injury – he turned to find Emily freeing the catch and swinging the door open, arms wide.

A matronly sort of girl, Emily Goodchild had steamed her way through university in haze of dinner parties and amusing incidents, which everyone talked about and no-one could quite remember when pressed. If her conversation lacked sparkle, she made up for it with an imposing manner and a superlative pair of breasts, which she took care to have always on display. She was fiercely possessive of any men she looked upon as being her 'admirers', a group to which George had belonged since the time he accidentally kissed her at an end-of-exams party two years before.

'Porge!' she exclaimed – it was her name for him, she had names for all her boys – 'What are you doing out here? Watering the garden?'

'No I –'

'Yes you were, you naughty boy! I saw you. Poor Porge. Too embarrassed to come in and ask for the toilet were you?'

'No I –'

'It's alright; you don't have to explain yourself to me. We were watching from the window,' she said, enfolding him in a bosomy hug. 'Happy New Year, darling. Happy Millennium or nearly millennium, or whatever it is. And don't worry about explaining why you're late, either. You know I don't care about things like that.'

'No, well, I will explain,' said George, returning her pressure as best he could. 'You see, I –'

'No, Porge, no. Not at least until you've had some wine.'

She glanced hopefully at his empty hands.

'Didn't manage to –' said George with the beginnings of a shrug. 'Sorry.'

'Oh don't be ridiculous, Porge. You know I don't worry about things like that. Wouldn't have expected it anyway.'

She turned and led him into the hallway and up the carpeted staircase, past prints of Cornish villages and an alcove containing a potted plant. Following Emily's behind as it swayed to and fro, contained in a tight, blue skirt, George was reminded unhappily of a pony-trekking trip he had been on as a child in Wales when, after hours of plodding behind the one in front, his pony had run amok and caused a brief stampede.

He had spent the rest of the day being sick in the holiday cottage bathroom.

'Just as well it's all very simple, instant food tonight,' said Emily as she let him into the strangely quiet flat. 'Not that it matters, of course. Not that it would matter in the slightest if all of it, every last bit, had burnt to cinders, because darling it's so lovely that you're here.'

'Yes,' said George, hopefully.

The hall of the flat was long and narrow, tricked out with cream fittings and flanked with uplighters at modest intervals. Through an open door half-way along it, George saw part of a table at which sat a number of people, denoted by various arms and legs. His heart sank. A dinner party. Of course, he should have known. They would have been sitting, politely, waiting for him, raising their eyebrows over the mixed nuts. And now he would have to play the buffoon, dappy George who once went to a tutorial in the middle of the night. (It was a story that was often told about him and made much of, despite there being a perfectly logical explanation.)

He coughed and took a step along the corridor, groping desperately for some phrase, some witty formulation, to make it all ok. Then he saw her. Closest to him and facing away, into the room, sat a tall girl with a slender back and a gracefully curving neck, her hair done up in a swirl: Jennifer.

'Ikea,' said Emily, mistaking his stare. 'It doesn't matter if all your furniture looks the same as everybody else's when it's all so nice.'

'Yes,' gasped George.

'Go on in, Porge' said Emily, giving him a motherly nudge. 'Get yourself some wine. I've just got to do a bit of the old domestic goddess routine in the kitchen.'

He went in. There were six of them, four guys and the two girls, ranged around the circular table set up behind the sofa, looking up at him, amused. Two of the guys he recognised as being rower-types from college – rugged and straightforward blokes who alternated their time between the bar and the gym – the other two, he supposed, Emily must know through work. It was the sort of thing she did: gather together a group of random, unconnected people and try to make them fit.

'Ah, George,' said one of the rowers – Geoff Hirschman was his name – with a broad grin. 'Glad to see you're improving. At least you're operating on the right half of the twenty-four clock now anyway.'

'Yes,' said George, sitting down at an empty place with a polite smile. Jennifer's eyes flicked up to meet his as he took his seat. He nodded hello and looked quickly down at his plate. It contained a slither of smoked salmon, lying on a bed of rocket and crowned with a solitary black olive. The salmon looked as if it had been there a while and was faintly brown at the edges.

'What's this about?' said one of the other guys, sensing a joke.

'Well,' said Geoff, easing into the anecdote as gratefully as if it were a hot bath, 'When we were at uni, George, regularly, used to turn up to lectures in the middle of the night, thinking it was daytime.'

The table erupted, drowning out George's protest.

'It wasn't regularly,' repeated George. 'It was only once. One tutorial.'

'Oh that makes it alright then!' jeered one of the others, a boy with spots and a very large nose.

'And there was an explanation,' said George.

'What was the explanation?' said the mousey girl sitting next to him.

'Well, I'd been doing an all-nighter –'

'My cousin did that once,' cut in the other guy that George didn't know, a blonde hulk of a man, sitting on Jennifer's right. 'He works for Goldman Sachs –'

'I work for JP Morgan,' said Geoff Hirschman.

'– And he ended up going to their Christmas party on the wrong day. What a fool!'

'No!' exclaimed the boy with spots. 'Bet his bonus went right down.'

'Nosedived,' nodded the blonde guy. 'Only got eight thousand in the end.'

Geoff Hirschman whistled.

George looked around the room and noticed an open bottle of wine on top of a table by the door. He went and filled his glass, carefully avoiding Jennifer's chair.

By the time that Emily swept in three minutes later, he was on his second trip.

'Good boy,' she said. 'Found the wine, I see. And have you been cosily introduced to everyone?'

'Erm, not really –'

'Oh, Rafferty!' said Emily, pouting at Geoff. 'Didn't you introduce Porge? Honestly, you boys are hopeless. Just as well God gave women breasts,' she said, running her hand absently over her scooped out neck-line, 'If it were left to men, the human race would have starved long ago.'

'Er,' said the spotty boy with a smirk at his neighbour, 'How does that follow?'

'Never you mind,' said Emily, primly.

The evening lurched on, gathering pace like a boulder rolling down a hill. Smoked salmon was followed by mushroom lasagne with spinach and parmesan.

'Delia's a life-saver, don't you find?' drawled Emily, setting the plates down.

George nodded, gulping his wine. How many had he had – three? Four? At any rate, thank God for it: it was helping to keep him sane; it was keeping him able to talk.

And, as it turned out, he was talking rather well. He'd managed several conversations without any awkwardness at all. In fact the other college guy sitting next to him, Ben, was quite interesting. Unlike the rest of the guests, who were all tied up in the city with banking and consultancy, Ben was pursuing journalism, working his way up through various trade publications and in-house journals.

'Who knows,' he joked, a mushroom balanced on his fork, 'By the time I'm forty I might have got as far as *Sink & Taps Weekly*!'

'Wouldn't have thought there'd be enough to fill a weekly thing on sinks and taps,' said George, taking care to set his glass down flat – it was empty again, extraordinary!

'Oh,' said Ben with a wry smile. 'You'd be woefully surprised. I've spent most of last week putting together a feature on the technology behind plastic clothes pegs.' He put on a gruff voice: ''Most people think plastic pegs work the same as wooden ones. They're wrong. We've spent twenty years adding an extra coil to the spring to make their purchase tighter. The result is a smart, durable pegging item with a grip that is second to none' – Dave Turnbull, MD, Level Pegging.'

'Wow,' said George. 'Intense.'

'Mmn,' said Ben. 'Woeful, really. What are you up to anyway?'

'Well, it's complicated –' started George.

'Porge,' said Emily, leaning across to re-fill George's wine glass over his protesting hand, '– Oh, ssh George, you're catching up after all – is a genius.'

They all turned to look at him. Jennifer met his eyes and looked quickly down at her plate, where most of her food remained, cut up very small. Her hand went up nervously and fingered the pearls around her neck. Later, she would tell herself that they – she and George – had had 'a moment' and try to work out what it meant.

'A genius, eh?' said Geoff with cynical amusement. 'Does that pay well?'

'Oh not bad,' said George. 'Only got bonused ten grand last year, though.'

They laughed. Everyone laughed. He was being a success; taking threads from previous conversations and weaving them into a joke – look at that! He must try to do that again.

'Porge writes books,' said Emily, proudly.

George nodded: he did. The room swam gently at the corner of his eyes, warm in a rosy glow.

'Novelist, eh?' smirked Geoff. 'Neither am I'

'No actually,' said George, stifling a belch, 'Factual.'

The blonde guy set down his knife and fork and reached for his glass.

'What about?' he said.

'A biographical study of Evelyn Waugh,' said George the familiar words tripping neatly off his tongue. He rewarded himself with a gulp of wine. Here he was, talking marvellously well.

'Who's she?' asked Geoff with a guffaw. It was a school boy's joke and George didn't dignify it with a reply: Geoff's power was fading.

'Do you write a lot of books?' said the mousey girl.

'One book,' said George. 'Probably.' And then, because he was enjoying being witty and clever and surprising, 'Actually, I'm thinking of going into law.'

Emily jerked her head like a large chicken.

'Are you, Porge?' she said. 'You didn't tell me.'

'Selling your soul, eh?' said Geoff nodding. 'It's the best way. Souls are overrated as it is.'

'Why are you changing to law?' said Emily.

'Well, it's not definite yet,' said George, picking up his wine, watching it shimmer in the glass, 'But my godfather's a big-cheese legal-egal –'

'Which firm?' interrupted the blonde boy sitting next to Jennifer.

'Farrell and Fortune – and they're offering me a sort of traineeship thing, you know. See what I think.'

George sat back in his chair with his wine. He'd noticed that the table was starting to sway a bit; he wanted to keep an eye on it, not talk for a while. Somewhere at the back of his mind he was congratulating himself for having hoodwinked them all so neatly. How surprised they'd be when he emerged as a great, grand guitarist, bursting with the rhythms of the age. And if it didn't work out, he could just follow the plan he'd described just now and no-one would be any the wiser. Genius.

He allowed Emily to re-fill his glass – he was catching up, after all – and looked around at the rest of them, at their dear, simple faces. Life was so straight-forward for them: profit and loss, money in, money out, supply and demand. How he envied them their dear, little lives. How he wished, sometimes, it could be so easy for him. Except not now;

because now he was out-thinking them all. They were in the box and he was outside it, looking down at them, like mice in an experiment, or dolls in one of those cardboard houses they used to make on *Blue Peter*.

Time creaked and Emily leaned forward again to fill his glass, her breasts grazing the African violet in the middle of the table. Dear Emily. To think he might have married Emily, if, after kissing her, he'd asked her out and they'd gone out for several years and if, after that, he'd proposed. He wondered what sex with Emily would be like. Vigorous, he imagined, and bouncy. A sort of naughty hockey game.

The table was lurching hugely now, everything bobbing as though on the crest of a wave. He needed to take control. A break – that would be the thing: go to the bathroom; regroup. He stood up and went to the door, walking carefully round the curve of the table. He really was doing very well.

'Everything alright, Porge?' said Emily when he got to the door.

'Just, the bathroom,' he said. Somehow the 'going to' got lost, but it didn't matter: language was, after all, only a vehicle to convey meaning – he'd heard that in a lecture once. Look at him: even when he was drunk, he was really very clever!

'At the end on the right,' said Emily, helpfully. Dear old Emily.

So, to the bathroom, by way of the wall and a tangle with the coat rack. The bathroom was small and pink with a carpet and flowers. There was a mirror above the sink and George caught sight of his face in it as he came in the door: flushed with blood shot eyes. Frankly, he looked a state, but it didn't matter: he was getting away with it. They couldn't tell.

He ran a tap and watched the water flow. Perhaps if he put some water on his face? He leaned forward and stopped. Disaster: the wave that had been rocking the table rushed into his stomach and surged up his throat. He staggered to the toilet and was sick once, twice, three times into the bowl.

He stood up and regarded the results: bits of smoked salmon and scraps of rocket leaves, the odd mushroom floating here and there. Strange: he thought he'd chewed them all up. He'd done well, though. Most of it in the bowl. Only a bit on the carpet. A wipe with the toilet roll and Bob's your uncle. Except Bob wasn't his uncle. He didn't have an uncle, thank God.

There was someone waiting in the hallway when he came out. He glanced over his shoulder. It was alright: he'd left the toilet clean. He stepped to the side to walk back to the dining room, but the person came with him, hands grasping. It was Jennifer.

'George,' she whispered. 'Are you alright?'

'Fine,' he returned, affronted that his expert vomit-cover had been blown.

'Not now, I mean generally. In life.'

He laughed in the sardonic manner you saw in the old films they showed sometimes in the afternoons. This was Jennifer – *Jennifer!* the girl who'd once thrown his mobile phone in the Thames – asking him if he was alright. He laughed some more, magnificently, like Humphrey Bogart. He nearly said, 'Here's looking at you, kid.'

But she was still talking: 'I mean… the law. You've always hated the idea of the law, your godfather. Copping out, you called it. Playing safe.'

'Not true,' said George, waving a cautionary finger. 'Not true. When I was younger, I thought it was a fine, noble profession.'

'But at college. At college you were so passionate about striking out, doing something fresh and new. It was what I… always admired about you.'

So that was it: she was worried about keeping her claws in him, stopping him from going it alone, changing. It was always the way with her, with women generally: somehow they didn't seem able to deal with anything new and unknown. Well, if she wasn't careful, she'd regret it. Maybe not today. Maybe not tomorrow, but soon and for the rest of her life.

'Jen, Jen, Jen,' he said, with what he hoped was a casual wink, 'It's all under control.'

'Because George, you're a special person.' Was she drunk, he wondered? 'And sometimes I worry about you.'

He patted her reassuringly on the arm.

'I know, Jen. Me too,' he said. 'But it's alright. We're fine. We're dandy. Our problems don't amount to a hill of beans in this crazy world.'

She stopped and looked at him.

'Why are you quoting *Casablanca*?' she said.

He nodded another wink in her direction; turned on his heel; turned too far and had to turn again, and went off back to the dining room. A hush descended as he entered. Everyone looked up. They'd been talking about him, deciding he was odd. Well, what if he was?

He quested around in his thoughts for something witty to say, something to rival that bonus crack he made earlier. His mind moved slowly, like a diver wading under the sea.

'Do you know,' he said, holding on to the doorframe. 'I was thinking just now about that phrase "Bob's your uncle". That's a funny one, isn't it? I mean, why would Bob being your uncle be a good thing anyway?'

He folded his arms in satisfaction. There. Not bad. Something to get the ball rolling anyway.

'It's to do with a medieval game around a maypole,' said the blonde guy with barely a glance at him. 'The winner was called the Bob.'

'But why "uncle"?' said George. He was determined to get his money's worth out of it.

'Just a turn of phrase.'

George scowled. There. That was just like them, just like that sort of people: squashing the interest out of things. Explaining fun away. The answer probably wasn't even right. They were wankers, the lot of them. All wankers.

Emily came up to the door with a pile of plates that looked as though they'd held puddings. How long had he been in the bathroom?

'Squeeze me,' she said, trying to get by.

'With pleasure,' said George, reaching for her nearest breast. Here was a joke they'd all laugh at!

Emily gasped and stepped back. A fork fell to the floor.

For a moment no-one said anything.

'Did you just –' Emily stuttered.

A chair slid back and the blonde guy stood up. He came over to George and took hold of his arm.

'Come on,' he said. 'I think it's time you left.'

'Ooh,' said George, grinning round the room. 'Hark at Policeman Plod here!'

No-one laughed.

'Come on,' said the guy again, manhandling George out into the hall. For someone who spent ten hours a day behind a desk, he was really surprisingly strong. A sort of blonde incredible hulk.

Emily put the plates in the kitchen and came to the door to see him out. She stood a little to one side, a quiet figure, smaller than usual.

'Don't you think you ought to apologize?' said the hulk to George, seeing her there.

George took a step towards her.

'S-sorry, Emily,' he said. 'It's not you, it's me. Sorry.'

He staggered forward and kissed her wetly on the mouth. He'd been aiming for her cheek, but it didn't matter. It was what she wanted, after all. She loved him.

The hulk pulled him away.

'Out,' he said, shoving George onto the landing and shutting the door, hard.

George stood, swaying, looking at the panelling and the gold numbers screwed in place: 22. His age. For a moment he thought about ringing the bell and demanding an explanation. It was clear that the hulk was trying to get Emily into bed. Surely he should warn her?

Then the moment passed and he found himself absorbed in the pattern of the wallpaper by the door: swirly print with tiny fleur-de-lys, like little grapes on vines. He turned and set off down the stairs and out onto the street. The night was fine: clear and cold with a sprinkling of stars blazing through the city glow. Perhaps he should forget about taking the tube and walk home. After all, he'd walked all the way here, hadn't he? Perhaps he should just strike out into the night.

But no, no, the tube was better. No point going crazy. The tube would get him home. And here it was: the friendly station with its blue and white sign, the people going to and fro.

Outside was a newsstand, selling papers even at this hour. George dug in his pocket for a fifty pee and selected a *Standard*. On the front page was a large picture of a familiar couple stepping out of a car: a tall man and a carefully-coiffured blonde. George blinked. People he knew? He looked again. The headline flashed before his eyes – 'COMMERCIAL BREAK-UP?' – black letters spidering across the page. Beneath the picture was a caption: 'Separation is temporary, says Trudy, prompting speculation that split is ratings stunt.'

George grinned at no-one in particular, delighted at the joke he had found. So David and Trudy were at it too, giving everyone else the run-around, playing the world for a fool. He stood, swaying, staring at the picture: the couple caught in the camera flash, arms raised as they stepped out of different sides of a car. You had to hand it to them: they certainly knew how to spin a yarn. Looking at the picture – the wavering mouths, the eyes glinting with unshed tears – you could swear it was almost real. Except that he knew what they were up to! He could see the wood for the trees! He could tell they were laughing, laughing inside as the world rushed to gorge itself on the stories they threw to it, an owner chucking an eager dog a bone. And why could he see this? How did he know? Because – haha! – he was at it too! Because they and he were one of a kind, masters of misdirection, merrily waving a pocket watch in front of the eyes of the crowd, whilst changing the slant of the universe behind the scenes. Such genius! Such bravado! Such sheer and utter wit! All the world's a game and all the men and women merely players. And no-one knew! No-one even knew! He laughed and threw the paper down. Let someone else find it and not see the joke.

Tripping through the ticket barriers, George went down onto the platform. There he found an obliging bench, slumped, and fell asleep.

3

'George?' A pause and the clink of crockery on a tray.
'George?'

George groaned, tried to sit up and banged his head on
the wall. Pain tightened around his brain like an iron helmet,
two sizes too small. Impressions of possible rooms, possible
people with trays rushed in upon him: matron throwing back
the curtains in the san; his grandmother, a distant, floral
fragranced memory, beaming over a plate of jammy dodgers
arranged oddly side by side; some gentle, unfeasibly beautiful
stranger – leggy, bright and blonde – com to live with him and
make it all alright.

'Yes?' he croaked, alarmed to find his tongue dry and
rigid in his mouth, like the desiccated kipper someone had
fished out of the bins once at school and tried to make him eat.

The door opened and his mother looked round it.

'Oh, so you're alive then,' she said. 'Cup of tea?'

George nodded weakly. She came and put the mug
down on the table beside his bed and stood looking down at
him, dangling the tray. She was in jeans and an old jumper,
which must mean it was her morning off, or else the weekend.
George concentrated and tried to think what this might tell him
about where he was in the parade of days. But it was no good:
time lay scattered around him like the debris of a party when
the curtains are opened in the grim light of day.

'So,' said his mother. 'Working today?'

George made a non-committal grimace. Visions of
streamers and trays of cava and monstrous faces leaning in to
kiss him flashed before his eyes. Perhaps this was New Year.
Was this New Year? But something was not right: the images
felt stale – a copy of something he'd remembered before – they
ran too slickly through his mind: New Year was no longer
new. What then?

'You must have had a lot to drink last night.'

George managed a nod. This was one thing he could
testify to with near certainty. Either that or they'd got him
playing cricket again. Perhaps both.

'Luckily,' said his mother, eyeing him, 'The police have said they won't press charges.'

George blinked.

'Police?'

He tried to sit up again but it was no good.

'What police?' he said weakly.

'Yes,' said his mother. 'I thought you wouldn't remember.'

She turned and went to the door.

'Drink your tea,' she said.

'What police?' said George as she went out. 'What police?' he called again as she walked down the stairs. His voice was thin and feeble, making him sound like a Victorian invalid. A Victorian invalid in a bath chair. A criminal Victorian invalid.

He glanced around the room at the skylight, the faded blue wallpaper, his guitar propped sturdily by the cupboard. There was his book-shelf stacked wonkily with books, his desk and computer, and the endless drift of papers piled up here and scattered there. No signs of criminality here. No, visible signs, anyway. Nothing more incriminating than the stack of magazines poking shyly out from under his bed and, he reassured himself, you could hardly cite those as evidence of a criminal mind; even the one with the horsewhip was really remarkably tame.

Yet something in the heap of papers banked up around his desk snagged him, made him blink, and look again. Wasn't there something about today –? A glimmer of a memory rose to the surface of his mind, a piece of glass glinting on the bottom of the sea. A woman's voice – nasal – and something about a book. Thoughts bubbled. Shit! His tutorial! Wasn't it booked for today? At two? His eyes searched wildly for the clock, hands scrabbled madly at the duvet as he learnt the horrid truth: shit – it was already half-past twelve! Heaving, eyes narrowed against the light, he scuttled from bed and dug around in the drifts of things for some clothes. He shook his head at himself as he banged into his bookcase, sending a shudder through the files and papers heaped on it and his desk, where, somehow, he noticed, the envelope had lately taken up residence, propped against the computer, its blank face scuffed and creased into a permanent frown.

He found something that would do for a sock under the keyboard and hopped up and down the room trying to drag it on. Inside his head, his hangover romped like a three year-old child and he spat violent nonsense syllables with every bounce. He had got consistently worse at rushing since he left school. That was the trouble. Once upon a time he'd have been out of bed and ready within three minutes of the bell. Mind you, he reflected as he turned the sock round and tried to approach it from a different angle, that was largely owing to something ominous whispered to him by a freckled boy on his first day in the place. Thinking back on it, he couldn't remember the exact utterance, except that it contained the words 'what for' and that this somehow conjured a vision of an alarming, paddle-looking thing in his brain – something like a cricket bat with the back taken off.

Peering bewilderedly at the sock, which was now beginning to look suspiciously like a woollen hat, George's eye caught the sneer of Evelyn Waugh, leering down from the photographic portrait his parents had proudly bought, framed and hung above his desk after he got his degree: a welcome home present; a surprise. Today, Evelyn was looking particularly smug – a hint of amusement playing around his plump, cherubic lips, a gimlet glimmer in his eyes – as though he were taking especial pleasure in watching George squirm.

'Oh fuck off, you bastard,' spat George, throwing down the hat and turning desperately for the bathroom. 'You're hardly one to talk.' He put a hand to his head and closed his eyes. 'Anyway,' he moaned, 'It's all your fault. You and your fucking dad!'

And, in a way, it was true: for if Arthur Waugh hadn't bought the plot of land just up the hill near the heath back in 1897 and built the house that squatted there now, hunched and apologetic among its neighbours like someone's nephew at a fashionable party, six year-old George might not have stumbled on it one innocent kite-flying day with his father.

Had the Waughs chosen to settle instead in Finchley or had Evelyn opened a draper's shop or a school for orphans instead of plying his pen, George might not have stood, wide-eyed, staring up at the white walls and boxy windows of the house, whilst his father, talkative for once, expansive, told him that this was the home of Evelyn Waugh, author of many books. And then George might not have incubated the obsession that was to skew his childhood and cast a shadow over his student years. He might by now have been a ruddy-faced backpacker with a pair of Birkenstocks and a rucksack, or a motorbike daredevil brought in to do all the stunts on films. But then – there was always this possibility – he might very well have been bent, retching, over the toilet bowl with an hour to go until a tutorial on quite another subject and another non-existent essay to hand in. It was important not to get things out of proportion.

Straightening up, he caught sight of his face in the bathroom mirror: his cheeks red and blotchy; his eyes bloodshot; his hair standing on end as though trying to get as far away from his head as possible. A vague memory of the previous evening drifted into his thoughts; a splinter of timber from a ship-wrecked boat bobbing to the surface of the sea. Hadn't he been in a bathroom last night? A pink bathroom with floral tiles? Floral tiles and a pink, sick-smattered carpet? Where in God's name had that been?

He picked up the air freshener his mother insisted on, even though it was his bathroom and she never came in there and sprayed it liberally around.

Then he stopped. Hadn't he done something last night? Apart from the vomiting. Hadn't there been something else, something terrible? He goaded his sluggish brain. Slowly, an image came to him of chunky thighs and substantial buttocks swathed in a tight, blue skirt, climbing the stairs: Emily Goodchild.

Oh God, he hadn't pinched Emily's arse, had he? Was that why the police got involved? Because he'd become some sort of sex pest? Because he was a pervert? Surely not. Not even he. That was the sort of thing he would definitely have remembered. Still, he must have behaved pretty badly. He'd have to do something to make up for it. Some sort of flower or plant – girls liked that sort of thing.

George staggered back into his room and met Evelyn's stare, which was now an open gloat. The bastard was relishing every second.

'Fuck you!' he launched at him again, and went back to digging for clothes, fighting back the riot of Waugh emotions that could still from time to time catch him unawares.

As a child, the thought of having a famous writer living just up the road had been painfully exciting for George. Discovering 'Underhill' was the most interesting thing that had happened thus far in his existence, measured out as it was in crumpets, cartoons and trips to Watford Playdome. Evelyn Waugh, the first famous person to make an appearance in his life, albeit indirectly, seemed hopelessly exotic to George; a person sporting a brand of being more scintillating than anything his parents' rounds of Nescafe and afternoons spent watching the *Antiques Roadshow* could hope to be.

As he got older and began to be allowed out on his own to post letters and buy sweets, George started to make pilgrimages to the house of Evelyn Waugh. Running along the high street and up the hill, he would loiter around the garden gate, hoping for a chance meeting and an invitation to tea in the grand library and drawing room which so clearly lurked behind the house's modest façade. Scouring his parents' bookshelves for Waugh's books, and rummaging through the twenty-pee boxes in Cancer Care, George had, for several years, to make do with *A Handful of Dust* and an incomplete copy of *Vile Bodies*, originally belonging to someone called Martha Pratt. These he read repeatedly, grappling his way through the sparkling sentences again and again, until they ran smooth and plain as a stream in his mind. Sometimes he would copy them out and his mother would seize on them and mistake them for his own. He still cringed when he remembered the day she advanced, beaming down upon him like the headlamps of a four-by-four on a dark country road, waving a scrap of paper she had found in his waste-paper bin, which bore the legend: "I wonder to what enormity that mad teacher will be driven next."

'Enormity,' she had said, eyes glinting. 'Enormity is a very big word for a little boy.'

He had felt too awkward to admit that the sentence was actually taken from *A Handful of Dust* and that he had simply plugged the word "teacher" in instead of "father". She had framed it soon after that and hung it in the kitchen above the fridge, and every morning as he ate his frosted flakes, it had glared down at him, until he went away to school.

Sometimes when he wrote Waugh's words, hunched on the bed in the little box-room that was his before his parents shelled out for the loft extension to allow him more room to 'work', George actually felt as though they were coming from him and not something he'd read at all. It was only when he looked back on what he'd written that he realised it was borrowed from the books he'd scoured almost since he was old enough to read. In many ways, it did not matter; it was the act of writing, not the words he wrote that held the power; that moment of pure potential, when meaning fought for expression, wriggling itself into the awkward vehicle of words and escaping onto the page. Staring at the scrawled sentences once the frenzy was over, they seemed to George to be nothing more than the tyre tracks of some rapid get away; the main event having passed.

'This must be what it's like for Evelyn,' he used to whisper to himself, clutching the ragged scraps of words, beaming at the thought that he was like his hero and that his hero was near.

Throughout his childhood, the fantasy of meeting Evelyn Waugh obsessed George. He imagined the walks they would take, the discussions they would have, but, more than this, he imagined the instant sympathy that would flare between, from one outstanding spirit to another. At Sunday lunches, under the indulgent smiles of his parents and oblivious to the well-meant enquiries from his godfather about school-work and sport, George would sit and think about the sumptuous feast going on up the hill, the roast goose and selection of cold meats – for Evelyn Waugh's tastes were luxurious and strangely old-fashioned – and wonder how long it would be before he was eating Sunday lunch there himself. He half-suspected that Evelyn Waugh might ask to adopt him and he had made up his mind to say yes. It was simply a case of waiting for fate to present the opportunity when the two of them could meet.

In the meantime, he did all he could to prepare himself. He asked for all the books for birthdays and Christmas. Hunched over them far into the night, he committed large chunks of prose to memory, ready for the day when Evelyn Waugh would take him under his wing, leading him from his parents' gas-fireside to taste the wonders of the world. By the time he was ten, George could recite long and bewildering passages from all the books to the pride, and occasional embarrassment, of his parents and latterly himself. The memory of his recitation of the defloration of Nina Blount at a dinner party for his father's associates was still enough to make him stop dead in the middle of the street and bend double, furiously biting his fist.

But by far the most intense and violent emotional event came with the death of Evelyn Waugh, in a dastardly introduction to *Brideshead Revisited* read when George was twelve. The shock of that day still jarred in George's memory and stood out as his one pure encounter with pain, beating even the loss of his front tooth during a sports lesson at school. It hurt him to think of it even now: the sneering matter-of-factness of the academic's preamble; the joyless trudge through a wasteland of comparisons, each gone into and examined in yawn-making detail. And then the blunt pronouncement of Waugh's 'untimely death in 1966', dropped in and passed over with casual brutality, as though it were a fact that everyone knew. George had stared at the page as the world slid sideways and a pain, like a wound from a pickaxe, blossomed in his chest. For a while he sat, propped on his pillow, his bedside lamp warding off the shadows in the corners. Then, padding downstairs on bare feet, he had gone to his father's study.

His father sat, poring over papers in the yellow glow of his lamp, huddled behind the desk that always seemed too small. Behind him were the books he had accumulated during his time in London: earnest books with weighty titles; books about money and fraud and tax laws; tomes steeped in the serious things of life.

George stood for some minutes watching his father work, trailing his pen down columns of figures, his hand darting in occasionally to highlight an inconsistency or pick out a flaw. At his elbow sat a half-full glass of sherry, glimmering in the light. To George it seemed alive and trembling, a mocking reminder of one who now was not.

At length, reaching for the sherry, Geoffrey French looked up.

'Evelyn Waugh's dead,' said George quickly, not waiting to be asked why he was awake and out of bed at this late and adult hour.

'Yes,' said his father, taking a sip from the glass. 'I must admit I've always thought so.'

He gave his son a brief smile, then turned his eyes back to the page before him, leaving George to trail back to his room and the bed and the book that looked suddenly faded, dead and false beneath its orange cover.

It was enough to stop him reading for a summer. Left to his own devices, the whole thing might have ended then and there. But the upset had come too late to stop the Waugh effort altogether. George had already been recognised as a clever boy by those around him and noises were being made about significant schools. Tutors were hired and, with merciless coaching, and a little shuffling from his godfather, George managed to secure an assisted place at a prestigious boarding-school near Bristol.

And so began a game whereby George insinuated himself into a world that wasn't his; doing enough to get by but never too much; going all in on a hand that held only one decent card. He learnt the lingo, grew his hair, effected the casual, shrugging stance the older boys sported about the place with one hand in their trouser pockets, as though perpetually impatient but not bothered enough to say so. At times, when the headmaster strode up through the great, wood-panelled hall, when once – glorious! – he hit a six during a cricket game on a cloudless afternoon, something of the old Waugh feeling, returned: that sense of greatness at his finger-tips, round the corner, in the next room. This was a place where things happened, he told himself as he slouched about the place, this was where life, really truly might start.

But there was something about it all that missed him. There was something intangible that shut him out; something unspoken that mocked him; something that was nothing to do with the brand name on his trainers, the family caravan in Rhyl or his ignorance of rugby, but yet fed off all these things. For a while, he put it down to the fact that he was a bookish boy in an extremely sporty school. But it was more than that: the spirit of the place somehow shrank from him, eluded him, would not mix.

His parents didn't help. Despite most parents only putting in an appearance at school matches and speech day, they made a point of making the five hour round trip on an almost weekly basis, frequently bringing his godfather with them, to watch whatever house match, concert or play George had a miniscule part in. There were times when, looking across the cricket pitch at the three lonely figures standing next to the groundsman beside the pavilion, George could hardly prevent himself from shouting at them to go home. As it was, he was barely civil to them afterwards at the tea, and frequently found himself mumbling angrily at his shoes in response to their enthusiastic enquiries. But they didn't seem to get it and persisted in creaking in at the school gate in the old Cavalier to cheer noisily whenever he managed to hit the ball.

As he got older, he threw himself into his work, drawing on all those years of Waugh obsession to woo the English Department and carve out his niche. His name on the wall was his ambition, his name on one of those antique wooden boards they had to call a specialist sign-writer in to update every year. He got it too, twice in fact, 'G. French, G. French' up there in the lobby for all to see. Gold letters. And yet, standing on the stage in the main hall, clutching the Piffle Prize, clapped by the whole school, with the headmaster's words of praise echoing in his mind, there was still that sense of something eluding him somewhere, something not quite granted, out of reach. Still, driving out of the gates for the last time in the back of his parents' car, looking back at the grand, Gothic buildings, he couldn't shake the feeling of someone who, after hours of panning for gold, has been left with a tray full of mud.

It was a feeling, this missing of greatness, that continued to haunt him throughout his student years. Even as he graduated, coming out into the indifferent sunlight outside Senate House, he thought he glimpsed it in the back of an academic gown disappearing round the corner of the street. Still, months later, it taunted him: in certain songs; in Shakespeare; in that moment of invincibility before the hangover sets in. It was this that haunted his dreams of life, of great and devastating art. It was this that caused him to struggle, panting and nauseated, into a pair of dirty jeans. And it was this that, as he snatched up his bag and hurried from the room, made him turn, grimace and give the finger to Evelyn Waugh.

*   *   *

The University of Lewisham and the South East Region occupied two terraced houses at the end of a street in Penge. Established three years previously by the ambitious head of a sixth form college, it had quickly gained a reputation for rapid, effective degree conferral and the large bust of the founder, which leered out from a bay window at passers by. It catered for a wide range of students, many of them foreign, and offered a gamut of courses from Medieval French studies to a diploma in advanced knitting. The university's particular strength was having secured the patronage of Barbara Windsor, who regularly attended charity dinners on its behalf and took care to drop its name whenever a microphone was thrust in front of her face. Already it was known, somewhat erroneously, as the fast-track to fame for aspiring soap actors.

Despite being half an hour late, George found a 'Do Not Disturb' sign slung on the door-handle of the English, Languages, Politics and Modern Dance Departments, which were all contained within one front room. Panting, he sank onto a cracked plastic chair in the corridor outside. At least he would have a moment or two to collect his thoughts and marshal his excuses before he had to face his tutor. Better think of some problem he could say he was wrestling with, something earnest and knotty to do with Evelyn Waugh. Masculinity. That was always a safe one: serious yet reassuringly vague. Slightly personal and so unlikely to prompt too many probing questions, yet very fashionable, very now. Oh yes, he could rant on about masculinity in Evelyn Waugh for, well, a good five minutes. That just left the problem of the other fifty-five.

He shifted uncomfortably in his chair. Thankfully, his headache was beginning to recede, although, given the thoughts that rushed in to replace it and the agitation of his feelings, he was not entirely sure that this could be called a good thing. Partly, he was angry with himself for having come at all. Why hadn't he stayed in bed, phoned up, said he was ill? After all, it was true, wasn't it? Certainly truer than the last two times he'd pulled it off and the girl had happily bought it then, even advising him to make up some honey and lemon to aid his recovery. Perhaps he should do it now: say he'd taken a funny turn and leave. It wasn't too late. Except that, if he were to do that, he would have missed every one of his tutorials scheduled until the end of his course and, even by George's standards, that smacked slightly of taking the piss.

He was also partly angry with himself for having failed to come up with the essay or whatever it was he was supposed to be handing in. Not that he hadn't put a lot of thought into it. Christ, it was a wonder his brain still worked, the high level of thinking he'd been putting it through these last through weeks! And, after all, that was the lion's share of academic work, wasn't it? The thinking? The visible part, what you got on the page at the end, was only, what, five percent? A bit like an iceberg. And he'd been up against it, hadn't he? What with Christmas. And the New Year. The millennium no less. And being ill today – how could he have known that was going to happen? How could he have factored that in? A hangover – you couldn't legislate for things like that. And it wasn't just the hangover. Now he came to think of it, he hadn't been fully well for, oh, quite a number of weeks. It was a wonder that he'd managed to do any sort of thinking at all, really. It was a miracle he'd managed to get here, given the state of him! And still they expected him to slave away, putting his poor, beleaguered brain through its paces again and again and again? Squeezing out thoughts at the risk of life at limb? Christ! What sort of monsters were they? What sort of inhuman –

A cough. George looked up. The girl behind the desk at the end of the corridor was looking at him. He flushed. Had he been speaking out loud? He listened anxiously for the echo of his own words. Impossible to be sure.

'Better go in,' she said, nodding at the door. 'He sometimes gets distracted.'

Briskly and capably, George went to the door and knocked. There was no answer, so he knocked again and, turning the handle, nudged his way through into the room beyond.

The Department of English, Languages, Politics and Modern Dance was a small office in marked disarray. Filing cabinets spewed papers onto the floor, piles of books teetered and, on the desk in the centre of the room, ashtrays over-flowed and mingled their contents with an assortment of pens, pencils, rulers and household paraphernalia. There was a cheesy, saw-dusty smell in the air which, combined with the nest-like appearance of one corner where papers were banked up around a couple of grubby cushions, lent the whole room the impression of a giant hamster cage. Heady fumes issued from the gas fire, linting up the wooliness of George's thoughts, and above the mantelpiece, hung a circular, plastic clock, stopped for ever at twenty to five, the second-hand twitching like the leg of a dying fly.

Assuming the room was empty, George turned to go, stepping towards the door just as a gentle snore alerted him to the presence of a pair of legs protruding from under a newspaper in the far corner of the room.

'Dr Worthy?' said George.

The newspaper rose and sank to the accompaniment of another snore.

'Dr Worthy?' said George again, stepping over gingerly to tug his tutor's arm.

The newspaper slipped to reveal John Worthy's face, framed with tufts of greying hair, the eyelids flickering.

'Dr Worthy?' said George again.

'Not a doctor actually,' mumbled the sleeping man. 'They never gave me the…' His eyes popped open. 'Ah!' he said, starting from under the newspaper. 'James! Excellent!'

He fumbled the paper closed folded it, flashing the headline "WE DID IT IN THE AD-BREAK, REVEALS SEX-BOMB PSYCHOLOGIST", and stuffed it down between his chair and the wall. Then, smiling awkwardly at George, he stood up and hurried over to his desk, motioning for George to sit in the orange chair facing it.

'James,' he said again, sweeping aside a toothbrush and shaving kit to get at the documents in front of him.

'Actually, it's George,' said George. 'George French.'

'Ah, yes,' said the tutor, fitting a pair of glasses to his nose and peering hopefully at a bank statement. 'Moliere? Camut?'

'No,' said George as his headache rumbled like the drums of a distant army threatening a renewed assault, 'My name is George French. I'm an English Literature student.'

'George French. That's right, that's right,' said the tutor, lifting a stack of papers and squinting underneath. 'The war poets, isn't it?'

'Evelyn Waugh.'

'Waugh! Of course!' said the tutor with an uneasy chuckle. He opened a drawer and turned out a pile of forms. 'Something about masculinity, wasn't it?'

'As a matter of –' said George.

He caught sight of a call-girl card lying on top of a copy of *Plutarch's Lives* on the desk. "Something for the weekend" ran the caption in bulging, pink letters above a picture of a busty blonde, tilted to reveal the black leather strap running up the middle of her arse. Noticing his gaze, John Worthy reached out and snatched the card up.

'Fascinating, aren't they, the *Lives*?' he said, tucking the card clumsily into his jacket pocket. '*Plutarch's Lives*. So many lives in them. Don't you find?'

'Yes,' said George.

'So, said the tutor, jumping up and hurrying over to one of the filing cabinets to start to rummage through the drawers. 'What are you doing at the moment? Are you doing… anything?'

'Well,' said George. 'Obviously this course. And I'm thinking of perhaps writing a book. Or I might –'

'Uhuh,' said the tutor, leafing through a tattered ring-binder upon which someone had once scrawled the legend: "Car Insurance". 'Interesting. And, er, do you get enough to eat?' He looked up suddenly. 'Er, sorry, do you… are you living somewhere?'

'Actually, I'm living at home,' said George. 'With my parents.'

'Mmn,' said the tutor, turning his attention to the contents of an old leather satchel with a broken strap. 'Sensible, sensible. Things can get a lot worse. People don't realise.'

Dropping the satchel, he stood for a moment gazing round the room, his teeth pulling fitfully at his bottom lip. At last, his regard fell upon a ghoulish wooden object propped against the wall on one of the filing cabinets. He picked it up.

'Er, do you like this?' he said, snatching it up and brandishing it.

George peered: it was a heavy, troll-like thing with a gurning face and squat body that had possibly once adorned a tribal mask.

'Mmn,' said George. 'It's very –'

'Isn't it?' said the tutor regarding the object with pride. 'Got it from a car boot sale. Managed to beat them down. Might even be able to sell it on myself.'

Catching something in George's expression, he set the troll down and hurried back to his seat with the air of a schoolboy caught passing notes when the teacher's back was turned.

'Now,' said John, tapping his fingers on the desk and glancing hastily around the room. 'War poets, er, Evelyn Waugh. Waugh, the unsung poet of war. Hmmn?'

'In a way,' said George.

'Wonderful,' said John. 'Well, you'll never guess what's happened. The thing is, I can't seem to find your excellent, er, essay. Which is a shame because I read it and I remember being particularly...'

He trailed off, as though transfixed by a spot on the ceiling. On the clock above the mantelpiece, the second-hand twitched. John jumped, as though suddenly startled. He looked at George.

'Anyway,' he said. 'I'm sure it was –'

George coughed; clearly he would have to say something.

'The thing is –' he said, catching sight of a copy of *The Beano* protruding from a filing cabinet. Hadn't they stopped selling it years ago?

'The thing is –' he tried again, groping for the correct words in the gloomy recesses of his brain, a dim warren of archives lit by a buzzing fluorescent bulb.

'The thing is,' said John Worthy. 'It doesn't really matter.' He closed his eyes and shook his head. 'I mean, of course it matters. Of course it's a crying shame, but, when all's said and done, well,' he waved a hand vaguely in George's direction, 'Let's face it, you were hardly going to fail this thing were you? That Chinese girl got through last year and she couldn't even speak English. And anyone can see you're a bright sort of boy.'

'But,' blurted George, 'I didn't actually do the essay. That's the thing. I haven't written a word.'

'Oh well, that's a relief,' said the tutor, fitting his glasses to his nose and reaching for a form. 'What do you want me to put? Long-term illness or something worse?'

'I'm sorry?'

'What about "A baby was sick on the manuscript"? I used that one once and the best thing about it, as I recall, was that on that occasion it was actually true.'

'But –' said George.

'I always find that glandular fever ticks all the boxes. Shall I put that?'

'But –' said George.

'Or gastric flu?' continued the tutor. 'There's a lot of it about…'

'But,' blurted George, 'Shouldn't you just put that I failed to do the assignment? That I haven't met the requirements of the course?'

The tutor regarded him over the top of his glasses: a seagull watching a child with its sandwich, working out where to strike.

After a moment he said: 'Why on earth would I want to put a thing like that?'

'Well,' said George watching a fly that had been wheeling around the room batter itself against the glass of the window and sink, twitching to the sill below, 'Because it's true?'

The tutor shook his head.

'But surely the point –' continued George.

'The point,' said John Worthy, 'Is to do enough to appear to be taking it seriously. No one really cares what you do, as long as you look like you mean it. Just keep your head down, turn something in on the appropriate day – some time in June, I think it is – and, er, Bob's your uncle. You'll have a diploma, we'll have something to report to our trustees, and your parents'll have a certificate to put on their wall. Perfect.

'In actual fact,' he reached down and picked up a box of beribboned scrolls from under the desk, 'You could probably take your diploma now. Would you like to?' He

shook the box invitingly. 'I mean, of course it wouldn't be…
but then most employers don't… Anyway, it's here if you
want it. Only for goodness sake make sure you get the right
one. We had a Dance student leaving last year with an MSc.
Very awkward.' He peered warily at the scrolls. 'In fact, look,
here we are: blue, English. That's you. Take it and have done.'

So saying, John Worthy pulled out a scroll from the
box and handed it across the desk. George sat staring at it, the
creamy, ridged paper reminding him of another
communication waiting for him at home: the letter, which, he
had noticed this morning through the fug of his hangover haze,
his mother had propped conspicuously against his computer. A
feeling of greyness washed in. So it had come to this, had it?
All that promise, all that preparation, all that tuition and extra
work? For this? So that he could sit here in this dirty, little
room and have qualifications handed to him like sweets?
Success was supposed to be hard wasn't it? Success was
supposed to be worked for. And yet here it was, falling open
like a rotten nut at his feet. Here was the future handing itself
to him on a plate, ready seasoned and heated up like one of
those ghastly meals-on-wheels they brought his grandfather,
loaded with mashed potato and mushy peas and things he
could easily chew. And all the while he sat at home while the
world went on elsewhere. Like a pensioner. Like Sue-down-
the-road or – worse! – like Sue's infernal cat. Fed and watered,
sitting at the window in a quiet close, mewing at the birds it
would never catch.

He shifted in his seat and started as his eye caught a
familiar shape balanced precariously on a pile of books on the
shelf behind John Worthy's head: a block of wood with its
plastic emblem of the soaring arrow and below it the Latin
motto, *Nec tenui ferar penna*; a house trophy from George's
old school. Doubtless just another of the tutor's car boot sale
purchases, it was nevertheless alarming to see such a familiar
object in this squalid little room. It was a warning, a reminder:
there was greatness out there to be got, it seemed to say, it
required only a brave heart and a bold sword to find it. Perhaps
this time he would achieve it? He was young, after all, and

clever. Perhaps this time it would not get away. But first he must get away; get away from this rat's nest and its drowsy horrors; get far away to somewhere he could think.

George coughed and looked once more at John Worthy who sat furtively in his chair, eyes stealing to the bottle of cheap whisky balanced on one of the cabinets at the side; a hamster crouching in its cage, beadily eyeing the nuts. So people lived like this, did they? Well, not him.

'Actually, I'll leave it,' said George, pushing the scroll across the desk.

John Worthy blinked.

'Oh, you want to complete the course, do you?' he said 'Very honourable, I'm s–'

'No,' said George, 'I think I'd better just leave the whole thing.'

'Oh,' said John again, glancing nervously at the box, 'But… Hmmn. Better if you could see your way to taking one of these with you, really. It skews the figures otherwise, you see.'

'No,' said George, 'I –'

'You don't have to be stuck with the English one if you'd rather not. I mean, I know I said you had to take the right one, but as long as it's roughly the right one I'm sure no-one would mind. Let's see, what else could you have?' He rummaged through the cluster of scrolls, peering at the ribbons. 'What about Early Computing?'

'No,' said George, 'Really, I –'

'Colonial French? Golf in the Middle Ages?'

George stood up.

'Really,' he said firmly, 'I think I'd better be going. Thanks all the same.'

With a last glance at the trophy perched on the shelf above the desk, he turned to leave.

'Well,' said John Worthy, staring sadly at the scroll, 'If you're sure. I suppose I'll have to give it to the receptionist again, although I don't like doing that – there's bound to be a scandal one of these days.'

'Goodbye,' said George, heading out of the door and along the corridor past the receptionist, who, he now noticed, had an impressive selection of coloured ribbons blue-tacked onto the wall above her desk.

*   *   *

His mother was sitting at the kitchen table poring over the crossword, a cup of tea beside her, when he got home. She looked up, glasses balanced school-ma'amishly on the end of her nose. Had she been sitting there waiting for him, George wondered, fingers drumming the pine finish?

'You went out,' she said, quietly. 'I thought you were supposed to be working today.'

She looked back down at the paper, her pen trailing up the side of the page and darting in to complete a word. On the wall behind her, hung the tyrannous sentence in its floral frame.

'I was,' said George, standing in the doorway. 'I did. I had a tutorial.'

'Oh,' said his mother, jotting down letters on the margin of the page. 'How did it go?'

'Fine,' said George, stepping over the threshold to the cupboard to get a glass. 'Actually, I gave up the course.'

'Uhuh,' said his mother, 'And – ' She stopped and looked up at him sharply. 'What do you mean you gave up the course?'

'I gave up the course,' he repeated, warming to the sound of the words. 'Finished. The end. No more course.'

She threw down her pen.

'Oh George –!' she began.

'No, Mum,' he held up a hand like a traffic cop in some hard-hitting American drama, 'It's alright –'

'But this is a disaster!'

'Really, Mum, it's for the –'

'What am I going to tell everyone at the January party?'

He frowned. 'What January party?'

'*The* January party! This Friday. Everyone coming, all our friends. All wanting to see you and hear your news!'

'What news?'

'Well how you're doing, what you've been up to. I don't need to remind you, do I George, that there are a lot of people concerned about you, a lot of people who've invested a lot of care and hope in your future.'

She certainly didn't need to remind him: they sent him Christmas cards every year, often with pound coins sellotaped inside.

'Well, you can tell them what you like,' he said. 'Why not tell them the truth? That I've given up the course, that I wasn't enjoying it and anyway it turned out to be a pile of poo.'

'George!'

'Well it was. Anyway, poo's not a swear-word.' He stepped towards the sink before adding: 'Anyway, I'm twenty-two.'

He turned on the tap and watched as the water swirled into the glass. No-one had said anything to him about a January party. How come they thought it was ok just to assume he'd turn up?

'Anyway,' he said, squinting out of the window at the garden beyond. 'I might not be around this Friday.'

'Oh?' said his mother, laying the newspaper down. 'Well where might you be?'

'I might be out.'

'What, out like you were out last night? Out getting drunk?'

'Possibly.'

After all, he might, mightn't he? Someone might call and he might get invited out. It was only Wednesday now. Anything could happen.

'I see,' said his mother in a small, sighing voice. 'Well, of course, I can't make you come. You're old enough to do what you like.'

He turned.

'I might come,' he said quickly. 'I'll just have to see.'

His mother nodded, her neat bob giving a reproachful twitch. She looked up at him over the top of her glasses.

'Where were you last night, anyway?' she said.

'Out at... with friends,' he said.

'I see,' said his mother. 'Friends. Was it the friends who put you up to the drinking?'

'Put me up to the... Christ, Mum! How old do you think I am?'

He turned back to the window. Outside in the garden, the apple tree nodded blindly to itself; an old man agreeing with something someone said to him many years ago. That really was rather poetic. He should find a way of working it into a song.

Behind him the paper rustled as she folded it up.

'You know,' she said, 'You won't be able to behave like this when you're at Fortune's. Robert's put his neck on the line to sort that out for you. You won't be able just to drop in and out as you please.'

George didn't reply. He was watching a sparrow balancing on a rosebush outside and a song was forming in his mind:

'Blackbird singing in the dead of night,
Take these broken wings and learn to fly...'

He stopped himself: no, too late – someone had done that one before.

She was still talking: 'And drinking won't wash there either. Hungover, incapable, slinking home at all hours of the day and night –'

He turned round suddenly.

'I thought it was the police,' he said.

'Er, sorry?' she said, frowning.

'I thought it was the police who brought me home,' he repeated, his voice rising. 'That's what you said this morning. That they decided not to press charges. That's what you told me!'

'Well –' she put a hand to her hair.

'There weren't any police, were there? There weren't any police, last night! That was just something you said!'

'Georgie,' she said, pushing back her chair and standing up. 'Just calm down. The point is –'

'No!' shouted George, stamping his foot. 'The point is you have to realise I am not a child any more!'

With that he slammed down his glass and stormed from the kitchen. Running up the stairs, he stamped his feet as hard as he could. Let her hear how he was no longer a child!

He stood on the landing outside his room, twitching. God, he wanted to go back down there and give her a piece of his mind! Or, no, explain things calmly, make her realise. He could see it all – how it looked in her mind. He could see all of it: the narrow little plan, the sniffish way she'd decided it, sipping her tea. 'I'll just make him think the police were there,' she'd have thought to herself, 'Just to show him what might have happened. Just to make the point.' As though she could somehow see more of the world than he could! As though she were on some sort of higher plane looking down at his life, at the way his mind worked!

He waggled his arms in desperation, contorting his face to utter a silent moan, a mime artist trapped behind a wall of glass. He needed to get out. That was the truth of it. To get out, get away from all these people with their plans for his life, with their maps of how things should be. Everything had to be managed and orchestrated by them. Everything had to adhere to the rules of their game. There was no room for anything else. No room for that moment of blind glory in the blazing summer sun. No room for inspiration. How on earth could genius touch him when he was shut in every evening watching repeats of *Agatha Christie's Poirot*?

Turning his head, George caught sight of himself in the mirror on the bathroom wall. He was red and panting, his nostrils flared, his shoulders heaving like those of a baited bull. Watching himself grow slowly calm, he noted with detached interest the bubble of saliva on his chin. He remembered that he needed a drink of water and hadn't brought the glass.

Well screw them, frankly. Screw them all. He'd sort it out: he'd get some wild, outlandish job – a dustman, or a cleaner, or a casino croupier – and move away; or, better still, he'd go and live in Spain and write them extravagant letters about how well he was doing with no return address. He'd train as a matador and pick olives in the mountain groves! And then, once he'd got into the rhythm of things, he'd make a killing with his songs for acoustic guitar, and he'd become world-renowned, and everyone would want a piece of him. Then they'd see.

Nodding once at his reflection, George went into his room. The letter sat, propped up on his desk, leaning on his computer. He stopped. A smile spread across his face. Or... how was this for playing them at their own game? What if he took the traineeship – the poxy, money-grubbed, favour-ridden thing – and made of a go of it, just for as long as he needed to save up the money to launch his music career? Hell, if he did that he could move out even now! Get one of those swanky, corporate apartments. Bring girls back. He could even – and this was where it got very clever – form a band with a sort of legal twist to the name: *Legal Tender* or *Pending Release* or something equally witty and sharp. That would really rub their noses in it. Ha!

George strode across the room and tore into the envelope, splitting its gizzard with one swipe. He pulled out the paper – cream and finely ridged – and spread it before his eyes:

Dear George

Re: Application for traineeship at Farrell & Fortune

Thank you for coming to see us last month and for your interest in a traineeship with the firm. We were impressed by your enthusiasm and obvious interest in the law.

However, we felt that, given your commitment to your postgraduate studies and to the completion of your book –

neither of which bears much relation to the work you would be undertaking here – you would not be able to vouchsafe the time and attention that the role demands. It is therefore with regret that we have decided not to offer you a placement at Farrell & Fortune.

May I take this opportunity to wish you every success with your work and future career?

With all best wishes

Jonathan Farrell

George laid down the letter and looked up at the picture of Evelyn Waugh. He could swear the bastard was laughing.

4

She'd begun tidying round him at four: plumping up cushions, straightening pictures, sweeping magazines into the rack by the door. The Hoover had already been round, leaving its tracks in the carpet. There was a smell of furniture polish in the air.

George shifted along the sofa so that he could see past her bottom as she bent, rubbing furiously at scratches on the coffee table that had been there since he was a child. It had been an emotionally draining afternoon and he wasn't in the mood for a row. At half past two, soberly dressed and with make-up that only seemed to enhance the marks of sorrow and sleeplessness on her face, Trudy Donovan had appeared on television for a ground-breaking interview with Crispin Guru Murphy. Sensitively, yet searchingly, he had led her through the labyrinth of her emotions to probe the trembling, raw mass of her hurt. Every circumstance surrounding her husband's infidelity, every wayward glance, was handled and set down as reverently as the effects of a dead person once the curtains have been opened and the coffin carried from the house.

'When I thought about it, I realised I'd known the truth for years,' Trudy, had confessed, peering out from under lashes that did credit to Max Factor, who were sponsoring the interview. 'I'd known that he never really loved me, that he was just pretending for the sake of his career. I suppose I was silly to let it go on so long, but it's amazing what you can put up with day by day and, really, it's only now, looking back, that I can see how awful it truly was. There were three of us in that marriage – alright, not always the same three, but still, usually three or more – and it was, well, pretty crowded.'

Outrage had been added to outrage, insult to thoughtless insult, until at last even George found a tear trembling in the corner of his eye. At last he could stand it no longer. There was nothing for it but to pick up the phone and leave three, if not four, very heart-felt recordings of his name, address and telephone number.

'I hope that's not a premium rate number!' his mother had called from the kitchen, cloth in hand.

Now, recovering, he was watching *Countdown* and the conundrum was proving particularly tough. It was going to need all his concentration if he was to have a hope of beating the buzzer and, of course, this had to be the moment that his mother chose to blitz the coffee table, oblivious to the emotional roller coaster he had just ridden and his need for a clear view of the screen. Oblivious, too, thank goodness, he thought as he craned his neck to see past his mother's jiggling skirt, to the fact that Carol Vaudeville was wearing a particularly slinky top which he was anxious to remember for later on.

His mother swept on around the room, shifting ornaments, setting out little pots for nibbles and snacks. Now and then, she glanced at him, eyes narrowed, as though daring him to get up and make a break for the door, to ruin her party before it had begun. She'd been like this for several days, ever since he had suggested he might not attend the January party, the highlight of her entertaining calendar, the crowning of the year.

'Easily the liveliest gathering held this side of the library from one year to the next!' he'd actually heard her gabble to one of her cronies on the phone the week before.

George sighed and stretched out as his mother turned her attention to the ornament-stand at the far end of the room, leaving him a clear view of the screen. In actual fact, he hadn't made any firm decisions about where he was going to spend the evening. No-one had rung, of course. Not unless you counted one wrong number and someone intent on bumping up the number of text messages on his monthly mobile deal. 'But who would I send them to?' he'd asked the cold-caller – Taz – with genuine interest, 'Who is out there to text?' There was no point in bumping up his text messages unless they bumped up his life as well.

He lay on the sofa as his mother attacked the papers on the bureau. It was unsettling watching her: the waspish movements of her hands combined with her angry, darting glances at him. It was as though she were trying to tidy his very thoughts. If only she could see how he truly had her best interests at heart. If only she could see how he longed to come to her party, to play the perfect, dutiful son. Indeed, whether he stayed here or went out somewhere else, it would always be with a view to what was best for her; after all, if he went out and met some new, amazing people and became famous through that, think of the parties she could have then! Think of the stories she would have to tell! And if he stayed here and helped with the washing up, well, that was good too. Either way, she couldn't lose. Poor, dear, bustling mother. If only she could see how closely he considered her in everything he did. He sighed sadly and adjusted the cushions behind his back. As it was, he would probably end up staying for his mother's party after all: it was starting to rain and he hadn't managed to catch *Neighbours* at lunch.

'You might help!' blurted his mother at last, staring at George with a reddening face. It was a point of principle with her that, in truly harmonious families, people did things for each other without needing to be asked; she always became furious when she had to nag.

'How?' said George, looking around with a genuine shrug. 'You've done everything and it's only half-past four.'

It was true: the place was spotless. It always was. What was he supposed to do? Hoover it all again just to keep the peace?

'Well,' said his mother, temporarily at a loss. 'What about tidying your room? That's certainly well overdue.'

'Oh right,' said George. 'Because people are going to be partying in my room, are they?'

'There might be coats,' she said sniffily.

'The coats'll go in your room. They always do. 'What's the point of carrying them up two flights of stairs to put them in mine? Come on, Mum.'

'Don't you tell me to come on!' she said throwing down the black sack into which she'd been sweeping most of the papers. 'Don't you dare tell me to come on! I'm not the one lying on the sofa watching *Blankety-Blank* –'

'*Countdown.*'

'I don't care what it is. The point is –'

Out in the hall, the phone began to ring. She stood looking at him.

'Look,' she said at last, 'There'll be people at this party, just remember that!'

She flounced from the room to the phone.

George rolled his eyes. What had he done now? Had she expected him to go and answer the phone? What was the point of that? It would only be one of her friends asking if they should bring sausages on sticks or pineapple bites. How should he know? Anyway, he was sitting down.

By six o' clock, when George's father got home, his mother's *Smooth Classics* compilation was rubbing nastily against the strains of the *Neighbours* theme tune from the TV. Coming into the living room, loosening his tie, Geoffrey French nodded briefly at his son and stood staring at the screen as the credits rolled.

'Good day?' he said at last.

'Yes,' said George blankly. 'You?'

'Oh, you know,' said his father with a shrug. 'Could be worse.'

George did know: his father had taken over the family paper firm two days after his sixteenth birthday and had run it much the same ever since. Apart from one secretary, he worked entirely on his own, in a small red brick office somewhere in the back streets towards the east of the city. When he was younger, George had thought the building must be a front for something – money-laundering or a nest of spies – so suspiciously unexceptional did it appear. That was until he had spent two dreary weeks doing work experience there after his GCSEs and found that the office did exactly what it said on the brass plate by the door. No hidden agenda there, no ulterior motives: the place was the Ronseal of the business world.

His father coughed.

'What have you been up to?' he said. 'Working hard?'

'Erm,' George hesitated. What should he say? That he got up at twelve, looked at some porn, spent forty-five minutes lying on his bed trying to throw balled up tissues into his bin, and, for the last three hours, had been stretched out on the sofa watching *Countdown* and Children's TV? Besides, what was there to work at now the course was at an end?

'In a way,' he said at last.

'He hasn't,' said his mother, popping her head round the door. 'He's been lying there watching television all afternoon.'

His father looked at him.

'Well,' he said hopefully, 'I suppose you're only young once.'

'I think he's depressed,' muttered his mother in a whisper designed for George to hear. 'He doesn't get up, doesn't eat properly, doesn't go out –'

'You won't let me go out!' called George. 'I tried to go out, I was going to go out tonight, but you wouldn't let me!'

'– I honestly think that if I didn't ask him to get up so I could Hoover under him, he would never move at all!'

'Mmmn,' said George's father. His eyes wandered to the bureau. 'What happened to the bank statements?'

'I moved them.'

'You moved them?'

'I threw them away.'

'Jean! They were supposed to go in the file!'

'How was I supposed to know that!' she said, turning and stamping off to the kitchen.

'You weren't!' he protested, following her out of the room. 'You were supposed to leave them alone!'

George slipped off the sofa and away up the stairs. He'd just remembered he had an elderly, half-finished pack of fags left over from a night out after his finals hidden in his sock drawer. He might smoke them out of his skylight, watching the black-hatted figures making their way to Friday evening shul through the streets below and pretend he was a gritty, English actor contemplating his next difficult role.

*   *   *

The doorbell rang at twenty past seven. George looked at his radio clock and groaned. What was it about older people that made them so eager to get everywhere on time? At the parties he went to – well, at the two or three he'd attended since he left university – punctuality was a positive vice; turning up on time meant that you were a bit too keen, a bit too needy, a bit too ready to be entertained. Before the last party he'd been to, a low-key affair at a friend of a friend's in Leyton, he'd spent twenty minutes watching television in the window of Dixons just so he wouldn't be the first to arrive. When did this change, he wondered? When was it no longer the done thing to slope in the door two hours after the start of a party, frowning as though you'd rather be somewhere else? Did having children do it? Was it a generational thing? Maybe it was something they taught them once upon a time at school, along with heraldry and walking around with a book on your head.

'George? Could you get that?' called his mother from downstairs.

George grimaced. He knew she was down there, straightening the vol-au-vents on the platters behind the kitchen door, poised to sweep out and welcome the first of her guests. His father was probably at a loose end too; skulking in the study, nursing a sherry and working himself up to playing another game of solitaire on the battered old PC. He could easily step out and release the catch on the front door. But he wouldn't. He'd delay coming out of the study as long as he could. It would be left to George to take the coats and smile and make polite conversation about traffic, television and sodding Evelyn Waugh.

He slumped off his bed and down the stairs. The doorbell rang again.

'George!' called his mother.

'Yes!' he shouted. 'Alright!'

He undid the catch and the front door swung open to reveal two small, bespectacled people on the step. Standing behind them, peering over their heads was a similarly bespectacled and somewhat spotty boy. George stood and stared at them. There was an awkward pause.

'Jim! Margaret!' cried George's mother, sweeping forward, arms outstretched. 'How wonderful to see you! Come in, come in!' She stepped aside nudging George out of the way. 'And this must be Andrew! Goodness me! George, you remember Andrew, don't you? You used to play together in the park!'

George stared blankly at the young man's shiny face: pale and pudding-like with a suggestion of buck-teeth. 'Er,' he said.

'Of course you do! Andrew's an engineer now.'

'Actually more of an astrophysicist,' interjected the boy abruptly. 'I do dabble in engineering, yes, but really it's more of a hobby.'

'Andrew's been running his own radio station out of our garage since he was twelve,' said the small woman, whose rigid bob looked as though it had been fashioned out of horse hair and glued to the top of her head. 'He's like his father: into everything!'

'Well,' said the small man, pushing his glasses up his nose with an awkward flinch. 'Like me before I got distracted.'

'Yes,' giggled the woman.

'I'm also interested in String Theory,' continued Andrew. 'I'm looking into ways of applying the Sparks solution to a wider frame of reference.'

'Well!' said Jean French with a meaningful glance at George. 'Isn't that impressive!'

George looked again at Andrew. Now he came to think of it, he did remember a small, weedy boy who had wet himself one day on the roundabout and had to be taken home.

'Let me take your coats,' he said.

The door-bell rang again as George was coming down the stairs, and he went gratefully to answer it, leaving his mother to entertain the Adams family in the lounge. Sue-down-the-road was standing on the step, flushed and wearing a red, tasselled jumper, festooned with gold thread.

'I hope they're alright,' she said, holding out a foil-covered dish. 'I burnt the first lot and I might have left these ones in a bit long.'

'Sue!' cried Jean, sweeping forward again. 'How good of you to come! And so early too!'

'Kosher sausage rolls,' said Sue, handing over the dish. 'Using lamb. Just in case anyone's…you know.'

'Oh,' said Jean, 'Lovely.' She lifted the foil and peered beneath it. 'Actually, we were going for more of a Chinesey theme with the snacks. But, well, anyway, thanks.'

She turned and swept the plate off into the kitchen, washing her hands before returning to her guests in the lounge.

'So,' said Sue, turning hopefully to George, 'How's it all going now? How's the course?'

The party began to fill up quickly after that. Guests spilled into the dining room and the hall and the doorbell rang so frequently that even Geoffrey French was forced out of the study to stand duty as a host. George circulated with a bottle of wine, brandishing it like a talisman whenever anyone threatened to involve him in anything more than a superficial conversation. He got trapped a couple of times. Once by an old primary school teacher, who insisted on taking him on one side and dispensing clichés about grasping the nettle and taking the bull by the horns; once by a retired colleague of his mother's, who kept asking him the same questions using slightly different words, as though George were a safe that would crack open and reveal its contents if only the right combination were found.

'So you're studying at the moment?' he said, chewing a crispy wonton wetly beneath his moustache.

'Well, I was,' said George, 'But I stopped a few days ago. Decided it wasn't for me.'

'But you're doing a course?'

'No, I was. I gave it up.'

The man nodded, swallowing thoughtfully. George opened his mouth, ready to make his escape.

'What subject is it again? Ancient Greek?'

'No,' said George, shifting his weight onto the other foot. 'It was English literature, but –'

'Mmn, mmn,' said the man nodding vigorously and reaching for a sweet and sour nibble on a plate that was travelling past. 'And there was someone you were interested in, wasn't there? Who was it now?'

He frowned and pushed a battered shrimp between his lips.

'Well –' said George.

'Daphne Du Maurier!' he cried, spattering George's arm with crumbs.

'Evelyn Waugh,' said George.

'Oh well,' said the man, shrugging, 'Close. She was a fine sort, Daphne Du Maurier. Used to sunbathe naked on the cliffs, you know.'

George nodded. It was something this guest always managed to bring up at every party he attended. He looked down at his arm and tried to brush the worst of the batter flakes off.

'So,' said the man at last, bringing his gaze back to George from some far away point halfway up the banister, 'You're doing a course on Evelyn Waugh?'

George stayed with him for several minutes more. He didn't mind talking to him. In many ways he preferred answering the same question over and over to the well-meaning interrogations which most of the other guests tried to subject him to. Faced with their beaming persistence and boundless enthusiasm for news about his life, he was beginning to feel like Dustin Hoffman, trapped inside the opening party scene of *The Graduate*. The whole experience wasn't helped by the occasional sight of his mother, chin raised, jewellery glinting, passing round versions of him with the cucumber and sweet plum sauce.

'Yes,' he heard her saying as he was returning to the kitchen for a fresh bottle, 'Well, he's got lots of options at the moment, lots of things he could go into. He could pursue the book, or look out for another course, and then there's always the option of a placement at Farrell & Fortune, his godfather's firm. Difficult when you're brilliant at so many things. Personally, I think he might opt for medicine in the end.'

George shuddered as he put the wine bottle down on the side. That was another thing: so far, he hadn't managed to work up to telling them he hadn't got the placement after all. How to break it to them that their darling Robert hadn't come up with the goods after all? How to understand it himself? He looked to the left and saw his reflection, pale and insubstantial, in the kitchen window against the night. Above him was the framed sentence he had stolen from Evelyn Waugh as a child and above that the kitchen clock showing the time as a quarter to nine. The tube rumbled past outside: a steady, hollow sound, dying into the blankness of the Sabbath night. In the houses all around, Jewish families were breaking bread and saying prayers, the men solemn, the women sitting modestly by, all sealed within the circle of their Shabbat candle-light, yet spreading an inscrutable calm, which seemed to wrap the world in quiet. For George, growing up here, Friday evenings had always felt like this: no matter how gladly he threw himself into them they always carried a note of gravity; a widow at the second Christmas after her husband's death, endeavouring to pull the cracker and join in the fun, yet breaking off and staring wistfully into space.

But away, somewhere away beyond all this, up the hill, past the house of the bastard Waugh, there was the city and life happening, pulsing, playing itself out. To think that he was stuck here, handing round plates of his mother's sweet and sour prawns, whilst away, over the hill, people were connecting and mingling, weaving a great net around the future and pulling it steadily near; whilst there were artists – real artists! – communing together in words and music, touching greatness itself! There were people out there with dreadlocks! People living on the dole! People – he'd seen *Withnail and I* – who did nothing all day except for drinking lighter fluid and thinking bold artistic thoughts! He gazed longingly through his pale face at the purple night sky. Somewhere out there, the course of life was being irrevocably altered tonight and here he was, stepping out of the kitchen to take round another bottle of wine.

He was just backing away from a woman in a black twin-set bent on finding out how many hours a day he spent at his desk, when a misplaced foot stumbled him and sent him tottering against a broad shoulder and a strong, well-wadded arm.

'Careful there,' said a familiar voice, whilst a hand reached round to relieve George of the wine bottle. Turning, George found himself face to face with his godfather.

Despite the fact that they were now practically the same height, George had never lost the feeling that he was looking up whenever speaking to Robert Bude. Generously built, although not fat, the man filled a suit and a room with a sense of command and authority which had awed George as a child and even now was impressive. When he was younger, George had assumed that he too would one day use his wine glass to describe a circle that somehow drew everyone in to what he was saying; that he too would listen politely to another's point of view and then respectfully, yet devastatingly, correct them. It had seemed that this massive self-assurance must be part of growing up; something acquired in the hazy stretch between boyhood and adulthood along with stubble and wisdom teeth. Yet, now, watching his godfather serve himself a glass of wine, George felt further from it than ever. He doubted he would ever attain that mammoth confidence that revealed itself everywhere about his godfather's person, right down to the neat twist he gave the bottle to stop it dripping wine onto the carpet, just as he doubted that the patches of sandy bristles on his face would ever level themselves out into the even, manly covering that suffused his godfather's cheeks. When he thought about his godfather now, it was impossible to see how he had ever been anything less than he was, as though he had risen into himself like an inflatable dummy George had seen blown up from a canister at the start of a school fête. Beside his godfather, George would always be a small boy, cramming candyfloss into his mouth, gawping.

'So,' said Robert, handing back the wine and stretching out his fingers to grub amongst the nibbles on the side. 'How's it going? Still working hard on the book?'

'Oh well, you know –' stammered George. 'Difficult.'

'Mmmn hmmn,' said Robert looking over George's shoulder and away around the room.

'The thing is,' said George. 'I'm not sure if I –'

'I'm proud of you, you know, George,' said Robert, bringing his attention back to his wine glass. 'You've got ambition, you know that? Drive. Keep your eye on the ball, play with a straight bat and the world's your oyster.'

'Mmnn,' said George.

'You're a real credit to your parents, you know, particularly considering their humble beginnings, the way they struggled – where is your mother, by the way?'

'Oh, I think she's –' said George, waving a hand vaguely in the direction of the hallway.

'Excellent,' said Robert, 'I must just –'

And he was gone, his large back moving off across the room, edging out of sight. George blinked. It was not exactly how he'd imagined the first meeting with his godfather since his rejection from Fortune would go. He'd pictured the scene a number of times, running sentences he might say through his mind. He'd practised being aloof, calm, indifferent. At times he'd thought he might laugh it off as if he didn't care, make out that he was relieved. And once or twice, in brave, angry moments, he'd blustered at himself in the bathroom mirror, asking how he could fail to recognise his potential, how on earth his firm could afford not to give him a chance. Still, something he hadn't bargained for – perhaps the only thing – was this awkward shuffling from his godfather, this quite uncharacteristic sloping off. It was almost, well, it was almost as if Robert were cross with George himself. Either that or there was something he wasn't saying. Some inadequacy in George, perhaps? Somewhere at the back of his mind, that uneasy sense of greatness missed, forever darting from him, glowed, sparked and flickered into life. Was this what they knew about him? Was this what they saw?

The flames grew steadily, searing through his thoughts. He shook his head to quench them, and stood, staring absently around the party. They were all here, the birthday card-senders, the well-wishers, the people he'd had to scrawl thank you letters to from the moment he could hold a pencil. In any moment, they would start to descend, hands clutching, eyes peering. He would have to think quickly if he didn't want to

drown in a tide of benevolent curiosity. On the other side of
the room, he noticed Sue-down-the-road and Andrew standing
awkwardly next to mantelpiece and the imitation antique
clock. They looked uncomfortable and out of place: a couple
of second-hand dolls put on the shelf by mistake in *Toys R Us*.
He felt strangely sorry for them. Perhaps he should go on a
rescue mission and offer them a drink, give them all a bit of a
break.

He took a step towards them and –
'Porge!' said a familiar voice.
Bewildered, George turned to be confronted by a
generous bosom spilling out of a gaping shirt, dark hair falling
to the shoulder and eyes, small and heavily lashed, staring
eagerly at his face. Images of the other evening flashed
through his mind. What was it he had done again? Touched
something? Made a mess?'

'Emily –' he said, his mouth groping for something
appropriately gallant and vague to say. It was a position he had
found himself in on more than one occasion during the time he
had known her: a nagging sense of having fallen short of a
standard set without his consent.

'Porge,' said Emily, hurrying forward, hands clutching
a nearly empty wine glass, face flushed. 'Your mother's told
me everything; that it's all fallen apart. Oh Porge, I'm so
sorry!'

She rushed towards him and threw herself on him, her
hands gripping him under his arms. There was a sharp smell
about her, as though she had steeped a lemon in alcohol for
several weeks and then smeared it liberally on herself.

'Well,' said George, pulling free, 'It's not exactly a
question of things falling apart –'

He looked down at her. Her mouth was smeared with
lipstick and there was a dusting of sparkly powder around her
eyes. He frowned.

'How did you get in touch with my mother anyway?'
he asked.

'Oh Porge, it was the funniest thing! My mother's
hairdresser's daughter got married and at the wedding it turned

out that there was someone there who used to work with your mother! How random's that?'

'Extraordinary,' said George. Their vile connections again, he might have known.

'So of course once we found that out I just had to get in touch. And that was when she invited me to the party. And that was when she told me, Porge, how it's all gone wrong.'

'Well,' said George, 'As I say, it hasn't all gone wrong.'

'Oh Porge!' said Emily, flinging the hand holding her glass against him. George looked down as a splash of red wine joined the grease stains from the old man's batter on his shirt. 'Brave Porge! Wonderfully strong, inventive, brave Porge! You don't have to worry about acting the hero with me. As soon as I heard what had happened, I knew how you must be feeling. I mean you had the course and the promise of the book, and now what have you got?'

'Yes,' said George, glancing around the room for something to save him, an escape route. Andrew and Sue-down-the-road were beginning to look positively tempting. 'But –' He caught sight of his mother walking across the room, followed by Robert, his hand on her arm. Something about the way they walked, the touch of his hand, made him pause.

'I'll tell you what you've got,' continued Emily, 'Nothing. That's what. And it's all very well being brave, Porge – it's marvellous to be brave – but the point is, what are you going to do? You can't go on being promising for ever, you know.' Here Emily paused, sweeping back her hair and thrusting her bosom forward before going on: 'It's something I've only recently realised myself. When I was younger,' she said, moving her hand from her hair down her neck and allowing it to trail casually over her breasts, 'I suppose I thought I would always be young, would always have it all before me. But then, you know, you hit twenty-two and, well, you suddenly realise things won't always be as they are now. I mean, I might only have twenty more years left in which I can still have children! So, you see, Porge,' said Emily taking a step towards him, breasts trembling, 'You and I are more similar than you might you think.'

'Yes,' said George with a cough as his mother and godfather slipped into the kitchen and pushed the door to. 'By the way, I meant to apologise for the other night. I think I –'

'Oh Porge!' bubbled Emily with a laugh that shook her generous frame. It's utterly understandable! Completely forgotten. Given everything that's happened, I'm surprised you didn't throw me on the couch and ravish me there and then!'

'Er,' he said, 'Would you like another drink?'

Her eyes sparkled.

'Oh, would you Porge?' she said, shakily holding out her glass to where she imagined his hand to be. 'That would be splendiferous.'

As he set off, he heard her turn and speak to the person standing next to her: 'Hello, I'm Emily. I'm in corporate PR.'

'George!' said a woman as he stepped into the hall. 'I hear you're thinking of going into accountancy –'

'George!' said another as he passed the banisters. 'You're mother tells me you're considering teaching English as a foreign language. I should introduce you to –'

But George wasn't listening. He by-passed them all, carrying Emily's wine glass to the kitchen at the end of the hall. The door was ajar when he reached it, a small strip of light showing the edge of the surface and one or two of the bottles ranged along it. The room seemed strangely empty, removed from the party babble, and, as he stepped through, a hurried movement caught his eye: two figures stepping quickly apart, faces turning towards him. He knew the bright, swirling colours of his mother's blouse before he saw her face, mouth open, eyes moist. Next to her stood his godfather, one hand, the hand that had grubbed amongst the savoury nibbles, still resting on her arm. George stood for a moment, staring at them, and in that moment, another moment came crashing down upon him: a moment containing blue sky, and railings and manicured grass; a moment containing a kite and buckle shoes tripping between its tails… and hadn't there been – what if there'd been? – of course there had been two figures, never noticed before, standing dark against the scene. A split second – frozen now like single frame of footage in a police reconstruction – before the hand that bumped and propelled him, turning him to face the house of the famous author and the stories that stretched across its years. The two moments slotted together, like the pieces of coloured film they had showed them in primary school which could be laid one over the other to spell out words, and suddenly the meaning was clear. For, after all, hadn't he known the truth all along? Hadn't he seen for years that his parents didn't really love each other, that they were pretending for the sake of his father's career? Almost from the moment he could talk, he had known that there were three people in his parent's marriage and it was, well, pretty crowded.

A crash drew his attention, and, looking down, he saw with interest the remains of Emily's wine glass shattered at his feet. He stood and watched himself looking at it, at the heap of see-through fragments, cracked and winking in the light. Strange to think that glass was made from molten sand. He looked up again, slowly, and again, it was as though he were watching himself, standing looking at them, at their eyes, blinking.

'I beg your pardon,' he heard his voice say, calm and terribly English, like the straight man in a *Carry On* film.

Then he turned, ever so calm, ever so polite, and made his way out into the hall. He walked slowly along the carpet, feeling, strangely, as he had when, at the age of eight, he had first made tea for his parents and carried the trembling tray in from the kitchen whilst they sat making bright conversation ever so slightly too loud in the lounge. He was carrying this reality, carrying it. Any false move and he might drop it and it would break.

A woman, a small creature with curled, grey hair, stepped in front of him and began to talk. He watched her mouth opening and closing, framing and releasing words like so many bubbles of hot air. Then, from afar, he heard his mother's voice, bright and polished as the silverware in the dining-room cabinet, and felt her hand on his shoulder.

'You'll have to excuse him, Anne,' he heard her saying, 'He's not quite himself at the moment.'

And so he brushed her off and stepped onwards and up the stairs because he was not quite himself.

'Oh dear,' he heard the grey-haired woman saying as he rounded the corner of the banister onto the upstairs landing, 'Attack of the teenage mutant ninja turtles is it?' But in his mind all he could see were pictures of blue sky and kites, of hands on shoulders and hands on arms, and all he could hear was Emily's voice repeating 'you hit twenty-two', 'you hit twenty-two' until he couldn't be sure whether it was cricket she was talking about, or driving, or some random game involving smacking plastic rabbits on the head.

George reached his room and shut the door with a bang. The thud of it jumped him back into himself, sending the images crashing into the darkness like a tower of invisible plates. He looked around him. Yes, it was all still here; the books, the papers, the posters, clothes and junk. Strange, how you could see something like that, how the universe could shift, and yet your 50 metres swimming certificate could still hang on the wall. Hours, days, weeks of nothing and then this: a flurry of wisps of knowledge, darkening the sky and heralding a storm. Here it was at last, the great grand drama, the secret sorrow casting its ghastly shade, the rot at the root of it all.

There was a pounding on the door.

'George?' His mother, anxious, sharp. 'What's the matter with you? George?'

'Go away.'

'George, if you'll just –'

'Go away.'

'George –'

'Go away. Go back to the party. Go back,' – he bit the words – 'To your guests.'

He went to the window and looked out at the row of gardens behind the house, leading up to the tube line: trugs and trellises; greenhouses shielding rows of peeping seedlings; order. And then his own garden, his parents' garden, beneath the window, shady and ragged, frowned upon by the apple tree over which his mother could never quite get control. Unweeded, grown to seed, with rank upon rank of gross, sprawling greenery possessing it day by day. He saw again the stepping apart, the hand on the arm. They were down there, having a party. And all the while, there was this. For years there had been this. Again the egg-blue sky, the little hands clutching the kite. And for this he had been steered towards the house, the endless hours of dry books and bespectacled men, plugging away foolishly at thoughts that were brittle and moth-eaten in reality's headlamp glare, building his house of cards atop academia's teetering Babel Tower.

Looking around the room now, at his books and papers, the coloured folders, they all seemed nothing so much as childish toys, pacifiers to keep baby quiet while his parents got on with the real business of the world. They were nothing but a huge distraction, a sop to his pride, so that he could get on with making his Lego castle by himself, turning, only now and then, to Mummy and Daddy for applause.

And it had worked. God, it had worked. Images crowded upon him: Christmases and birthdays, meals out; hands on arms and meeting on doors, fingers mingling around the sherry glass. How had he not seen it? How had he not seen the way they were engineering it all before now? All those polite conversations around the dinner table, those thoughtful, modestly expensive gifts. All those meals when Robert had taken George out to little wood-panelled places with sawdust floors that hadn't changed much since he was young. All those cricket matches spent ensconced grandly in the long-room at Lords. All those elicit pints brought slopping from the bar – 'Don't tell your mother,' Robert would say as George reached up to take the glass that was almost too big for his hands. And all the time, beaming in the flicker of the muted candlelight, smiling in the summer sun, he'd really been itching to get back to grunting and sweating with George's mother; to spread her messily on his desk, amidst affidavits and writs and petitions for divorce; to have her, gasping, over the fax machine. That one may file and file and be a villain!

He saw the letter, lying on a heap of papers at his feet and picked it up, feeling the rich texture of it between his fingers. No wonder he hadn't got the placement. It all made sense now. After all, they'd hardly want him hanging around the scene of their crimes, would they? He could just see them now, riding each other over the photocopier, putting the water-cooler to misuse. The whole thing was sick and unnatural and weirdly skewed, an amateur dramatics production in which everyone was playing the wrong part, his mother moonlighting as Mrs. Robinson when she should have been playing the queen. His poor father! And yet, should he feel sorry for him? After all, hadn't the hand directing George, pushing him to turn away on that flawless summer day, been his father's? Hadn't his father, doubtless, now, slipping from the party for some of his single malt whisky and five minutes in the study with the paper, simply let things happen as they had? Sticking to his crumpled suits, dusty accounts and the office with the plastic pot-plants, hadn't he simply resigned his right to protest? Declared with too low a score? Left the way clear for his wife to play the field? Christ! What hope was there for him coming from such a home?

George bent down and picked up a book, a large, weighty tome of a thing: *The Collected Letters of Evelyn Waugh*. Ha! He'd given them a collected letter or two! He flung the volume across the room, watching it flap like a turkey before it crashed into the frame on the notice-board and fell to the floor, cuffing the computer on the way. A thin crack spread across the glass of the picture. Above it, Evelyn Waugh's eyes stared out at George, chastened.

'Porge?'

George turned. Emily stood in the doorway, framed by the landing light.

'You didn't bring me my drink,' she said.

She stepped forward into the room. The orange glow from the street lamps eased itself over her face, her breasts.

'Oh,' said George, running a hand over his forehead. Evelyn Waugh's eyes stared out at him across the gloom like the eyes of a gagged torture victim, brimming with mute appeal. 'Sorry I –'

'It's alright, Porge,' said Emily, shutting the door softly and leaning against it. 'You don't have to worry about me.'

'Actually, Em,' said George. 'I'm not really in the party mood this evening. Think I'd rather be –'

'It's alright, Porge,' said Emily, her voice sinking into Cadbury's Caramel softness. 'I know exactly how you feel. You're upset. You're angry. The last thing you want is to be making small-talk with a bunch of people twice your age.'

'Mmn,' said George as Emily stepped towards him, wobbling on heels that were slightly too high. Looking down, he realised he was still holding the letter. He folded it quickly and thrust it into the pocket of his jeans.

'And I also know,' said Emily, putting her hand up to finger the pendant around her neck, 'That the reason you're upset has nothing to do with not finishing your course or not getting that placement thing.' She reached the windowsill and turned to lean against it, next to him. 'I know what's really eating you.'

'Er, do you?' said George. He felt the letter, a firm, forbidding square against his thigh. They really must have taken him for a mug, letting him apply like that, knowing all the while that they would turn him down.

'Oh yes, Porge,' said Emily, reaching out to run her finger along his forearm and down to his hand.

George folded his arms, ducking Evelyn Waugh's stare. The bastard could hardly mock him now, after all he'd only ever been another pawn in their game.

'You're sick of everyone not listening to you, Porge' said Emily, reaching up to finger a button on her shirt. 'You're sick of them all – Jenny, your parents, everyone – not realising that you've moved on, that you're a man.'

George nodded absently. What they didn't realise was that he'd moved on, that he was a man. They thought they knew him; they thought they could see around the edges of his life. Well they were wrong. Oh yes, there were things they didn't know about him, other sides.

'I know you're a man, Porge,' said Emily breathlessly.
'I *feel* you're a man.'

George stepped away from the windowsill. Really, he
should start being different right now, he supposed. Storm out!
Have somewhere fabulous to go. Where? That was the only
thing.

'Oh, Porge!' said Emily, releasing the button. 'I won't
let them treat you like a child!'

George started and looked down at her, shocked to find
that she was still there. She stood before him, shirt gaping to
reveal her large, rounded breasts encased in a generous black
bra.

'Er, Em,' said George with a cough, 'I think your
shirt's come undone.'

'Touch them, Porge,' said Emily, stepping towards
him. 'Touch me.'

'Er –' said George again.

'Don't be shy, Porge,' said Emily, reaching out to take
his hand.

George backed away.

'Er, look, Em' he said. 'That's very sweet of you and
everything, but –' He caught sight of his guitar, propped up in
the corner. For Christ's sake, he was in London, wasn't he?
The place had to be heaving with opportunity, with artists just
waiting for him to come along! Why waste anymore time?
'Actually I'm just on my way out.'

'Out, Porge?' said Emily. 'But you don't go out.' She
narrowed her eyes and leaned in. 'Out where?'

'Well, it's a sort of a par –'

Emily's eyes brightened. 'A party! Oh Porge, how
marvellous! I'll come too!'

'Well,' George coughed. 'When I say party, I really
mean more of a gathering.'

Emily opened her mouth to speak.

'For boys,' he added quickly.

'For boys?' said Emily, frowning. 'What sort of a party
is that? Oh Porge, they're not gays, are they?'

'Er,' said George, 'Not as far as I know.' He went and picked up his guitar. 'Anyway, the point is I'm actually rather late so –' He stepped to the door and opened it. 'Bye,' he said and went out, leaving Emily gaping below the mutilated picture of Evelyn Waugh.

Downstairs, the party was in full swing. Guests packed the lounge and the dining room and were spilling out into the kitchen and the hall. One or two had given up standing and opted for perching on the stairs, nursing their drinks between pin-striped knees in bizarre imitation of their student days.

George stepped through them on his way to the door, manoeuvring his guitar over their heads.

'Oooh,' said one woman. 'Are we going to have a song?'

'No,' said George.

'Are you a musician?' said another. 'You must speak to my husband Paul, he conducts the Finchley Choral Society, you know. Hang on a second. Paul!'

'Actually, I'm just going out,' said George, elbowing his way towards the door.

'What, another party is it?' said a man with mammoth eyebrows. 'Too boring for you, are we?'

'Actually yes,' said George, staring at him. 'Yes you are.'

The man blinked.

'George!' called a voice. 'George! Stop right there!'

George flinched: his mother. He had to get out before she caught up with him and it was all over.

He forced his way on, past a fat woman eating a pickled gherkin – surely that wasn't an oriental snack? – until he reached the door. His hand was on the catch. If he could only get the door open wide enough against the crush of bodies to get his guitar and himself through, he would be free. He looked back. His mother was battling her way through the crowd, arms flailing. In another moment she would be upon him. Panic seized him: he had had nightmares like this.

He turned back to the door and began wrenching roughly at it, fighting against the bodies that pressed, leaned and sprawled. He heard his mother's voice again, nearer now, much nearer. God, any moment now and –

'Porge!' a scream, shrill and primal, resonated in the hall. All heads turned, all sounds ceased save the droning of Pachobel's *Canon* from the stereo in the lounge. At the top of the stairs, stood Emily: hair wild, shirt still undone.

'Good Lord,' whispered one of the men near George. 'I didn't think Jean went in for strippers!'

'Porge!' Emily called again. But it was too late: taking advantage of the lull, George had slipped round the front door and out into the night.

He stood on the doorstep and breathed for a moment, absorbing the sounds of the evening: the rush of cars past the end of the road, the strains of music from the kosher wine bar, the rumble of an approaching tube. He was pathetically, unreasonably happy; excited as he had been once during a game of Hide and Seek at primary school, when he had lain for ages on top of a flat roof, out of eyeshot of the bumbling 'It'. Through his mind ran the old negro strain: 'Free at last, free at last/ Thank God almighty/ We are free at last.' He was almost tempted to break into song. He grinned and gripped his guitar. Well, that would come, it would all come. He was young, he was in London, and the night was all before him. What couldn't he achieve?

He walked to the garden gate and out along Newbolt Close, savouring the cold breeze on his skin, the scent of promise just around the corner, of greatness waiting to be got. He wished that he had cigarette so that he could smoke and look intense. So much for the suburbs and their dreary dramas and affairs, George French was starting to live!

As he passed Sue's house he noticed a small, feline form sidle out onto the pavement and slink along under the hedge.

'Toffee?' said George, looking down. 'What are you doing outside?'

The cat froze and peered upwards, its muscles poised to run. George glanced at the house. The lights were on and music – surprisingly contemporary for Sue – was playing somewhere inside. Sue must have given up on the party, George supposed. Well, he didn't blame her. Stuck with that Andrew, no-one could have lasted more than half an hour. He looked back at the cat. Really, he should grab it and go and knock on the door; but there was something about the wild glint in its eyes, the terror flattening its ears, that made George hesitate. The cat needed no second chance: thrusting its bouffant tail in the air, it set off up the street at a run, its fur streaming behind it in the breeze. Skidding round the corner at the end, it headed off in the direction of the park, disappearing into the night.

5

'So,' said Trudy, running a hand over her carefully coiffed hair, 'It all started the night you found out that your mother was having an affair?'

'That's right Trudy,' said George. He was older, but he didn't look it, only slightly more rugged with a leather jacket and light stubble peppering the lower part of his face. 'My parents were having a party and I walked in on my mother and the man I thought was my godfather having a private moment in the kitchen.'

'That must have been terrible for you,' said Trudy, shaking her head at the camera.

'No, actually,' said George with a wry, measured smile. 'I think it crystallised quite a few things. Made it clear that I needed to do something more; needed to get out.'

'But, I mean, walking in on your mother like that. How must you have felt?'

'If you want the truth: bored,' said George. There was a titter of laughter off-set, not too much though – he was known for his dry sense of humour, the world-weary way he looked at life. 'Seriously,' he continued. 'I mean, I looked at her and I just thought: "Is that all you can find to occupy your time?" I just knew that there was no way I wanted to be stuck in a mundane job stealing extra-marital kisses behind the fridge-freezer in thirty years' time.'

'So you took a bad thing and turned it to your advantage?' said Trudy, leaning in so that her cleavage peeped from inside her soft, velvet top. Her breasts really weren't bad for a woman of her age.

'Well, yes,' he said, shrugging modestly. 'I suppose you could say that.'

'That's extraordinary,' simpered Trudy, 'But then you've always been quite unusual haven't you? Didn't you once turn up to a tutorial in the middle of the night?'

George opened his mouth to frame a witty yet suitably powerful reply and suddenly became aware that a man over the other side of the caf' was staring at him. He ducked his head and stared into his coffee, trying to ignore the sight of his guitar propped up against the steamed-up glass beside him. He had to admit, he did look a bit foolish sitting here at half-past nine on a Saturday morning with a guitar. Like some sort of bizarre wandering minstrel or a character from Children's TV threatening at any moment to break into song. Why hadn't he thought to bring the case?

Avoiding the man's gaze George sipped his double-strength latte and stared out beneath the plastic sign at the street beyond. He hadn't been to bed all night but he didn't feel tired, more sort of insulated: wrapped round with cotton wool and wadded against the world. There was a lightness to everything, as though all of it – the tatty shops outside, the rundown cinema turned evangelical church on the corner with its faded banners extolling the healing power of prayer – were somehow not solid, not real, but happening only in his mind.

He didn't know exactly where he was, but one thing was clear: should the whole singer-songwriter malarkey not work out, he could probably do quite well starting a café chain in West London and making his name like that. He'd had to walk for hours just to find this place through streets and streets of terraced houses, past parades of shuttered shops given over almost entirely to betting and borrowing, as though people round here did nothing but lose money and try to claw it back. How delighted they'd be when he breezed into their lives with his jazzy café-cum-restaurant-cum-bar. The Saviour of Harlesden, they'd brand him, the answer to youth crime. Already he'd spent some time racking his brains to try and think of any pianists he knew called Sam.

He stretched grandly, pleased at the easy, fluid sweep of his thoughts. He was thinking marvellously well this morning. His mind felt cold and clear as a mountain lake, perfectly reflecting the sky. It was being free that did it, that was the thing. Free of all those queries and questions and expectations. Free of vol-au-vents and small-talk and the nightmare of pelting forever around the sand-strewn track after the ever-escaping hare. Free of convention and the perpetual, pointless game. Free of it all! Free! Think of that! Sweet

Moses, he could start writing a poem right this minute, so unfettered and astonishing were his thoughts.

Well, all in good time. One thing after another. He must be careful not to get caught up in that must-do mentality that had scuppered him once before. He was already stealing a march on the day just by sitting here, drinking his coffee. He smiled to think of all those people from the party with their toupees and teasmaids who would be up and off to garden centres later in the day. He was beating them all now. The rest of the world was still asleep. In fact, the street outside looked almost dead. Only a homeless woman, hunched in a massive coat with a fistful of bags, and a turbaned shop keeper, rattling up the newsagent's shutters, hinted that the day might be nearly here.

He stretched out and took another sip of coffee, smiled complacently across the room and –

'Jennifer!'

He'd seen her coming in, a tall, willowy girl with glinting chestnut hair, but it wasn't until she put her bag down at a neighbouring table and turned to look at the boards above the counter that he realised who she was.

She looked round, confused.

'Oh hello,' she said, flushing.

'What are you doing here?' said George, shoving back a chair, motioning for her to sit.

'I'm meeting someone,' she said. She looked at the chair he had placed for her and glanced quickly at the door. 'I'll just get a –' she said, gesturing towards the counter.

George watched her go up, her fine form moving beneath the fabric of her skirt. She was well-dressed. She was always well-dressed: modestly but with allure, like one of those secretaries in the adverts who went home at the end of the day, slipped off their dresses and shook down their hair. He'd done well to get her. And here she was, turning up just as he was starting out on his bold new directions. It had to be a sign.

'So,' he said as she came back to the table, carrying a trembling cup. 'You're meeting someone?'

'Oh, you know,' she said with a shrug. 'Shopping.'

George smiled. He did know. It had been a recurring theme in their relationship: Jennifer would plead poverty when he proposed nights out, yet somehow always find the money for a new pair of shoes. Looking back, it had been rather endearing.

'Funny place to choose for a spending spree,' he said, nodding at the street. 'Isn't it all charity shops round here?'

'Oh, there are places,' said Jennifer, quickly. 'If you know what you're looking for.' She lowered her bag to the floor. 'So, how are you?'

'Oh, you know,' said George, running a hand over his hair. 'So-so.'

'Did you get back alright the other night? I was worried about you.'

'What other night?' said George, watching Jennifer's long, slender fingers lift the cup to her mouth. She could have been a pianist, she really could.

Memory nudged him, 'Oh, the dinner party. Oh that was fine. Absolutely nothing. Actually, I'm used to it.' He yawned expansively. 'Haven't been to bed tonight yet either.'

'Oh,' said Jennifer, 'Well that explains it. I thought you were looking a little... tired. Where were you?'

'Just out,' said George casually, looking out of the window. 'Walking around. Watching the sun rise.'

It wasn't quite true: shortly after he'd stormed out of his parents' party he'd got on a bus and fallen asleep, riding it two or three times round its route before the driver cottoned on to his presence and turfed him onto the street. He'd then spent a nervous hour dodging plastic bottles, fag packets and eggs being thrown at him from a car of lads that had spotted him and tailed him all the way from Willesden Green. Since then he'd been wandering around trying to find somewhere to get a drink. Still, she didn't need to know all that.

'Oh right,' said Jennifer, glancing up as the door opened to let in two women wearing headscarves. 'And, er, are you still living at home?'

'Technically,' said George. 'Although I'm thinking of moving out.'

'Oh right,' said Jennifer, stirring the spoon round in the cup. 'Are your parents buying you a place?'

'No, I'm going to rent,' said George flinging his arm out expansively and narrowly missing his guitar, 'Actually I'm hoping to get into the music world.'

'Hmmn,' said Jennifer. 'But won't that be very difficult without a proper job? I mean renting's very expensive, George. It's throwing money away. You don't realise until you do it.'

The hectoring tone was coming into her voice now, the one she'd always used to point things out to him: know-it-all with a whining edge. George's jaw stiffened.

'I'll manage,' he said firmly. 'There are lots of cheap places.'

He'd seen them out on his walk this morning: grubby houses with letting cards in the windows, rooms from fifty pounds, just the sorts of places a musician or an artist or a budding personality might live. And he already had a head start: he had at least a hundred pounds in the bank and his allowance was due in in a couple of weeks' time. Not that he wanted to be beholden to that, of course. Oh no, he would do it all himself. Still, it was nice to know there was a safety net, should anything go wrong.

'Besides,' he continued. 'I can always get a part-time job if I need to. I'm not completely useless, you know.'

'I never said you were,' said Jennifer. 'I merely suggested that you should think about it carefully. It's much harder to back out once you've got a contract and a landlord to worry about.'

'Yes, I know all that,' said George impatiently.

'I'm sure you do,' said Jennifer, 'I was just saying –'

'Look!' said George, a red image flashing into his mind, something to kill the argument dead. 'I can't go home, alright? My mother's having an affair.'

Jennifer gasped. 'Oh George! That's awful! You poor, poor thing. With who?'

'With Robert,' said George slowly. 'My godfather.'

'Oh George!' gasped Jennifer again, reaching out to touch his arm. 'A double betrayal! That's absolutely terrible!'

He nodded, it was terrible. Funny he hadn't remembered it before. He forced his mind back to the evening before, to the scene in the kitchen, the alarmed faces looking towards the door.

'Mind you,' said Jennifer, releasing his arm and turning her attention back to her cup. 'I must say I'm not surprised. I never did like that Robert much. Very fat fingers.' She shivered. 'And of course I do see now that you've got no option. There's no way you can stay in that house with that going on. I'd say come and stay with me, only –'

'Good morning.'

George turned and squinted up at the figure which loomed above them, blonde with its hair glinting, halo-like in the brightness from the street.

'You both look very serious,' continued the figure. 'What's the controversy?'

'Oh, Edward, hi,' said Jennifer, flustered. 'George was just telling me, er, about his plans to move out and become a musician.'

George beamed at her. She was always good at that: social goal-keeping, finding a way of protecting people's confidences whilst making sure no-one felt left out.

'Well that is controversial,' said Edward, turning so that George recognised the blonde hulk who had thrown him out of Emily's party. 'How are you going to make that fly?'

Not by getting an office job and using management speak, George wanted to say, but instead he murmured. 'Oh, I'll make it work one way and another.'

'But you do know renting's really expensive -?' began the blonde.

'Mmn,' said George, sipping his coffee. 'Why are you here, anyway?'

'Oh, I live just round the corner,' said Edward, slipping his record bag off his shoulder and setting it down next to a chair. He was joining them. Well, wasn't that typical? Barging in with no sensitivity to the fact that, clearly, George and Jennifer had things to talk about, that they had a history.

'Mmn,' said George, making a show of glancing up and down the street outside. 'Classy.'

'It's not bad,' said Edward, slipping off his coat, 'For a first-time buyer. How's your head, anyway?

'Fine thanks,' said George, but the blonde didn't stay to listen, he had already stepped to the counter and was ordering a breakfast energy smoothie. Somehow that was typical too.

'What's he doing here?' hissed George to Jennifer. 'I wouldn't have thought this place would be his sort of –'

But the blonde was back.

'Sorry,' he said. 'Terribly rude of me. Do you guys want anything?' He glanced at Jennifer, who shook her head; then at George, who did the same. 'Sure?' he said. 'Sure you don't want to take advantage of a free cup of coffee? I could even stretch to a muffin if you're desperate. It's a tough old world out there on those streets, you know.'

'No thanks,' frowned George. 'I'm fine.'

'That's all, thanks mate,' Edward called to the man behind the counter before scraping back the chair next to Jennifer and sitting down.

'So,' he said, lifting the lid off his smoothie and stirring it round with a straw, 'Music, huh?'

'Mmn,' said George.

'What sort of music?'

'I'm not sure yet,' said George. 'Probably something with my guitar. I might not stick with just music though. I might branch out a bit, do some comedy, write a bit. Try things out for a while, see what fits.'

Jennifer beamed encouragingly at him. If the blonde hadn't been there, she probably would have squeezed his hand. Who could tell? They might have been about to have a passionate, tearful reunion where they'd have gone back to her place and spent the afternoon making tender, searching love. He thought wistfully of her thighs.

'Difficult when you've got bills to pay,' mused the blonde.

'Well people do,' said George.

'Do they?'

'Oh yes.'

'Really?'

'Oh yes.'

'Give me an example.'

'Well,' said George, frowning at a poster advertising yogic flying classes on the wall. 'I mean, take Evelyn Waugh. He spent years trying his hand at painting and furniture-making before it became clear that he had to write. His first book wasn't written until he was 27.'

'Mmn,' said Edward. 'But didn't Evelyn Waugh – forgive me, I know you're the expert – didn't he just take up the writing because it was the family business and everything else he'd tried had failed? Wasn't it a fluke that he turned out to be as good as he was?'

'Well –' said George.

'In fact, if I remember rightly, he didn't even like doing it that much, did he? It was journeywork for him.'

'Mmn –' said George.

'Didn't Evelyn Waugh marry a woman called Evelyn?' piped Jennifer.

George looked at her over the top of his coffee cup. Dear, sweet, pretty Jennifer. He could have kissed her.

'Yes,' he said. 'Yes, he did. Two Evelyns together: Evelyn one and Evelyn two.'

'Wouldn't that be strange?' said Jennifer. 'I'm not sure I'd like it.'

'Just as well your name's not Edward, then, isn't it Jenny?' said the blonde.

George cursed him inwardly. Wasn't that exactly the sort of chauvinistic, arrogant gag that someone like him would peddle? There was no way he could let him get away with it.

'Or George,' he said quickly.

The two of them looked at him. Something strange entered the atmosphere of the room. George blinked. Clearly, the lack of sleep was beginning to tell on him.

'Right,' said the blonde, picking up his bag and glancing at Jennifer. 'Are you ready?'

'Yes,' said Jennifer, standing up to put on her coat. George looked at her.

'You were meeting him?' he said.

'That's right,' said the blonde, dropping some coins into the saucer of Jennifer's cup. 'We're going shopping.'

'Oh,' said George.

'Lovely to see you again, George –' said Jennifer.

'Sober,' added Edward.

'Glad that everything's… starting to work out,' she said.

'Good luck singing for your supper!' called Edward, nodding at the guitar, as he held the door open and Jennifer walked through.

'Bye,' said George.

He watched them go, walking up the street towards the cross-roads, deep in conversation. He saw how it was. He saw exactly how it was: after Emily's party, without George there to protect her, the blonde had made some sort of insinuation to Jennifer. He'd picked up on her love of shopping – for he was clever – and assembled some pretext to see her again. Perhaps he'd told her he knew a good ladies shoe shop or a boutique specialising in bags. And even if she'd smelled a rat, Jennifer would have been too nice to turn him down. She'd have pretended to be pleased about it, made Edward feel that there was nothing she'd rather do on a Saturday morning than go shopping with him. And so she had come to meet him. And now all through today, he'd be oiling around, working his hideous charms. He'd probably buy her things: trinkets and baubles. Tacky little things that would nevertheless make her feel as though she owed him something. He'd lure her into a café on the pretext of another coffee and insist on paying for lunch. And then, as the day drew on, he'd find some reason to bring her back to his flat. He might suggest dinner or tell her she could try things on and look at them in the full-length mirror he undoubtedly had on his bedroom wall. And finally, once she was there, he would shut the door, turn the lights down and start oozing his way in between her thighs. And she, poor Jennifer, would be helpless in the face of it. In fact, she'd probably tell herself that she'd chosen this, that this was her fault, that by arranging to go shopping with Edward in the middle of the day, she'd somehow declared herself available, open and willing. And so he would have his wicked way. And so he might go on having it for many days to come.

George shuddered and put down his cup. Poor Jennifer. He would have to rescue her; that much was clear. He would have to sweep in and show up the blonde in some devastating and masterfully controlled scenario in which he picked apart the pieces of his lying life with all the precision and finesse of a television detective wrapping up a case. He would bring it all out to her. He would bring it all out to them all. They'd be stunned, amazed. And she, she would be so glad and grateful, she'd probably start weeping there and then. She'd probably beg him to marry her, declare a rampant desire to have his babies. And you never knew, he might say yes, after a suitably dramatic and agonising period of walking around on some cliffs, thinking, during which time, of course, she would realise just how dreadful life would be if he turned her down and beg him all the more. Or perhaps he wouldn't. Perhaps he would realise that to commit himself fully to his music and to the many thousands of people who depended on him for inspiration, he would have to live his life alone, only very occasionally indulging in frenzied one-night stands with a series of Russian super-models who had dedicated their lives to supporting his art.

Well, all in good time. First, he had to find somewhere to live and make his name. Simple. He stood up, snatched up his guitar and stepped out into the milky sunshine. He began walking up the street, between mothers with pushchairs and pensioners with sticks. What was it the blonde had said again? Good luck singing for your supper? The arrogant fuck! As though he would need any luck for that! Ha! As though George French needed any sort of fortune to help him on his way! He watched a nervous man lighting a cigarette, his fingers flicking at the lighter, once, twice, thrice. After all, how hard could supporting yourself be? All these people were managing. All these people were somehow getting by. And how much more equipped was he? With his excellent A levels and good degree? There really was no contest. He practically went to Cambridge, after all. They all said he could have walked it if he'd managed to get the papers in on time. They all – two of them at least – said he could have been top of his year. That had to put him ahead in the likely to survive stakes. He stepped aside just in time to avoid a pensioner on a scooter zooming to the post office. Besides, there were plenty of options. There plenty of things he could do which would earn him enough to stay afloat without tying up his time. Looking around at the shops selling exotic vegetables and sari-silk and cut-price electrical goods, at the market stalls and kebab shops with their steamed up windows and peeling signs, there had to be loads of possibilities just in this street alone. Probably, if he popped his head around the door of one of the newsagents, they'd make him manager there and then. It was a thought. But no, he had to be careful. He didn't want to get into all that climbing the ladder nonsense, that playing of the game. That was how they trapped you: making you feel you were on to something, flattering your pride. Well, he wouldn't fall for it. A simple job, that was all he asked for, something to pay his way. He could be a waiter or a shop assistant or a driver for a firm – after all, how hard could passing the driving test be? He could sign up to be a labourer or deliver letters or clean windows. For heaven's sake, he could shine shoes if it came to it! He smiled to himself. In actual fact, there might be something rather fun about shining shoes: doing something simple and repetitive and utterly unchallenging; starting one task and finishing it before moving on to the next. It would free up his mind to think about whatever he chose. After years of sitting at desks, it would be good to be doing something physical, using his body, feeling tired at the end of the day. And it would make for a hilarious chapter in *George French: A Life Worth Living*. The anecdote possibilities were endless.

When it came to it, he thought, turning into a shabby-looking side street, it might actually be rather fun to be poor.

Not for ever, obviously, not for a long time; but for a short while it might be rather stimulating to taste life unsweetened, to struggle and to suffer and to go without brushing his teeth. It would free him up, give him another window on the world. For he, George French, was made of stern stuff. For him it wasn't about the froth and fluff and comforts. It wasn't about breakfast energy smoothies. It was about the journey, the artistic freedom, the soul. Somewhere to hang his hat – that was all he needed. His metaphorical hat, at any rate.

He tried several places. At the first, a shabby end of terrace house with dirty net curtains and a badly spelled letting sign in the window, a series of faces appeared at the door, one after the other, each straining to understand him before waving him silent and going to fetch someone else. At the second no-one answered when he rang. And at the third he was shown in by a confused old lady who seemed convinced he was collecting for Christian Aid.

'I've come about the room,' he said, looking around the dingy hallway, layered with dust and stacked with yellowing newspapers.

'Oh, yes,' said the old lady, reaching for her handbag. 'It's for the Africans, is it dear?'

'The room,' said George slowly. 'You've got a card in the window?'

'Terrible time they're having out there, aren't they?' she said, fumbling with her purse. 'All those flies!'

'You see I'm looking for somewhere to live. A room to rent. You've got a sign.'

'No wonder so many of them come over here. Who could blame them?' she said, picking over the change in her purse. 'I don't mind in the slightest, so long as they get jobs. It's the ones that don't work I can't stand. Walking up and down the high street in fancy dress.'

She pulled out a coin and inspected it, holding it up to the light.

'Is it old money you're after, dear?' she said.

'No,' said George, desperately, 'The room.'

He was becoming conscious of time passing and that, in a few hours, it would be getting dark. A strange, unfamiliar headache was tightening itself around the back of his neck like the grip of a boxing glove.

'Well, here,' said the old lady, holding out a coin. 'There's fifty pee for you. Will that do it?'

'No, really,' said George, backing away towards the door.

'Come on now, dear,' said the old lady, advancing. 'People think because I'm old I don't know what I'm doing. I know what I'm doing. Take the milk money and we'll say no more about it.'

In the end, he had to take the coin and post it back through the letter-box after she'd shut the door. He walked off down the street, shaking his head.

He didn't bother stopping at the next couple of places with cards up. They depressed him too much and the signs looked as though they had been written twenty years ago by people who were probably no longer there. He walked up the path of one house only to turn back at the sound of a large dog, barking behind the door.

Finally, coming to the end of the road, he saw a house with a sign up behind the living room curtains: 'Rooms to let from £40 a week'. It looked newer than the others and he was encouraged by the mention of a price. It seemed business-like, efficient. Without much to compare it to, forty pounds sounded roughly reasonable. He did a quick calculation. If he had, say, £120 in the bank, he'd be able to put himself up for three weeks without earning a penny. And three weeks, well, that was ages. By the end of three weeks, he'd most definitely have achieved something. Just look at how much had happened in the last twenty-four hours! Life could grab him at any time – that much was clear. He just had to be open to it.

He rang the bell. There was silence, then the sound of footsteps heaving heavily to the door. The catch clicked and a face looked up at him.

'What?' said the woman through a mouthful of crisps. The packet crackled as her hand went in for more.

'I'm here about the room,' said George, gesturing towards the card in the window.

The woman craned her neck to see it, wisps of hair escaping from her greasy ponytail and blowing in the breeze.

'What about it?' she said, looking doubtfully at his guitar.

'Well, I'd like to see it,' said George, shifting uncomfortably.

'Like to see it or like to pay for it?' said the woman, narrowing first one eye, then the other.

'Like to pay for it. If I like it.'

'Hmmn,' said the woman darkly. 'We've had people seeing it before.'

She turned and led him slowly down a passageway suffused with a thick, meaty smell, as though a thousand fried breakfasts had been cooked in it and left to congeal. A bare bulb dangled, shedding an orange light, and underfoot the carpet crunched.

'Kitchen through there,' said the woman, waving a careless hand at a closed door. 'Hob free between 10.30 and 11 at night. Don't use the oven.

'Living room' she said, nodding at another closed door. 'Strictly out of bounds. My husband's signed off permanent sick. He does most of his work in there.'

Reaching the stairs she turned.

'If you're not going to like it, you better say now,' she said sternly.

'Well,' said George, 'I can't honestly –... I mean, I'm sure it'll be...'

'Right,' said the woman, turning and addressing herself to the stairs. Muttering obscenities under her breath, she pulled her enormous frame up step by step, using the sagging banister.

At last, wheezing and clutching her crisps, she led George along the landing at the top to a door at the end. She turned the handle and stepped aside to let him through. George went in.

The room was a box room, about two feet longer than its sagging single bed and two or three times as wide. Light fell through a yellow net curtain onto a patch of greying carpet. There was a wardrobe and a tallboy supporting a small television at the end of the bed and a squat little table bearing a lamp. Dust lay thick on every surface.

'I'd say I'd give it a clean,' said the woman, munching, 'But I don't think it's very likely, do you?'

George agreed that it probably was not.

'To be honest, I haven't been up here in three months. Not since the last one popped his cl – er, popped off. I gave it a once over then.'

George looked around the room at the rose-patterned wallpaper faded and flaking off behind the door, at the grey blanket on the bed.

'How did the last lodger die?' he said.

'Natural causes,' said the woman, blinking. 'Such as what comes from putting a rope around your neck and kicking away the stool.'

'Oh,' said George.

He looked around the room again. It was dirty, miniscule and basic. Through the sepia filter of the net curtain, he saw rooftops stretching away and a tower block's menacing bulk. Flies stalked arthritically across the window pane. He shivered. The place was hopeless, godforsaken, the seat of someone else's despair.

'I'll take it,' he said suddenly, shocking himself with the sound of his voice.

'Will you?' said the woman with interest, regarding him over the top of her crisp packet. 'Then that'll be fifty-five a week with a week's rent in advance.'

'It says forty on the sign,' ventured George.

'It says "from forty",' corrected the woman with a fat smile. 'There's a difference.'

George passed a hand over his face. Numbers flashed before his eyes. With a hundred and fifty in the bank, he should be able to do it. And there was always his allowance to look forward to. Not that he wanted to rely on that, of course.

'What about the bathroom?' he said suddenly.
'Where's that?'

'Bathroom's five pounds more.'

'More?' said George. 'How can it be more?'

The woman folded her arms.

'I'm renting you a room,' she said. 'What you decide to do in it is down to you. If you decide to live here and use the bathroom, then you'll pay five pounds a week more. I am not a charity.'

She stuck out her bottom lip and blew away a wisp of hair which was straggling into her eyes.

'Alright,' shrugged George, a desperate, sinking feeling clawing its hooks into him and dragging him down. 'Sixty pounds a week.'

After all, there couldn't' be many rooms worse than this in London, it had to be one of the cheapest.

'Plus bills.'

'Bills?' said George, frowning. 'Bills for what? Surely that's the bill?'

'Bills,' said the woman, sucking in an ominous breath, 'For water, electricity, gas, council tax and sundries.'

'Sundries?' said George, thinking surreally of poppadoms and chutneys.

'Sundries,' said the woman, nodding.

'Well, what do bills come to?' said George, the £150 in his bank account shrinking before his eyes. Perhaps it was closer to £200 after all.

'Hard to say,' said the woman, fishing around in the bottom of the crisp packet for crumbs. 'Can't really tell what things cost until you've had them.'

George shrugged again, helplessly. If this was the price of independence, then he would have to pay it. It was what everybody did after all. Still, it did seem very hard that it should all cost so much. He was surprised people didn't make more of a fuss. They sat around at dinner parties talking about traffic and wrangles at work, sit-coms and politics, when all the time the light-bulbs over their heads and the radiators warming them were eating their hard-earned cash. Even just sitting, watching television, the metre would be ticking, the pennies mounting up. It was outrageous! No wonder people turned to crime! No wonder thousands languished on state benefits! What chance was there for anyone when around each and every single person stood an army of invisible money-lenders, each suing for his pound of flesh? What point was there in trying when the bastards would get their money's worth out of you, one way or the next?

Yet later, once he had paid the money and been given the key and was standing in the room alone, he couldn't help but feel a little proud. After all, he was doing it, wasn't he? He had taken the first step. Let it not be said that George French was lazy, let it not be said that he was putting off life. No longer would he dull himself with easy comfort, blunting his edge on home-cooked meals and bed after the ten o'clock news. No longer would he defer life with vague promises of future achievement, hovering like twelfth man on the pavilion steps in case he was called to play. Here was George French taking the first step on the road to freedom, setting his cap at success. Here he was getting out of the tiresome game, stepping off the manicured lawn and into the jungle beyond. In a little while, in a very little while, he would be famous and known and all this would be no more than anecdote-fodder, stories to tell on *Desert Island Discs*. But for now all he had to do was keep sharp, keep focussed and work on clawing his way to success. And he would start, tomorrow he would start.

He sat down on the lumpy bed and strummed tunelessly on his guitar. See how far he had come. It was almost as though he were living in a poem already: something by Philip Larkin or a piece of Geoffrey Hill's. How artistic his existence had already become! How poetic and impoverished and charming he was! He might even take himself out to dinner tonight as a reward.

6

The woman behind the counter eyed him suspiciously. George shifted and looked down at his rumpled shirt, the grey stains that were starting to appear on his jeans. He'd only been wearing them for five days but already they were starting to lose something of their sharpness and take on a dismal, grubby air, yellowing like the photographs left for years on the window-sill in his father's study, fading in the sun. Sleeping in them probably didn't help but somehow George had been unable to face getting into bed without a barrier between the greasy sheets and his skin. Still, it wasn't too bad; from a distance, in certain lights, he could still cut quite a dash. Only yesterday he'd caught sight of himself in a window coming out of Burger King and, for the merest sliver of time, had mistaken his image for that of a world-worn, jaded rock-star winding down from tour. And it wasn't as though he'd been neglecting his personal hygiene and appearance completely: he'd found a pound shop on the corner and had been getting clean socks from that.

'How much?' he said, nodding at the rows of computers, nervously fingering the change in his pocket – it was alarming how it seemed to diminish by itself, this money that he carried around.

'A pound,' said the woman, before going back to circle another answer in her magazine word-search puzzle. The page bent over the grip of her fingers and George saw that she had already found 'CUP', 'TIN', 'BOUNCE', and 'PEEPLE'. He left the coin on the counter and went to sit at a machine.

There weren't many other customers at this time of day, somewhere in between two and four o'clock, the dead hours of the afternoon. He wasn't exactly sure how late it was, having stayed in bed most of yesterday and as long as possible today so that he could avoid buying breakfast and start the afternoon two pounds up. Looking around, several others had been operating on the same policy. There was a small, dark-haired girl, clutching a bundle of baby and scrabbling furiously at the keyboard next to him. On the screen in front of her ran a long email in a language heavily reliant on j's and c's. It might have been Polish. Every now and then the girl paused to gather her thoughts, all the while yammering quietly to the bundle, which was white and small and peculiarly still.

There was a tall, thin man in a sandy-coloured jacket, hunched over a computer as though to guard it from view. Now and then, when he reached over for the cup of coffee balanced in the little holder at the end of the row, George caught glimpses of girls in leather basques and thongs gyrating on the flashing screen. The picture was grainy, the movement mechanical: a free site. George watched the man bent over it, mouth twitching, and it made him strangely sad.

He shook his head and turned his attention to his own computer, typing in the code and sitting back while he waited for the machine to crank into life. A sinister little counter appeared and established itself in the bottom corner of the screen, flickering with readiness to tick his hour away. George coughed and called to mind what he was trying to achieve: a job; something to remedy the downward trend of his nearly non-existent bank balance; something to buy him the space to pursue his artistic dream; a start. Not that he would need it for long, of course. Already he had made marked progress, lying on the bed in the lodging-house room, fingering his guitar. Yesterday he'd spent a whole hour working out two entirely new chords, bringing his repertoire up to a total of six – not at all bad for someone who didn't even take music GCSE!

And the thoughts that were coming to him! Great long chains of fine-spun gold reeling out of the foundry of his brain –

He paused, scrabbling hastily in his pocket for the notebook and pencil he'd bought yesterday in the pound shop. He must write that down. That was exactly the sort of inspired fragment that was visiting him on an almost hourly basis these days. He'd use it in a song or – for he was beginning to suspect he would do this too – include it in a novel or a ground-breaking play. God, he was so young and there was so much time and he was so fiercely, intensely clever!

He finished scribbling and looked back at the screen. Ah yes, the job. Preferably, it would be inspiring, but it didn't have to be. Preferably low in-put, but, again, it didn't have to be. In fact, he might actually enjoy something with unsociable hours and unreasonable demands, something that would find him sitting in an all-night café at five in the morning, spent. There was scope in that. He would have to be organised, though. There were lots of jobs – all sorts of zany possibilities – and he would be a contender for them all. So he would have to be exacting, demanding, rigorous; he mustn't let his head be turned by gimmicks and irrelevant fripperies. He'd know the right thing when he saw it, it was simply a case of keeping calm and using his hour to the max.

But it wasn't as straight forward as all that. For one thing, the computer he was working on, a grumbling old Amstrad, was painfully slow and he spent many of his precious minutes watching the blue worm growing in the bottom corner of the screen. For another, it wasn't entirely clear where to go to tap into the reservoir of work that had to be out there somewhere beyond the screen. Specific searches, such as 'bizarre jobs, London art' turned up a clutch of irrelevancies, whilst the results of a general search on 'jobs' were largely obscene. After a frustrating twenty minutes, George was still no nearer to getting paid than when he first logged on. He sat staring absently at the thin man, two computers down, who, having finished with the porno-site, was now busy checking the racing results. How did soon-to-be celebrities go about getting that first dead-end job? He racked his brains for examples. The papers were full of rags to riches tales of people getting spotted on the Deli counter in *Saverite* or handing out flyers on the Tottenham Court Road. He could understand the spotted part, but what about the step before that? How did people go about getting that first apparently worthless situation so essential to the biography of every famous person worth their salt? Surely you didn't have to go into places and ask for work? There had to be more to it than that. There had to be some sort of procedure that people followed, some sort of neat job-seeking ritual known to everyone but him. He goaded his mind back to his miserable half-hour with the Latin teacher who also gave careers advice in the musty little Careers Office at school. What was it she'd said again –?

'George?'

He ducked instinctively and looked up. A figure stood above him, dark against the light coming from the street. For one horrible moment, George thought it might be his father, discovered in some hideous double-life in and around the internet emporiums of west London.

'It is you,' said the guy, sliding down into the seat next to him. 'I thought it was. How are things?'

George thought frantically to place the slanted cheekbones, the beaky nose. Was this perhaps a private detective hired by his mother to track him and bring him home?

'Er,' said George, weighing up the distance to the door, 'Alright.'

The guy nodded. His eyes flitted to the screen.

'I didn't know you were a fan,' he said, indicating the picture of pop-star Sheena Sherine arching in pink PVC next to an article entitled 'Dry-clean to Diva-queen', which he'd been scanning for hints.

'Oh,' said George, quickly clicking close, 'I'm not. Just doing research.'

'Funny,' said the guy. 'So am I. What's yours?'

'Oh, you know,' said George, shrugging. 'This and that. Jobs mostly. You?'

He sighed. 'Oh, this ridiculous article on internet cafes and what people use them for.' He shook his head. 'Woeful, really.'

George smiled as everything fell into place: it was Ben, the would-be journalist from Emily's dinner party, the guy who'd been doing that dreary article on plastic clothes pegs.

'Who is it you're writing for now?' he said with a smile. '*Modems Monthly*?'

'No, nothing so thrilling. Just *The Times*, I'm afraid,' he said, making a face.

George nodded in sympathy. The local paper, *The Willesden & Harlesden Times*, was a notorious publication, perpetually on the brink of financial ruin and always scrabbling for news, often far beyond its geographical boundaries. Once, when at school, George had been on a trip into London with a coach-load of boys to watch an open-air play in Regents Park. The whole thing had been hi-jacked by a scruffy little man wearing a mac and waving a press card, who insisted on trailing them throughout the afternoon, asking numerous questions. The fact that he was a hack from *The Willesden & Harlesden Times* who thought he was covering a care-in-the-community trip to London Zoo was only revealed sometime later when one of the boys' parents sent in a cutting complete with a photograph of a group of pupils gurning in front of the bandstand.

George grinned. 'Bad luck,' he said.

'Thanks,' said Ben. 'I suppose it could be worse.' He glanced around. 'Listen,' he said. 'I'm supposed to be here interviewing users and all that nonsense but frankly, well, it's hardly the life and soul, is it? What do you say we cut and run to the pub up the road? I reckon I could cobble something together if you don't mind helping me make some rubbish up.'

'Well –' said George, his mind racing to the ten pound note tucked carefully into the pocket of his jeans. It was Monday. If he bought one pint – just one – he could probably make the rest of it last until Thursday. But then – the thought struck him like a blow between the eyes – what if Ben wanted to buy rounds?

'Oh, come on,' said Ben. He winked. 'I might even give you a mention…'

George looked at him. One pint wouldn't hurt, would it? And it was work after all, wasn't it? Talking to the press?

'Alright,' he said, shrugging – after all, his allowance was due in a week on Thursday and, who could tell, he might be famous by then.

'Good man!' said Ben, getting to his feet.

The two of them strode out of the café, leaving George's pound to ebb away slowly on the computer by the door.

*　　*　　*

The Wig & Bedpan at the end of the high street was somewhat different to the snug, oak-panelled establishments that George had frequented in his student days. Sandwiched between a kebab shop and *BetULike*, the place could hardly claim authenticity or picturesqueness among its qualities. Probably the only thing it had in common with the drinkeries George knew was the fact that it was tucked away. So tucked away, in fact, that, had it not been for Ben stepping off the pavement onto the patch of waste-ground in front of it, George may well not have spotted the pub loitering behind two recycling containers and the remains of a clapped out car. Originally a house, the building had been stripped and gutted, screwed around and tarted up, so that now, leaning giddily against its neighbours, larded with blue and purple paint, it resembled nothing so much as a Butlins' drag queen past his best.

Inside was little better. Posters for Bingo nights jostled with adverts for tribute bands on the walls and the carpet, an optimistic jumble of colours, shapes and swirls, was pocked and ripped by cigarette ash, stiletto heels and gum. Here and there, splinters of broken glass glinted, twinkling as they were caught by the light from the plastic Tiffany lamps overhead, which swung each time the doors opened or a bus rumbled past. Cobwebs festooned the corners and everywhere was the strong, rancid smell of cheese.

'Well,' said Ben, looking around, startled, and catching the barmaid's eye. 'Charming. What will you have?'

'Oh no,' protested George, trying, desperately to think of a way in which he could bring it about that he should only pay for himself.

'Nonsense,' said Ben, tapping the press card protruding from his wallet. 'Expenses'll cover it. 'Specially as you're helping me get my facts straight.'

George caved – after all, it seemed only fitting that *The 'Times* should pay him some sort of compensation for the term he endured having the defaced picture of him by the bandstand stuck to the houseroom wall. He glanced nervously at the clock on the wall as Ben handed over a note. If he could spin his pint out for a close on an hour, he might be able to say he had somewhere to be and leave without buying the next…

He shook the idea from his head: the thought was shabby, small and hollow-eyed; unworthy. Oh well, another week of crisps and bananas it would be then. Joy.

They picked up their drinks and went to sit by the window, through which sickly, yellow light trickled, spilling onto the table and pooling in patches on the floor.

'Well,' said Ben, nodding towards the bar. 'The pub might not be genuine, but there are certainly a few antiques knocking about.'

Over his head, George saw the barmaid watching them, her sinewy arms folded, her beehive rigid, looking for all the world as though she had been put in mothballs some times towards the end of the 1960's and only recently taken out of storage.

'Mmn,' he said.

'So,' said Ben, sipping his pint and leaning back in his chair, 'How's it all going? The book and all that. Evelyn Waugh.'

George stared at him. Had that really been the substance of things the last time he saw Ben? Living at home and that ridiculous notion of a book? God, how naive he must have seemed! How narrow!

'Actually, it's not,' he said. 'I've given it up. I've given it all up.' And then, because the rhythm of his sentences seemed to demand something more: 'I'm going to be an artist instead.'

He folded his arms, blinking. There, he'd said it. He'd told Jennifer and that bimbo Edward and now he was telling Ben. He'd said it again. And it was getting easier each time, like trying on a jumper that was stretching itself to his shape. It felt nearly, almost his. He was particularly pleased with the term 'artist', which was something he'd decided on only a few days before. It was more liberating than simply describing himself as a musician. It had greater scope.

Ben set down his pint.

'Are you?' he said. 'But that's fabulous! What sort of stuff?'

George blinked. 'I'm sorry?' he said.

'What sort of stuff are you going to do?'

George considered. This problem of definition again. How to explain the myriad thoughts and stirrings of ideas that wriggled and writhed in his brain? The perpetual aliveness to possibility that haunted him? Even the word "artist" wasn't large enough to contain the things he felt he could be. And yet people would tie you down. They would have you in a box, assign you a position, slot you into place. Surely this was the very sort of narrowness he must work to change.

'I'm not sure,' he said at last. 'I'm going to do something with music, but there'll probably be visual elements to it as well. And words.' A thought struck him. 'I mean, people are always so obsessed with putting things in boxes, with giving things names. What they should really be focusing on is the ideas underneath, the truth. The way it's done – the genre, all that – is kind of incidental.'

There, there was something in that. He sat back, pleased.

Ben frowned.

'So what you're saying,' he said slowly 'Is that the subject dictates the mode of its expression?'

George nodded. He supposed that was what he was saying, yes. Only put like that it seemed balder and more commonplace than the great internal expansion he felt going on inside his mind. He tried again.

'There's so much world out there,' he said, throwing out his arm. 'Too much for any one of us to process, too much for any one of us to say. It's a question of finding a way of capturing most of it, concentrating it down.'

'So expression is as much about what is unsaid as what is said?'

George gave up.

'Something like that,' he said. 'Anyway, the point is, I haven't decided yet what form my art's going to take. I just know I'm going to do it.'

He took a long pull on his pint before remembering that he would have to buy the next. Across the room, the barmaid took her eyes off them and zapped on the TV up in the far corner of the room. The screen flickered and a leggy, blonde figure appeared, sitting on a sofa, surrounded by a studio audience. At the bottom of the screen were a logo and the caption: 'TV ruined my life'.

'It's terrible,' a scruffy teenager was snivelling into a microphone held steadily by the blonde. 'I don't go out. Don't sleep. I forgot my name the other day when someone was talking to me.'

George squinted up at the blonde as she nodded sympathetically. There was something very familiar about the perfect sweep of her cheek bones, the chiselled poise of her legs.

'It's a common problem,' she was saying, turning confidentially to the camera. 'We live in an age where, more than ever, people are bombarded with –'

She shifted her legs, causing her skirt to ride an inch or two up her thigh, and George twitched in recognition. It was Lucy Thinkwell, the psychologist who had caused such a stir on *David & Trudy*. So, they had given her her own show, had they? Well.

'So,' said Ben, raising his voice to talk above the television. 'Where does the job fit in with all this?'

George took his eyes away from the screen.

'Sorry?' he said.

'The job research,' said Ben. 'Is it for your art?'

'No,' said George. 'Well, maybe eventually. Right now I'm just looking for something to pay the bills.'

Ben nodded as he drained his pint and set the empty glass down on the table. George decided to ignore it for a minute or two. He shook his head.

'The main thing is,' he continued, 'I just don't want to end up like one of those people the other night.'

'What at the Virgin Queen's?' said Ben.

'I'm sorry?'

'Emily,' said Ben, tilting his pint glass from side to side. 'Just a name I have for her.'

'Oh,' said George, 'But she's not... is she?'

'Come on!' said Ben. 'All that posturing and playing with her tits. It's obvious!'

George nodded dumbly. He supposed it must be. To all but him, that was. Clearly this was another of those things that everyone else seemed to absorb automatically, as if by osmosis, whilst he tripped blithely by. Would he ever learn it, he wondered? This art of knowing without being told?

'Still,' he said at length, 'I don't want to end up like any of them. Chasing after money. Playing the money game. From what I've seen, it can turn you into a bit of a cock.'

'That's where you're wrong,' said Ben, tilting his glass at George and squinting one eye, as though he were some American TV sleuth. 'It's not the money that's the problem: they were just wankers to start off with.'

George laughed. It was true: he could remember them sitting, Geoff and that other bloke, roaring in the union, flushed and boisterous after some match.

Right,' said Ben, standing up. 'Fancy another?'

'Oh,' said George, reaching reluctantly for his wallet. 'I should –'

But Ben waved him away. 'Forget it,' he said with a wink. 'Expenses'll cover it.'

'Oh,' said George. 'But isn't *The 'Times* in trouble?'

Ben shrugged. 'No more than usual. Not so bad that they can't stand us a few pints, anyway. Same again?'

George watched Ben go to the bar. He felt a sudden warmth as he saw him dealing brightly with the barmaid, his accents ringing oddly in the damp and dingy pub, not caring – probably not even realising – that when his back was turned she would look at the punter at the far end of the room and take the piss. For Ben, it was perpetual summer in Regents

Park and the rest of the world were picnickers dotted about him, benignly wishing him the best; his life was a never-ending birthday party and he the beaming tot poised to slobber over the cake. George sighed. If only he could throw himself so gamely into life. If only he could buy into it like that, plug away writing articles on lost cats and school fêtes, waiting for the day when a serial killer or local celebrity scandal might give him the chance to make good. After all, it must be nice to believe in things, to look at the system and not be appalled. Even if the ladder led nowhere, it was surely better to be on it, climbing, than muttering in the shadows whilst life slipped by. Better, surely, to be doing nothing than watching it?

And yet, he thought as he watched Ben turn and shamble back across the carpet, eyes fixed on the slopping pints held tightly in his hands, would he really want to step into that world? Would he really want to involve himself in all that again: playing the wide-eyed, eager young thing; racing around the dusty track after the scuttling hare, knowing all the while that it could never be caught? No, surely this was better: to stare reality in the eye and know it for what it was; to see the scenery wobbling; hear the pulleys creaking. At least when the curtain came down at the end he would not be in the least surprised.

'Anyway,' said Ben, setting down the pints and resuming his seat, 'Here's to the artistic dream.' He took a sip. 'And I must say you're looking very well.'

'Am I?' said George, glancing down at his rumpled shirt and stained jeans in surprise. Was it showing already? The glow of artistic freedom? The lightness that came with casting off the shackles of the everyday grind?

'Well, no, actually,' admitted Ben. 'You look pretty ropey, but at least you're in a better state than when I first met you.'

'Yeah,' said George, wincing. 'Sorry about that. I must have seemed like a real prat.'

Across the room, the barmaid eyed them, grimly screwing a cloth around the inside of a dirty glass. George picked up his pint and took a long pull.

'Mate,' said Ben setting his glass down recklessly close to the edge of the table and gesticulating widely with his hands, 'It's not me you should be apologising to. You nearly caused a marital split!'

'Marital split?'

'Well, whatever you call it when engaged people break up.'

'Between who?'

'That blonde guy and the tall, thin girl, the one who looks a bit like a goose.'

'Jennifer,' said George.

'That's the one. Funny nose. Anyway, the two of them had a real dust up after he kicked you out. Took themselves off to the bathroom. Wouldn't let anyone else in for half an hour. By the time they did I was seriously considering following your example with that bush by the front door.'

'But –' said George. 'When did they get engaged?'

'All pretty recent, as far as I know. They were off to get the ring made this weekend. He was talking about it before you arrived. Apparently he knows a place somewhere round here where they do bespoke rings spun out of a spider's arse, or something.' Ben frowned. 'What's the matter? Dodgy pint?'

'No,' said George. 'Just –'

He sat back and stared at the surface of the table, watching glimmers of light flicker on its pocked veneer. He felt nothing, he was only thinking: a collection of random, largely irrelevant thoughts that swarmed around his brain like flies. He was thinking that Ben had had a hair-cut. He was thinking that, from certain angles, the barmaid looked quite similar to someone, a celebrity whose name he couldn't remember. He was thinking that there had once been a fruit machine standing against the opposite wall – the outline was still visible upon the smoke-tinged paint.

'Excuse me,' he said suddenly, lurching up. 'Loo.'

Standing at the urinal, staring into the blank face of the tiles, he called to mind the last time he'd seen Jennifer, in the café that weekend. So they'd been engaged then, had they? Plighted? He'd thought that there had been something between

Jennifer and him that morning, that it had been the two of them against Edward, that third, that bumbling oaf. And all the while, it was the other way about; the kaleidoscope had shifted and the joke had been on him. 'Poor George,' they would have said between themselves, walking off down the road. And one of them would have made some laughing comment about the way he looked, the rumpled state of his clothes.

He dusted off a memory of Jennifer, laughing during a picnic – the only time they had attempted sex outside – and used it to prod at the numb, lumpish mass of his feelings. Nothing happened. The mechanisms of his body continued with their own gurgling processes, untroubled by violent twangs of emotion, unperturbed. So he didn't mind then. No, he didn't mind. Jennifer was engaged and he didn't mind. After all, it was hardly surprising. Hadn't the marriage business been the start of all the trouble with them; the cause of the phone-throwing and the screaming in the street? There was some ridiculous statistic she kept quoting about 60% of couples meeting at university, as though odds alone should dictate their fate. His pointing the idiocy of this out did nothing to deter her. For all her sparkling exam results and stellar dissertations, hadn't this always been the height of her ambitions: to settle down and churn out kids? And women were funny like that, weren't they? Once they got that sort of idea into their heads, once the urge struck, there was no stopping them. If you turned them down, they kept going until they found someone else who would play ball. One man was probably much like another to them: a means to a sticky, nappy-strewn end. So, really, he shouldn't see Jenny's rapid engagement, less than 10 months – 10 months! – after they broke up, as anything personal at all. In fact, he should feel sorry for Edward because clearly the poor bloke didn't realise that he was simply a pawn in Jennifer's game; a stepping stone to a promised land. It all came down to biology in the end. Well, thank goodness he'd got out. And thank goodness he was separating himself from that world of falling in and settling down. Settling. Yes, that's what it was: plumping, like some grotesque cartoon holidaymaker, for a patch on a crowded, pebbly beach instead of walking to the headland and discovering the stretches of white sand beyond.

He went to the sink and winked at himself in the mirror above it, taking in his pallid features, the bags under his eyes. Alarming what missing a meal or two and a few nights in a flea-ridden bed could bring about. Perhaps it was time to give himself a little talk.

Mirror-talks were something that George had fallen into doing when he was very young. In fact, he'd been in the habit of them since his first day at boarding school, when snivelling and homesick in the cold locker-room, he'd realised that his mother hadn't bought him any running shorts. Screwing up his courage in his small, pasty fists, George had steeled himself to brave the cross-country course in nothing but his pants and had scampered out onto the playing fields to whoops and guffaws, his bare legs twinkling in the autumn sun. The episode won him fleeting, legendary status. His name was whispered in the houserooms and muttered on the stairs, and older boys, unused to thinking of first years except in their most private moments, stared at him inquisitively as he walked by.

Since then, George had been in the habit of prepping his reflection whenever facing a task in which he thought his nerve might fail. Before tutorials, meetings and exams; before first dates and last dates and trying to ask girls out; before that fateful interview at the offices of Farrell & Fortune, standing in the glimmering unisex toilets beside a tropical fern.

Now, staring into the small, peeling mirror in the Wig & Bedpan's gents' loo, he set about talking himself into the role of artist. Resting one hand on the dryer, he took a square stance and looked himself sternly in the eye. He found an innocuous place to start.

'You look fine,' he told himself. 'On first impressions – walking along the street, sitting in a café – you could easily pass for a creative person. I'd probably think you were an artist myself.' He glanced down at himself. 'The shirt's good, if a little creased –' He ran a hand along the collar, feeling the textured material beneath his fingers and nodded: the shirt was good. He'd found it in a charity shop in Hampstead and it was vintage and trendy, if a little mad. '– The jeans are fine.'

He flashed himself a smile. 'If anything, the tortured look suits you. After all, it's not supposed to be easy, is it? It's not supposed to happen overnight. And already you're making progress. For goodness sake, you haven't phoned that number and left a message since you walked out of the party all those days ago. That's got to be a sign of something.'

He nodded at himself: it did. Even if the business of avoiding phone boxes was at least partly a money-saving manoeuvre, there had to be some significance in the fact that he was no longer seeking solace in the recorded voice and mumbling his details with that pathetic fledgling hope flapping faintly in his chest. He was no longer waiting on life, that was the nub of it; he was for getting out and making his own opportunities, being go-ahead.

'Now,' here he drew himself closer and fixed his eye yet more sternly. 'The art is the hard part. There's no denying that. You haven't got a lot of experience –' he nodded. He hadn't, it was true: apart from a B plus for a painting of some snow leopards and a passable stab at a Grecian vase, he had little to show for his three years of art lessons at school. '– But that could work in your favour.' Could it? He was fascinated to know how he was going to square this one! 'Because,' he coughed to give himself time, 'You'll be fresh. You won't be bogged down in theory and jaded the way a lot of would-be artists are. You'll see things with an honest, unprejudiced eye. You'll have something new to give.'

George grinned at himself. Of course! He'd be fresh. It all seemed so obvious now. He couldn't wait to hear what he was going to say next!

'Of course, it will be tough,' he told himself, kindly, adopting the tone of the agony uncle who had a regular slot on the *David & Trudy Show*. 'Not only will you have to create your art, you'll also have to mould yourself into the kind of artist you want to be. There will be black days, there will be days of doubt –' he hugged himself. How he wanted those days of doubt! That angst! '– But in the end you'll be the stronger for it. The suffering's all part of the process.' A thought dawned, breathtaking in its simplicity. 'The suffering is the process!'

Brilliant! He grinned at himself again, at his tortured, intelligent face grinning back. This was one of those moments that he should record and remember, store up and save for the future, for when they came to him, begging to know the secret of his inspiration, his extraordinary vision of the world. It was a turning point, a – what was the word they used again? – an epiphany. When he got back to the table he would have to write it down, tell it to Ben. In fact, he thought, rubbing his hands under the dryer's lukewarm dribble of air, it would be rather good to be going back to his seat with something to write down: impressive. Because that was the sort of man he was, the sort of artist. He couldn't be alone for five minutes without an idea bubbling out of his fecund brain. He strode out of the toilets, pushing the door back with a bang. Here he was, an artist, setting sail on inspiration's boiling sea!

Ben was scribbling something when George got back to the table. For a moment George felt disconcerted, stumped, until he saw that Ben was using an old-fashioned flip-pad with an elastic strap for a pen, similar to the ones used by journalists in period movies. Something about it, the earnestness of it, made him smile. Bless Ben. He really was taking it all very seriously, this reporter business. He hoped Ben got a chance to make his way.

Ben looked up as he approached, tucking his notebook back into his jacket pocket. He gestured towards the fresh pint arranged next to George's half-empty glass.

'Are you alright?' he asked.

George looked around, shrugging, as though unsure whether the question was addressed to him.

'It's just –' said Ben, 'Well, there isn't a history, is there, between you and that girl? Because, if there is, I can understand why you might –'

George smiled. He laughed. Were they still stuck on this? This tiny point of domestic arrangement? His soul swam, large and generous, around the dingy room. Here he was considering the world, and Ben thought he was hung up on Jennifer! As though that tiny alliance mattered one jot in the great march of humanity, the great parade of time! As though any of it mattered – his mother's affair, the rejection from Farrell & Fortune – when it was all so ludicrously small, a speck on a pin-head on the notice-board of life! But that was Ben all over, wasn't it? Concerned with the little things whilst the planets revolved unseen, whilst stars died and galaxies collapsed in upon themselves. And thank Heaven he was. Thank Heaven there were people busying themselves with the minutiae of the every day, looking through the microscope at life. How else would the buses run? How else would letters arrive through the post? And how would artists, such as he, find time to sustain their fragile, important thoughts? Bless Ben. Really, bless him. In him was the pattern of the survival of mankind.

'I'm proud of you, Ben,' said George, sitting down.

'Er –' said Ben.

'I mean, I know you probably don't feel as though you've achieved very much so far –'

'Well,' said Ben, 'I wouldn't say –'

'– But you have. You've taken the bit between your teeth and had a go at living. You've busied yourself with things. You've –' he paused. He must be careful. He must not say anything to belittle the path that Ben had chosen, to shudder the scenery of his world, of *The Willesden & Harlesden Times* and all that. And he had been drinking, he must take that into account. ' – Made a go of things,' he ended lamely.

'Well,' said Ben, tapping his fingers awkwardly on the table. 'Thank you.'

'And all credit you,' continued George. 'Because it's a hard world. A hard life. The more I think about it, the more I realise just how precarious it all is. Just how flimsy.' He nodded to himself and sucked on his pint. 'Things aren't straightforward anymore,' he said, warming to his theme, as Ben slid his notebook out of his jacket and fumbled for a pen. Good, he was taking this down. 'In days gone by, people knew what they were going to do. It was all laid out. I mean, take my great-great-grandfather. Now I don't know what he did – don't even know his name – but he was probably a peasant of some kind. And when he had a son there was no question of the son being an astronaut: he was going to be a peasant too. But now,' he gestured expansively, taking in the whole of the pub, 'Now you could be anything or nothing. And nothing leads directly on to anything anymore. Degrees are like…' he searched for an image. 'They're like bombed out staircases, pointing up at the sky, leading nowhere. Like in that novel by Evelyn Waugh.'

He nodded to himself again and picked up his pint.

'Muriel Spark,' said Ben. 'It's actually in a novel by Muriel Spark, *The Girls of Slender Means*.'

'Mmn,' said George, sipping his pint with a wave of the hand. After all, what did they matter, these finicky details? Let the little people look after them. He was on a higher plane, hunting truth to her hiding places, overseeing the world. 'Actually,' he said as he set his glass down, a blast of feeling from his marvellous epiphany by the hand-dryer blowing through him, 'Going back to art and what you were saying before, the more I think about it, the more I realise that suffering is the process. It's what creates the artwork at the end.'

'Uhuh,' said Ben, flipping through the pages on his pad. 'A bit like that quote from Shelley – how does it go again? Oh yes, 'They learn in suffering what they teach in song'.'

'If you like,' said George generously. 'It's about experiencing the difficulty of living and finding a way to express it.'

'Uhuh,' said Ben again, his biro spiralling across the page. 'It must be… very liberating coming to art without much formal training.'

'Yes,' said George, smiling. 'I think it will be.'

And he began to talk, ideas swirling in his mind like water round the plug-hole; sentences grand and lofty, great cathedrals of meaning and sound. He spoke of the ideas that plunged on him as he stood at bus-stops, the urgent, tingling need to express that seized him in the street. He described the sensation of seeing truth in a gesture and the slotting together of beauty from odd, ill-proportioned parts, as a jig-saw takes shape beneath a child's patient hands. Oh his mind was full! He spoke of the meanness of the money-grubbing, pavilion-pleasing game; the narrow little box society would squash him into and sit down hard upon the lid until he couldn't breathe and scrabbled against it, as, all the while, the hoards were hunched there, on top of it, reading the *Sunday Express*! He spoke of those people who would paper over possibility and send visitors round by another route, like a sign he had seen once in a museum, "Exhibit closed. The management apologises for any inconvenience." And there were ushers and little roped off entrances. Great conclusions came because surely this was what it was all about, this business of getting on: bamboozling people; pulling the wool over their eyes; letting them think they were making progress whilst quietly shutting off the exits? All these people – he laughed – all these people who thought they'd cracked it, who thought that successes were falling open in front of them as easily as Christmas chestnuts! Really they were babies, distracted by a dangling bauble whilst Mummy crept silently from the room.

And still he talked on. Sometimes he talked simply for the feel of the words on his tongue, for the satisfaction of reeling out the sentences. And everything he said Ben listened to attentively and wrote down word for word in his little notebook.

7

The poster had said the lunchtime open-mike session started at half-past twelve but, when George arrived ten minutes before, there didn't seem to be anyone around. In all honesty, the place itself was bit of a let down, a bit far removed from what he had hoped. Lying on the saggy bed in the lodging house, hugging his guitar, he had imagined a majestic, sprawling sort of a building, crowned with turrets and adorned with flashing signs. There would be several entrances, and roped off areas, and bouncers with heavy, black overcoats and multiple convictions for Grievous Bodily Harm. Queues to get in would stretch around the block as the punters – edgy, bohemian types probably with nose-rings – waited excitedly for a glimpse of the daring creatures who would be laying their souls bare upon the stage. There might even – although this was probably stretching credibility a little – be a bank of photographers by the door, ready to take pictures of the performers who would almost certainly imminently be stars.

The reality was somewhat different: stumbling through the double-doors of the pub somewhere around the back of Euston station, George was accosted by nothing more menacing than a sign advertising 'Thursday Bingo' where the 'o' had been scrawled into an 'e'. There was a woman hunched behind a table by the entrance, sulkily reading a magazine, and he gave his fiver to her. She took the money without a word and stared at him, jaws chewing lazily.

'I'm here for the music,' said George, clutching the neck of his guitar, hardly daring to utter the words. 'I'm a musician.'

The woman shrugged and looked back down at the problem page, tonguing her gum from one cheek to the other.

George went to the bar and got a pint, fighting down the mixture of panic and excitement which seethed incessantly in his gut. Looking around, he was pleased to see that the mean exterior of the building had been partly misleading. At some point the pub had been extended so that, behind the small, narrow bar in which he now stood, was another rectangular space with a stage at one end. Upon this, he saw with sickening relief, two young guys were setting up to play. Emboldened by the knowledge that he had indeed come to the right place on the right day – itself a considerable feat without a phone, watch or any reliable access to the correct time – he turned to the barmaid.

'What time's the music start?' he said.

'Why?' she said, watching him with a lizard eye. 'Have you got somewhere to be?'

'Oh no,' said George, mustering up a laugh, 'I just wondered, that's all.' He jerked the arm holding his guitar, wishing once more that he had remembered to bring the case. 'I'm here to play,' he explained.

'Hmmn,' said the barmaid, staring at him doubtfully. At last she reached up to a ledge above the bar and, sighing, took down a piece of paper and a pen.

'What shall I put you as?' she said.

'Er –' said George.

'Your name,' said the woman, pen hovering impatiently. 'What shall I put your name as?'

'Er,' said George again, flushing. He glanced down. 'How about *The Guitar-Man*?'

The woman wrote it down.

'You're on at the end,' she said, flatly. 'After *Gut-Wrenching Spunk.*'

George went and sat at a table. Shit. That was stupid. The Guitar-Man? Why did he say that? What sort of a name was that? That was the sort of name you could only carry off if you were an Elvis throw-back busking on the tube or really fucking good at the guitar. And even then...

He sipped his pint. It was watery and sour. The barrel needed changing or the pipes needed cleaning. At any rate, there was something wrong with it. Still; buggered if her was going to take it back, particularly not now he was the sodding Guitar-Man. Jesus Christ. He'd be lucky if he made it out of here with all his limbs still attached.

He shook his head and fought the flush that was rising creeping steadily up his cheeks to the roots of his hair.

Honestly, wouldn't you know it? A solid gold chance to be brilliant and he'd gone and cocked it up. All he'd needed to do was come up with a half-decent name and he'd have had an anecdote made for life. It could have been like one of those stories rock-stars told on *Parkinson*; one of those casual, off-the-cuff reminiscences that mixed humour and bravado to devastating effect.

'Yeah, I was playing a gig at a dodgy pub in West London – first gig actually – and I'd got my guitar and I was all psyched up and I'd even managed to turn up on the right day at the right time –'

'Yes,' Parky would have said with a waggish smile, 'Because didn't you once turn up to a tutorial in the middle of the night?'

'Yeah, actually. But there was a reason. So there I was, all set to go, pint of beer, packet of horrible peanuts, guitar – the works. And then this barmaid asks me' – and here he could have done her voice – ''What name shall I put you down as?' And I didn't have one. So I just said the first thing that came into my head, which was –' and here would be the brilliant name '– And it's stuck with me ever since.'

'Amazing,' Parky would say, sitting back in admiration.

Except he wouldn't. Because instead of saying some brilliant, cutting edge yet timeless thing, he'd gone and said –

George caught the eye of the big bloke in denim by the bar and looked away quickly. Talking out loud again? Shit. Not only was he the Guitar-Man; maybe he was also some weird bloke who sat in the corner holding imaginary interviews with himself? Christ, he was going to have to get a grip if he was going to pull something out of the bag. Seriously. Already he was beginning to wonder whether his idea of refusing to plan what he was going to do until he was actually on stage was really a goer. It had seemed brilliant back in his grey little room, a way of forcing genius, like writing up to an essay deadline at school; but now sitting here, peering through the open doors at the microphones and amplifiers and wires and drums and kit, he was beginning to feel the drift of doubt.

Having spent his last tenner on two weeks' supply of socks, he had been reduced to going into a bank and withdrawing the last dregs of money in his account. This came to £3.92, which the teller passed through to him wonderingly, handling the coins as though they were extraordinary fossil specimens very rarely seen. These he had eked out on chocolate bars, crisps and bananas from the newsagent's on the corner: small things that did not absorb all his fortune at once. Moments of panic descended on him, where he felt himself swaying dizzily on the brink of a huge abyss, but for the most part he was calm. After all, this was all part of the story, wasn't it? The rags to riches tale? And besides, his allowance was due in a few days time; that would help take the edge off things.

In truth, he was quite enjoying cutting life down to the bone, narrowing existence to the barest essentials of what it could be. Astonishing, really, to find how little of life was necessary, how much of what the suited people rushed here and there to achieve was excess to requirements, done purely for the sake of doing. He enjoyed watching them scurrying for the bus-stop and the tube, caught up in the cage of their doing, like hamsters running on a wheels, whilst he, outside it all, was free.

It left a lot of time for day-dreaming. His favourite was his interview on the *David & Trudy Show* – now presented by Trudy alone – where he sat on the famous sofa, pouring out his extraordinary story to Trudy's motherly bosom. She would be overawed and generous, respectful and probably a little bit in love with him in a platonic, unobtainable sort of way. Thereafter he would appear regularly on the show, featuring variously as an expert on literature, youth culture and bonsai topiary as occasions demanded. Sometimes the interviewer was not Trudy, but the lascivious Lucy Thinkwell, swathed in a skimpy red evening dress with a dangerous slit up the side, which, despite ineffectual tugging on her part, kept revealing hints of her suspenders when she moved. She probed him extensively on his development as an artist before moving on to interrogate the psychology of his personal relationships and intimate desires, searching him with her eyes. The end of these interviews was invariably frantic and messy and most certainly not suitable for broadcast on daytime TV. After them, George felt flat and anxious as the euphoria ebbed away and he needed to get out.

He walked a lot. At first he confined himself to the streets around the lodging house, familiarising himself with the high street and its wig shops and grocery shops and barber shops where dreadlocked men carved patterns onto the heads of muscle-bound youths. Later, he struck out further into the city, walking down over the railway lines, through streets of crumbling terraces, to the ranks of white Victorian houses beyond, ranged like wedding cakes along the sides of tree-lined roads. Tower blocks erupted among them like belches in long lines of elegant prose, and beyond the great glass office blocks of the centre reflected the world back at itself, like con-men mirroring their victims' mannerisms before stepping in for the kill. Where several stood together, a hall of mirrors yawned between them: two flatterers locked in an endless war of compliment and denial.

Imagining himself in a gritty, London film, something with lots of close camera-work and shots of alleys, he wandered the shopping streets where people swarmed, faces set, eyes sharp for a bargain. The mass of the crowd ebbed and flowed past him, a huge, organic, living thing. At ghastly moments, the people who milled around him, barging, pushing, speaking into phones, seemed nothing more than vermin, so many blind automatons getting what they could from the world; yet at other times he found a greatness in their existence, their plunging on into the oblivion of the moment to come. There was something poetic about these people living out their lives, weaving their way in and out of buildings that had stood for centuries; claiming them, using them, unconcerned. In another hundred years – less than that – none of these people would be here: an entirely different set would be trailing their way around the streets, eating and talking, sitting at desks, tucking themselves into narrow beds rocked by the shudder of the tubes. The buildings would still be here, yet their owners would no longer possess them. That fat man eating the burger would be rotted into earth, his suit a mass of dusty fibres; that woman with the shopping and the tiny buttocks jerking inside designer jeans would have paid time's debt and sunk to her grave, leaving vintage shoes and jewellery to be picked over by granddaughters with grasping, sweaty hands. Nothing would be owned by anyone here anymore. And yet somehow this handover, this appropriation of property, place and rights, would happen peacefully. The people of the future would come trickling into now and carry off the spoils of yesterday to hand on quietly in their turn. Already it was happening: every minute a child was born and someone whose feet once walked these grey, paved streets, who hands once pushed these doors, was sinking to the stream-bed of the past.

George sipped his pint, a smile spreading over his face. The possibility of beginning something right here, today, thrilled him: it was bold; powerful; startlingly fresh. To get to the end of today with a work of artistic genius already in the bag! Oh, it would be too sweet! He beamed around the pub. To think that this was it, that these were the people who would witness the moment when all those strong, artistic currents that had gripped and tossed him in recent days finally hurled him onto the shores of expression and sent him scampering into the forest of words. It had all been gearing up to this moment on this cold day in February when he, George French, assumed the gorgeous mantle of Art and began to create.

He looked up and caught the man's gaze again, fixed as a harpoon shot between his eyes, pinning him to the wall. He looked back down at the table. 'Stay calm,' he told himself, 'Stay calm. People look at people all the time.' But in his mind he saw all manner of newsreel violence playing itself out at terrific speed and heard the voice of the woman on *Crimewatch* narrating the nauseating tale of his final hours. He shook his head to be free of it and glanced up again. The man had transferred his gaze elsewhere.

He smiled. There: he was fine. He was at a gig and he was fine. At university he'd gone to gigs, oh, several times. Never thought twice. This one was no different. Except that it was at lunchtime. And in an hour or so's time, he would have to play, or speak, or whatever he was going to do. Perform.

He took another sip of beer – it was improving – and sat back comfortably, eyes roving round the room. So, here he was, living the dream. Well, starting to, anyway, he thought, watching a chunky man throw a dart into the wall above the board at the far end of the bar. Yes, it was true, alright: George French was on the move. George was on the way to doing something real and tangible and utterly independent. While his father arranged numbers into columns and shook his head, while his mother checked for commas and apostrophes in documents no-one would read, he, George, would be achieving something, making a name, forging a platform for himself in the world. Even his godfather, puffing cigars in the upholstered silence of his Holborn penthouse, could not claim to have reached the heights George would soar to. Oh, they could reject him if they wanted, they could shut him out. It just made things easier for him. He would not now have to have the difficult conversations three years down the line, when, having set the world alight as a brilliant legal brain, he would turn his back on a career in law, crushing all their hopes. This set-back would be the making of him: the coiling of a powerful spring. And after all, wasn't this what the real world was all about? Taking the knocks and carrying on regardless? Wasn't this life? Wasn't he, as an artist – look at that! See how naturally the word came to him – going to have to learn to live with rejection as one lives with a difficult relative: accepting it and smiling and not minding when it broke his most precious things?

Of course, such recklessness was not for the faint of heart. Such bravery wasn't for them. They would baulk at it, run a mile, like the 'creative writers' at that meeting he'd wandered into a couple of days ago. "Anyone welcome" the sign said, so he wandered in, hugging his cleverness to him, ready to dazzle and amaze. He'd expected to find a collection of unstable creatives lurking in the room beyond, people with hair dyed eccentric colours who smoked roll-ups and sat backwards on chairs, but instead what confronted him was a circle of earnest, bespectacled people, reminiscent of the students who always went to lectures at college and handed in homework on time at school. After sitting for a while listening to them talking in hushed tones about re-writes and pacing, he had ventured a comment about the vitality of the creative urge, only to have one of them, a woman with long, brown hair and a generous nose, turn to him and say: 'Not being funny, but don't you need to have an idea? To write, I mean.' He had left not long after that. Philistines! What did they know about the cut and thrust of creative life, the blind pure urge to express? With all their talk of re-writing and sixth and seventh drafts! How calculating, how cold, how anal in the extreme! He doubted they were even writers at all. They were probably medical secretaries on their lunch-breaks trying to have a crack at art. They probably thought it was glamorous to pass themselves off as writers, to play at literature. Poor, dull, misguided souls! Poor money-grubbers: too frightened to step away from the mindless game; too hobbled to sever the ties of conventionality; too rigid to cast themselves loose on the winds of invention like him! He doubted they'd ever published anything in their lives. And to accuse him of not having an idea! Oh, he had ideas alright! He was brimming with ideas! He could feel them fluttering and growing and deepening within him. And soon, when the time was right – in about half an hour, in fact – the chimes of his genius would strike, the mechanism whir, and the dial of his invention would register the most marvellous display. It was all very –

'Daniel?'

George looked up to see a slim, blonde girl in a purple, quilted coat standing in front of him.

'George,' he said, hopefully.

'Oh, sorry,' she said. 'I'm supposed to be meeting someone and I thought you might be him.'

'No, sorry,' said George. He racked his brain for something he could say to keep the conversation going, but already she was turning to leave. Her eye caught sight of his guitar.

'Are you playing?' she said.

'Er, yeah.'

'What's the name of your band?'

'It's –' he caught sight of 'Gittar-Man' scrawled on the list that had been tacked up on the wall by the bar – 'Just… George French,' he said.

'Cool name,' she said. 'I'll look out for you.'

George smiled and she turned and walked off around the bar to the other side of the room. There. Look at that: already he was making connections, networking; already he had a – dare he say it? – fan. A groupie at any rate. And a very good-looking one at that. If everything went well – and there was no reason why it shouldn't, he was pretty clever after all – perhaps he should seek her out at the end. Unless of course Daniel turned out to be the big bloke in denim and chains.

George finished his pint and looked around the room. There were a few more people sidling in now: skinny, shifty looking characters, eyes turned towards the stage. A thought struck him: perhaps there were journalists here? After all, surely this was the sort of place where new artists were spotted all the time? If he were a journalist, this was exactly the sort of place he'd frequent, eager to be the first to spot the next big thing. Looking at it – at its dingy walls and 'original features', at the sticky tables and battered chairs, at the dartboard around which ham-fisted players were slowly demolishing the wall – it was exactly the sort of place where unschooled talent might take its first teetering steps into the open. A shame, really that he hadn't thought to ask Ben along. It would have made a nice change for him from covering cats up trees and old ladies stranded on traffic islands.

He scanned the room, seeking out the mixture of scruffiness and poise which would denote a writer from the *NME*, a hack from *Time Out*, or, even, a young maverick from *The Guardian*. It was everywhere possible and nowhere obvious. The lanky chap with the satchel leaning against the wall by the door was a contender for a while, until a clutch of spotty teenagers accosted him and it became clear he was still at school; a girl in khaki with a hat at a rakish angle held his attention briefly until she looked at him and smiled; then there was a middle-aged man, lined and greyed with smoke, who seemed to possess an appropriately hackish world-weariness until he opened his mouth to reveal he had no teeth.

George stood up and went to the bar. From there he had a good view and was able to identify several likely targets dotted around the room. Clutching his glass – lime and soda-water this time to help eke out the cash – he made his way over to a group of earnest-looking young men in faded jackets smoking by the window. Standing behind one of them, a small guy with a weaselly face, George pretended to inspect a dirty patch of wallpaper, listening to catch their words.

'The thing about Bowie,' Weaselly was saying, 'Is that he's reinvented himself so many times it's impossible to know who he is anymore.'

'I disagree,' said one of the others. 'The last album was a stunning return to form, a startling new riff on old themes.'

George smiled to himself. Clearly he'd struck gold: these guys even talked in sound-bites. He turned and leaned against the window-ledge, watching for his opportunity to get involved.

'Piss off,' said the first. 'You just nicked that from the quote on the back of the CD!'

The others laughed. George laughed too.

'Yeah well, what if I did? It's only there because someone said it.'

'Yeah, Jules, that's *some*one. Not a runting little nobody like you.'

George joined in with the laughter again. If he was clever about it, perhaps he could swing the conversation round to Dylan and then work his own stuff in? He caught the eye of Weaselly and looked quickly away.

'Can I help you mate?'

Shit. George looked back and smiled. It was at times like this that he really wished he had a fag. He wouldn't look at all odd if he were simply smoking a fag.

'No, you're alright,' he said in a strangely Northern accent.

'It's just, you've been standing there a while. Is there something you want?'

'Erm,' said George. Oh well, now or never. 'I was just wondering,' he said, 'If you might have a spare fag?'

Great: not only was he a weirdo, he was also a scabber.

'Sorry mate,' said the guy, stubbing out his half-smoked cigarette and reaching into his pocket for another. 'I'm completely out.'

The others laughed.

'Right, well, thanks anyway,' said George, and turned away.

Let them laugh. They weren't to know that they had one of Britain's most creative and promising artists in their midst. They weren't to know that he was thinking so far beyond them that such insults barely penetrated his consciousness. Christ, he better be good today.

A chord struck up from the other room, followed by a clatter of drums, and people started to move through. With a sinking feeling, George went to pick up his guitar. He was suddenly afraid that they might be very good, these boys who had spent the best part of an hour tweaking knobs on their guitars, and angry at himself for feeling that way. He edged through into the back recesses of the room.

The first song unrolled itself slickly, the voices of the boys intertwining to form patterns on the even canvas spun out from their guitars. In the middle, when the red rat-a-tat of the rhythm guitar eased off, ushering in a blue mood, the other boy picked up a saxophone, spattering the room with squiggles of sound. High notes, low notes, brash, guttural blurts and then, at last, the mournful melody creeping in, dragging its widow's weeds, alone.

The next act was even better, and worse. She was girl in her late teens, dressed in a skimpy white sack of a thing that collected over the lean curves of her breasts to fall to the middle region of her thighs. When George saw the leers spreading on the faces of the men ranged about the room, he hoped that perhaps here was a performer with only limited and obvious talent. But it was not to be: from the first wild whoop the girl uttered down to the last plaintive moan, she held the audience captive, causing even the most persistent of the gawpers to close his eyes now and then to savour the purity and freshness of her tone.

But it was the third act that really set alarm bells ringing for George. Desperate by now to see someone lowering the bar a little, he was relieved when a little bespectacled man in a torn shirt clambered onto the stage. Here, at last, surely, was someone who *The Guitar-Man* could show a thing or to?

The little figure did not disappoint. From the first tremulous chord, it was clear that the music industry would not be moving over for *Uncle Paul*, as he had billed himself. Trouble was, the audience knew it too. The introduction of the first song was barely played out before the heckling started, with voices rising quickly to drown out the strains of the guitar. A feral mood entered the room. Around George, jaws clenched, fists tightened and eyes glinted. Up on stage, the little man played gamely on, but the audience was having none of it, working as one to silence him. The feel of the place reminded George of a documentary he had seen once about the gladiatorial fights in Ancient Rome and the way the crowd turned at the first sight of blood, baying for the kill. He left the room and escaped to the toilets shortly after someone lunged forward and sloshed *Uncle Paul* with a pintful of beer.

Locking himself into the disabled cubicle, George stared at his reflection in the mirror above the sink. He sought frantically for the comfortable words, that vein of casual wisdom that usually saw him through at times like these. But there was nothing. The best he could come up with was some mutter about the audience not being the right sort of crowd and even he wasn't buying that. Panic shot through him like lightening cracking along his nerves. Christ! What had he been thinking, coming here with his three-quarter size guitar and his five and a half chords? Did he really think he'd get away with playing some nonsense to the crowd out there, those hard nuts with their skinheads and 'HATE' and 'FEAR' and 'MUM' tattooed on their knuckles? (He'd seen this on some bloke who stood next to him at the bar and for some reason it had been the most terrifying thing of all.) Fuck! Those bastards would eat him alive!

He took a deep breath and found that he was shaking. Well, one thing was clear. He wasn't playing here today. Oh no. Not for a million quid. Not for a record deal and – Well, maybe for a record deal but not for anything that was going to happen to him in that room right now. It was a no-brainer. *He'd* be a no-brainer if he didn't get out of there sharp.

He unlocked the cubicle and stepped gingerly out into the room beyond. There was no-one around. He breathed again. It was alright. He just had to stay calm and slip out while they were all looking the other way.

Stepping out into the corridor, he noticed that the pub beyond had gone quiet. The uproar was over then. Well that was good. Maybe the blonde girl had come on again and they were all back gawping at her. He hoped so: it would set the wind fair for him to make a clean get away. He pushed open the door.

'There he is!' called a voice.

Heads turned to look. In the midst of them, George saw the barmaid pointing triumphantly in his direction.

'The Guitar-Man!' she announced proudly, as though she had just solved a crime. 'Come on,' she beckoned to George. 'You're up.'

'No,' said George, waving his hands in front of him. 'Really, I –'

'Oh go on,' said the barmaid with a crocodile-like smile. 'It'll be fun.'

'Yeah, go on!' called another voice.

'You only live once!' piped up a third.

George considered. Perhaps he could have a crack at it after all. Who could tell, it might prove the making of him. Maybe this was the moment when all those hidden oceans of feeling surged up into one great crashing wave –

Then his eye fell upon the girl in the purple coat, standing looking up at him with big, beseeching eyes. The thought of her watching him whine and strum about the stage proved too much.

'No,' he said firmly. 'I really can't.'

'Oh go on,' they implored, bulging towards him now.

'No,' he said, backing away into a large figure, which let out an unfriendly noise.

From somewhere, a hand arrived on his shoulder.

'Really,' he said with a nod calculated to imply that if he had seemed to be ribbing them earlier, he was now in earnest.

The hand on his shoulder tightened its grip. Hands were coming at him from all directions now; flailing, seeking a purchase. Christ, what did they think he was? A bundle of bargains in the Boxing Day sales?

There was only one thing for it. Gripping his guitar, he lowered his head and ran. Careless of chests and stomachs, of groans and gasps and elbows jabbed into him in return, he charged bull-like through the mass of bodies towards the door. There it was, trembling with the passing traffic, daylight glinting through the glass. He was nearly there, nearly free of these hands that gripped and grasped at him, these nails. He surged on, straining, his arm reaching out to slam through the wood and glass and out in the air beyond.

He touched the door, could feel it giving before him, when – disaster! – something snagged around his foot and instead of the final stride he felt only chaos and free-fall and the tipping point of the roller-coaster. Helpless, George fell, smashing face down onto the concrete steps beyond, the world blanking, but not before, sailing over his head, like some great misshapen goose, he saw his guitar soar out into the lunchtime sunshine and land under the wheels of a bus.

8

George frowned and then winced as the bruised skin around his eyes contorted, making his face a mask of pain. He read the blinking message again: 'Insufficient Funds'. Christ! If there were insufficient funds, why didn't they just fill the thing up with cash from the other side of the wall?

He winced again and fought back the silly, irrational urge for tears. He was not in the mood for this today. He had not been in the mood for much, in fact, since the guitar incident, when, coming to on the steps of the pub, he found that, rather than rushing to his aid, the hundred or so punters at the gig had simply stepped over him and pissed off home. Back at the lodging house, he'd even discovered a footprint placed square in the middle of his back. The only person who had shown him any sympathy at all was his landlady and that had been of a most fleeting kind.

'What? Mugging was it?' she said regarding him through the banisters as he slunk up the stairs to his room.

Mutely, he indicated that, yes, it had been that, or at least something as bad, something equally traumatic.

'Hmmn. There's a lot of it about. Have a Wotsit.'

She thrust the packet at him and watched as, lower lip trembling, he selected a crisp and popped it into his mouth. It was his first food of the day.

'Rent's due on Thursday,' she observed.

He inserted his card again and went through the familiar steps. The screen flickered through its phases, each message following the next, until, as George reached out to take his cash, it flashed up once again the ominous "Insufficient Funds".

George flinched. A seed of doubt, insubstantial as dandelion fluff, blew into his mind and stuck. Surely the insufficiency couldn't be more to do with him than with the machine? The message stayed flashing on the screen, relentless. He thought quickly, but no, it was impossible: it was the third Thursday in February; his allowance should be in.

He looked again at the screen, hoping wildly that the message might have changed. It remained the same. What then? Should he try the process one more time? Perhaps it would throw up a different result if he pressed the buttons softly, asked for a different amount of cash? He tried, insanely glad for a moment as the machine hesitated before flashing up the tyrannous "Insufficient Funds".

Behind him, a queue was beginning to form. People coughing and shuffling, evidently annoyed. He thought again: it was the 17th of February; it was a Thursday; his allowance should be in. The logic was impeccable, each statement necessitating the next. Why then was he repeatedly running up against this brick wall? He looked around suspiciously. Was he the victim of some elaborate practical joke? *Trigger Happy TV* or that show that used to be on – what was it called? – *Beadle's About*. Perhaps, any minute, one of the people standing behind him would rip off a latex mask to reveal himself to be someone familiar – Noel Edmunds, perhaps – holding out a plastic award? He strained his eyes for the sight of cameras poking round corners or reflected in the windows of the shops across the street. But there was nothing: only the large, reddening face of the man waiting immediately behind him, a most un-show-biz sight.

'Look mate,' said the man, meeting his eye. 'Not being funny, but it's not a telly. Stop fiddling with the buttons and let the rest of us get on with our lives.'

Inside the bank, George did his best to put on his credible face. People tended to look suspiciously on you, he had found, when you were covered in bruises, as though you were not the victim but the aggressor, liable at any moment to lash out. By the time he got to the front of the queue, he had already taken against the woman behind the counter, a thin, pouting girl with giant hoop earrings and hair scraped back. There was something about her manner, the way she stamped forms and scribbled names and stared busily at the screen, that suggested she enjoyed nosing into other people's affairs, particularly when they were difficult and involved. He would have to bypass her, he decided, and find someone more suited and able, someone less likely to smirk at his plight and with the authority to sort things out.

'Can I speak to a manager?' said George, stepping forward to the counter as the last customer, a fat woman in a monstrous track-suit, picked up her bags and sloped off.

'Why?' said the girl lazily, chewing a gobbet of gum.

'Just –' said George, reigning himself in as the rippling frustrations of the morning gathered themselves into one tidal wave. 'Look, just get me the manager, please.'

The girl stared at him as, with one bony, manicured finger, she indicated the "Manager" badge on her lapel.

'Oh,' said George with a start. He stared at her uneasily. She couldn't have been more than twenty years old.

'How can I help?' said the girl with a pinched, missish little smile and a disdainful glance at his clothes.

George's fingers tightened on the edge of the counter. If only she knew! If only she really knew what he thought he was going to be!

He leaned closer and said quietly, 'I was expecting some money in my account today and, well, it's not there. And without it –' A ghastly void yawned before him. '– I'll be stuck.'

'Hmmn,' said the girl. She took his account details and brought up the information on her screen. 'Hmmn,' she said again. 'No, it's not there.'

'Well, where is it?' said George, all sorts of possibilities of fraud, theft or error careening through his mind. Wasn't this the sort of thing they were forever warning you about on the news? He made a quick mental note of the bank manager's build, the colour of her eyes.

'Direct debit's stopped.'

'I'm sorry?' said George.

'The direct debit,' said the girl slowly, taking the gum out of her mouth as though to make the meaning doubly plain, 'The thing that was putting the money in your account every month. It's been stopped.'

'But, but, that's not possible!' stammered George, leaning across the counter to try and get a look at the screen. The girl angled it further away from him.

'Well,' said the girl, yawning – evidently his predicament was small fry to her – 'That's what's happened. Now, is there anything else I can help you with?'

'But that means I've got no money!' spluttered George.

'Actually,' said the girl, 'It means you've got less than no money. You're overdrawn by thirty pounds and ten pee.'

'But,' said George, hands flailing as the world tilted crazily around him. 'I don't… I don't –'

'Have an overdraft facility?' suggested the girl. 'No, that's right. That's why we charged you thirty pounds when you took out three pounds and ninety-two pee with only three pounds and eighty-two pee in your account.'

George gaped.

'But I thought I had ninety-two!' said George. 'The cashier said I had three pounds ninety-two!'

'You must of misheard,' said the girl with a shrug. 'Shame.'

George gaped again.

'And I should advise you,' continued the girl manager, 'That there will be further charges should the money not be repaid within twenty-eight days of withdrawal and that interest on the money will be charged.'

George blinked. In his mind interest had always been something that banks paid to you. It was obscene to think of it working the other way round.

'So hang on,' he said, gripping the counter and holding himself straight. 'You've charged me –'

'Thirty pounds.'

'Thirty pounds because I went over my limit by –'

'Ten pee.'

'Ten pee. And now you're going to charge me until I pay you back.'

'That's right,' said the girl, as though talking to someone unusually slow.

'Well, but hang on, said George. 'Isn't that a bit unfair?'

'It's the rules,' said the girl with a shrug.

'But,' said George, 'I haven't got any money.'

The girl shrugged again, jangling her earrings from side to side. 'Not our problem,' she said.

George stared. Surely it was their problem? They were a bank, after all, weren't they? Surely money or the lack of it was their business, the bread and butter of their days? He was their customer. And they, they had robbed him.

George glanced around quickly. Did other people realise that banks did this, he wondered? That they robbed people blind? That they came and took their money in the night? Yoked them up to unasked for obligations? Bled them slowly dry? It was outrageous! He couldn't let them get away with it. Something must be done.

He opened his mouth to speak.

'Next,' said the girl, smiling pleasantly at the man behind George in the queue.

'Now hang on,' said George, stepping forward again. 'I'm not finished.'

'Look, sir,' said the girl, her tone a masterful mixture of boredom and deference, 'I've explained the situation to you. The direct debit has been stopped. If you want to know the reason for that I suggest you speak to the person in question.'

'Ha!' said George. Speak to his father when it was they who were robbing him, they who were plunging him into crippling debt? A likely ploy! A diversion tactic of the first order! But they hadn't reckoned on who they were dealing with. They hadn't realised that they had someone of his intellect on their books: George French, an artist of quite extraordinary insight. The little people might not be able to defend themselves, but he would not be thrown off!

'But you've stolen my money!' he shouted loudly, looking around the bank. 'You've robbed me blind!' He noted the hush, the awed silence that fell over the customers. There were astonished – moved – to see someone fighting their corner, someone making a stand! Any minute now they would shrug off the shackles of their down-trodden lives and rush to join him and it would be like a scene in one of those great, epoch-making films: *Braveheart* or *Sparticus* or *Shrek*.

Someone coughed.

'Calm down, sir, said the girl patiently.

'No!' shouted George – God, he was magnificent, wasn't he? – 'I won't calm down! I won't let you get away with this…' He rummaged for a word large enough and cutting enough to stop the known world in its tracks, 'This skulduggery!'

Yawning, the girl reached beneath her desk and pressed a button. A moment passed, during which the cougher, wheezing, was forced to go out, then a burly man in a forbidding black uniform appeared from a side door. George sized him up. So he was for it, was he? His neck on the line? Was he afraid? He probed his feelings. No. This was the fight he'd been waiting for for, well, all his life, it felt like. Brain versus brawn. His moment to do something extraordinary. God, was he ready!

He opened his mouth to speak but before he got a chance, the security guard grabbed him by the shoulders and began marching him towards the door. George struggled.

'Unhand me!' he shouted, blinking as he heard his voice: strained and ridiculous, like something out of a black-and-white film. What was it people normally said in these situations? Let me go? It sounded a bit weak. What if he tried growling and swearing and looking mean?

But it was no good: there was nothing he could do against the iron grip of the security guard dragging him to the door. After a moment, he stopped fighting it. So they were arresting him, were they? Well, let them! What did he care? Wasn't he already mired in ruinous debt? What more could they do to hurt him? He would go down fighting! He would start a one man campaign to expose the machinations of banks from behind the prison bars! He would call it: Campaign Against Banks! CAB! Yes! He could see himself now, holding court on the evening news, speaking to a cluster of microphones and a cheering, banner-waving crowd. 'Free

George French!' the slogans would read 'Down with banks!' Sod music! Sod art! He didn't really like galleries anyway. Clearly this was the method by which he would make his mark; clearly this was the way he would rise to fame and earn his place on Trudy's couch. There were so many glamorous possibilities! He could style himself as the maverick celebrity who spoke his mind, could carve out a career as an after-dinner speaker and aficionado of panel shows. He could even – here was a thought – become a sort of columnist-cum-presenter figure, building on his controversial beginnings to become known as a witty commentator on current affairs. Who wanted to be an artist when you could present *Have I Got News for You*?

The security guard bundled him through the double doors and out onto the steps of the bank. George squinted and raised one hand, ready for the cold clasp of hand-cuffs, the flash of paparazzi bulbs. He writhed for the cameras as he was manhandled down onto the pavement and deposited, finally clasping his hands and raising them in a gesture of mute appeal. He opened his eyes in time to see the broad back of the security guard retreating up the steps. He glanced quickly around, wide-eyed and staring. There was no-one in the street except for a handful of shoppers, a *Big Issue* seller and a beggar going through a bin.

'Er, hang on,' he called as the security guard reached the door. The man turned. 'Well,' George coughed. 'Aren't you going to get the police to arrest me?'

'Why?' said the man, looking at him narrowly, 'Are you a criminal?'

'Well,' said George, flapping a hand in the direction of the bank – there was a term for what he'd done, wasn't there? Something along the lines of... 'Creating a disturbance?'

The man looked between George and the bank and chuckled. He lumbered back down the steps. George steeled himself, ready for the pull of rough hands, the ride in the police car between two sneering officers. He was not afraid.

'If you ask me, mate,' said the man, patting George gently on the arm. 'What you need's a doctor.'

So saying, he turned and walked back up the steps. George watched, gaping, as the heavy wood door closed behind him. Unbelievable that they could let somebody create a nuisance like that and then do nothing about it. He could have been anybody! He could have been some nutter! And they just let him get off scot free! If he'd been in the bank under other circumstances – paying in a cheque or whatever else it was people did – and someone had behaved like that, he'd have wanted them dealt with. Taken out and taken away – no messing about. But instead they'd popped him outside the door and left it at that. Worse, they'd made a joke of it! Telling him he needed a doctor! As if that great oaf knew anything about it when he was clearly on illegal steroids himself – had to be to get muscles that size. The whole thing was a shambles! It couldn't be allowed. He'd put in a complaint! Write to the MP! Or, better still, he'd start a demonstration right here, this minute! That would teach them to leave potential nutters wandering around loose on the streets!

He opened his mouth to shout and his stomach growled. On second thoughts, why didn't he go and get some breakfast and then come back and give them what for? He'd be much more formidable with a plateful of bacon and eggs inside him and there was a café over the road that did a mean fry-up for only three pounds. He'd had his eye on it all week. That would set him up. That would make him equal to anything the bank clerks could throw at him. His mouth started to water. Oh yes! He could certainly spare three pounds of the allowance money to –

Something lurched in his chest, shuddered, and broke, sending the implications of the last half hour flooding coldly through him. The allowance money hadn't come through, had it? There was no money for breakfast. There was no money for anything at all.

He felt quickly in his pockets, cursing himself for the extravagance of previous days. He had ten pee – what that all? Yes, ten pee between himself and ruin. It was nothing at all. It was about as much good as a spider's web to a man falling off a cliff. Oh why had he bought that extra chocolate bar, that lottery ticket, instead of just going to bed? How foolish to pin all his comfort on the hope of his allowance coming through! He saw himself as he had been yesterday, tripping down the aisles in the newsagent's, picking out his favourite brand, throwing in a packet of crisps on a whim. What a clueless, mincing idiot he'd been! How pathetic! How naive!

As if rebelling of its own accord, his stomach, which had been grumbling away to itself for several hours, seethed and surged, sending a wave of hunger through his frame. God, he was going to have to get some food soon! If only he could think of something. If only he could make a plan! But try as he might, his brain kept returning to the idea that he should buy something and then remembering that he couldn't, like a goldfish swimming round and round its bowl.

He looked frantically up and down the street. The day was continuing much as it had before: people going here and there, babies crying. Extraordinary that it should do so, that things should just carry on, when he stood here, starving. Starving. The word sent shivers through him and he sat down suddenly on the cold steps of the bank, his breathing ragged. He needed to think. He needed not to panic and he needed to think.

He caught sight of his reflection, small and distorted, in the shop window across the street.

'Don't panic,' he whispered to himself. 'You're fine. You're not the first to be hard up. Don't panic.' An old lady with a shopping trolley trundled past, looked at him, and carried on. 'You'll find a way,' he told himself. 'You're determined, you're young and' – this old chestnut again – 'You're very clever.'

He hugged himself. Strange how that knowledge wasn't as comforting as it had once been. What did it really mean after all? That he could turn in a decent essay on *Paradise Lost*? That he understood the true definition of "dramatic irony"? What use was that in this world of deposits and jobs and getting enough to eat? He searched back inside himself for that feeling of calm assurance, that glowing self-pride that had come now and then from the admiring smiles of teachers, the tutors' enthusiastic words. They had told him on the strength of his Waugh dissertation that he would go on to achieve great things. Really, he couldn't see why they should think so: it was like expecting a champion show-jumper to excel at crazy golf.

He glanced up and down the street. Money. What was it people did when they wanted money? A blue and white sign swam into view. Of course: the Job Centre! Why spend hours blundering about the internet when there people paid to fit him out with a job? Probably if he went in now they could get him a good six hour shift for this afternoon – certainly plenty to buy a meal. Silly of him not to think of it before!

He went in and waited impatiently in line on an expanse of stained carpet, before a bank of windows. At last the buzzer sounded, and he bounded forward to the third booth along. He opened his mouth to launch into the list of his requirements – something part-time, undemanding, relatively decently paid – just as the figure behind the glass exclaimed:

'Jeremy Fairclough! In the name of sanity! What are you doing here?'

George peered through the dirty glass and made out the features of his former tutor, Dr John Worthy, beaming from behind the counter. He was thinner now and stubbled round the face, but it was still unmistakably he.

'Er,' said George, blinking. 'I might say the same about you. What are you doing here? Aren't you supposed to be teaching?'

'What, at the ulcer?' said John Worthy with a wave of his hand. 'Oh no, they kicked me out. Something about living in the room. A ruse if you ask me. They spotted me as a maverick the day I arrived, they'd been trying to do away with me since then. Word of advice: whatever you do, try not to stand out too much – most people are appallingly badly equipped to deal with difference.' He picked up a pencil and, fumbling, broke it in two. 'But you,' he said. 'Weren't you supposed to be a successful author by now and working on your second book? What was your subject again? Evgeny Kissen?'

'Nearly,' said George. 'I gave it up.'

'You look awful, by the way.'

'Oh,' said George, staring into John Worthy's blood-shot eyes. 'Do I?'

'Mmmn,' said John, gnawing at a hangnail. 'Atrocious. What have you been eating?'

'Well, not a lot,' admitted George. 'Actually, that's why I'm here: ideally I'd like to find some kind of job.'

Blue-tacked onto the counter window was a poster showing a man beaming behind the wheel of a London bus. The slogan read: "Give a man a fish and you feed him for a day. Teach him to fish and you involve him in a declining and poorly rewarded industry. Be smart: drive."

'Ah!' said John his face brightening. 'I've got just the thing! Been wanting to try it all day!'

He turned to a battered computer on his right-hand side and began to press buttons, his hands trembling. On the grey metal cabinet behind him, George caught sight of the little wooden trophy that must have come once from his old school and made its way through car boot sales into his ex-tutor's hands. So he had brought it with him then, this last remnant of that grubby little room. Funny the things that people held onto when everything else was turning to shit: passengers sitting in the first class lounge of the Titanic, grasping their tea cups as, around them, tables slid and skittered and smashed into the walls.

'It's a job-finder programme!' continued John Worthy excitedly, the reek of whisky coming and going on his breath. 'I ask you lots of questions and it assesses all the answers and then tells you what you're most suited to do. The Swedes swear by it.'

'The thing is,' said George, 'I've already got a sort of long time idea about what I want to do. I'm going to be some sort of celebrity-artist. What I need is money. Pretty fast. Sort of straight away, if we're honest.'

'Still,' said John Worthy, eyes fixed excitedly on the screen. 'Better to find something stimulating, wouldn't you

say? Why stack shelves in Sainsbury's when you could be a…
I don't know… a mental health nurse?'

'But I don't want to be a mental health nurse,' said
George.

'Just an example,' said John Worthy beginning to type.
'Now, what's your favourite colour?'

'Er,' said George, aware of time passing, aware that
now there was only time for him to work a four or five hour
shift today. 'Is that relevant?'

'Of course it's relevant,' said John nodding vigorously.
'You wouldn't want to be stuck in a work environment with
the colour you hated, would you? Particularly with you being
an artist. It might kill the muse stone-dead!'

George shrugged. 'Er, blue?' he said.

'Light or dark?' said John.

They went through a range of questions, some
personal, some trivial, some openly bizarre. George reflected
on his childhood, his friendships, and his attitudes to restricted
parking and Sunday opening hours. At last, clicking a final
button, John Worthy sat back with satisfaction and
pronounced:

'Mental health nurse!'

George frowned. 'But I've already said I don't want to
be a mental health nurse. I've already said that. Anyway,
doesn't that involve a lot of training? I need money now.'

'Not as much training as you might think, actually,'
said John Worthy, stroking the stubble-growth on his chin,
'But still, I see the problem. Mmn.'

'What are the other options?' said George.

'Oh there aren't any other options. That's it. Mental
health nurse. That's your dream career.'

'But it isn't,' said George.

'You say that now…'

'No,' said George firmly, 'It isn't.'

'Well,' said John Worthy, raising his eyebrows. 'The
computer's not usually wrong. But if you insist, we could
always run the test again.'

'Well, alright,' said George. 'But is there some way you could make sure it rules out any of the caring, nursing-type roles?'

'There's a 'not comfortable with disabled people' box,' said John Worthy. 'Do you want me to tick that?'

'Well,' said George, 'It's not that I'm not comfortable –'

'Well, you must be a bit, mustn't you?'

'No, it's just that I –'

'Do you want me to tick it or not?'

'Alright,' said George sighing, 'Tick it.'

At the window next to him, a large woman was shouting angrily at the red-faced clerk. The room was starting to feel prickly, hot and oppressive. George was beginning to regret coming in. Not least because, sitting here facing John Worthy, was unsettling his thoughts. He kept catching his mind free-wheeling off along the tracks of a parallel reality, where he was a hard-working post-graduate student who would shortly be going home for his supper. His stomach rumbled at the thought of his mother's shepherd's pie and he had to think very firmly and coarsely about what he saw going on in the kitchen to make it stop.

John ran the test again and sat back to wait for the result, drumming his fingers on the papers strewn over his desk. At last it came:

'Mental health nurse,' he announced again, proudly.

'But that's ridiculous,' said George.

John shrugged. 'It's what it says.'

'Are you sure this isn't just some ploy to encourage more people into nursing?'

'Well, there are shortages,' admitted John. He leaned forward. 'Look, I tell you what, have you thought about looking out for those cards in shop windows? That's often a great way in.'

'Or,' said George in exasperation, 'I could just go and get a job presenting the *David & Trudy* show. What about that?'

John Worthy blinked. 'Well, if you –'

'Oh forget, it,' said George.

He rolled his eyes and stared beseechingly at the little wooden trophy propped up against the back wall. Would it ever come again, that moment of vision, power and clarity? That pure concentration of potence, opportunity and execution? Even now he could feel the warmth of the sun on his face, the easy swing of the bat, the thump of hands commending a job well done. He was capable of greatness. He had done it before, he had achieved it. Then why could it not come again? And come quickly, because now he was getting tired.

John Worthy caught his gaze.

'What, this old thing?' he said, glancing behind him at the squat little block with its arrow soaring to the sun. 'You'll laugh, but this is probably my greatest achievement to date. My only achievement some might say.'

George frowned and looked at him, nonplussed.

'How do you mean?' he said.

'Old school, you see,' continued John Worthy. 'Cricket match. Never much of a player myself. But then one day, standing at the wicket, ball comes in and' – he clicked his tongue to make an approximation of the noise of leather on willow – 'I hit it over the boundary and away for a six. Marvellous feeling. Superb. If I'm honest, nothing has ever been quite as good again. Still,' he sighed, 'I'd sell it to you for fifty quid if you think you could give it a home.'

He stared intently from behind the glass and George was alarmed to see moisture gathering in the corners of his eyes.

'No,' said George, edging back in his chair. 'Really, I –
'

'Twenty,' said the ex-tutor.

George shook his head, panic gripping him round the throat.

'Fifteen. It's real mahogany, so I'm told.'

'No,' blurted George, standing up.

A dizzy feeling was upon him, sickness washing in and out. He felt as if at any minute the room might swivel, shrink or stick him like a mammoth sheet of flypaper, leaving him twitching, faint and mired; unable to get free. He stared down at the faded man looking up at him from behind the glass with sad, imploring eyes, and was reminded of a programme he had seen once about Battersea Dogs' Home and the six month rule. Nausea bloomed. Without another word, he turned and strode gasping from the room, past the leaflets and the posters and the phone booth by the door.

The street outside felt cool and welcome and he gulped in the city air. He walked quickly, his brain pulsing. Nightmarish visions swung on the chandelier of his consciousness: himself trapped forever in a never-moving queue; himself sprawled in the gutter whilst the wheels of traffic thundered by; himself in twenty years' time, whisky-sodden and wizened, fumbling at a keyboard in a dank and airless room... The image of the trophy swam before his eyes and he wretched. To think! To think! Was that what it came down to then? Was that where he was headed? Sitting behind a smudged glass screen, waiting to be claimed by life? Sinking slowly into incoherence? Surely not! Surely that wasn't him?

He stood for a moment at a pelican crossing, feeling his pulse rate subside. A cooler, calmer drift of thought washed in. No, no, it was alright. Because that sort of finish, that sort of decline came – surely? – only to people without any sort of aim or goal. Without any sort of direction. And he had direction. Christ did he have direction! He was heading – striding! – out of the mindless, soulless game! He was radical, utterly radical. That was the thing. No wonder there were moments of doubt: he was blazing a trail across a dark, uncharted galaxy; he was – no point being coy about it – a pioneer! Such black times came to all revolutionaries: Jesus Christ, Mahatma Gandhi, Ian Botham... the list was endless. But he would have to be careful; he would have to listen to himself more, stay alert, if he was going to last the course. He was quite possibly a genius and like all geniuses, he must be nurtured, protected and – this was crucial – not rushed.

He walked on through the winding streets, enjoying the pavement, firm beneath his feet: a foundation. Really he'd been expecting a bit much of himself lately, driving himself too hard. It was time he cut himself a bit of slack. Probably he was barking up the wrong tree pursuing this idea of work in the first place. After all, with all this worrying about where the next meal was coming from, there was no way he could focus on bringing out his art. That was the real trouble: here he was, a creative genius, beset by nagging trivialities when really he should be living and breathing truth. He shouldn't know what day of the week it was. Let alone be scrabbling around trying to find a job in *Burger King*! Whoever heard of such nonsense? Whoever heard of great art among the onion rings? No, what he needed was some means of income which would let him fix his mind on what really mattered and leave the world to itself. He needed a patron. That's the way these things always used to work, that's what made it happen for people like Michelangelo and Keats. A patron. Where was he going to find one of those? He thought quickly, but the prospects weren't great: none of the people who presented themselves were either approachable or likely to say yes if they were asked. Most sympathetic people he could think of were celebrities and there was no reason why they should listen to him. They probably received letters from nutters every day of the week. How were they to know he was the real deal? Besides, he didn't have the money for stamps.

Patrons. Come to think of it, you didn't hear so much about patrons these days. What was it people did instead? His brain idled for a moment, an engine lacking the clutch's bite. Then it came: grants, of course. He'd get a grant. There had to be loads available for someone like him, someone of his calibre. There always were, weren't there? School had been bursting with them: prizes for creative writing; bursaries for art; fee reductions for the boy in each year who could throw the hunting cane   an ancient piece of wood said to belong to the founder of the school – furthest. There'd even been a Gap Year Honorarium for the senior boy who wrote the best essay about where he intended to spend his year abroad. The money was meant to defray the travel costs, but, by long tradition, it was usually spent in The Artichoke, or 'Choke as it was affectionately known, buying drinks for everyone who had gone to the trouble of writing the essay without managing to scoop the prize. Surely the world beyond would be no different? It was simply a case of knowing where to look. And there were things available, weren't there? Arts prizes and, oh, the Arts Council! They gave grants to anyone and everyone nowadays, didn't they? People making sculptures out of plastic bottles and rubbish of all sorts! Good Lord, they were probably sitting in their offices, praying for someone like him to put in an appearance! Probably if he turned up in person they'd give him the money right away. Well, that was that sorted then: he'd get on to it as soon a possible, put in an application at once.

He walked on. Very lucky, really that John hadn't turned up anything of interest. Just think! He might have been sucked back into the world of work by the backdoor. He might, even now, have been typing up his CV! Horrors! Wasn't that just what they would have loved to see – his parents and godfather and the whole vol-au-venting lot of them: George bound into a faceless, decent job; dutiful; plodding. Good Lord, how he hated them! Well they would see the truth of it. He'd get the funding and his brilliance would be revealed. And then he'd make art about them too! Ha!

And stopping his allowance too! That was just the pits, wasn't it? That was too much. As though they could just shrug him off like a piece of cast-off clothing. As though they could duck out of their responsibilities when the going got –

Suddenly, a thought struck him. What if the stopping of the allowance was a mistake? After all, it was hardly likely that his parents would leave him stranded, was it? Alright, so he'd left the party a bit suddenly and hadn't been in touch since, it was hardly extreme was it? He'd heard of people doing much worse. And they'd be horrified – wouldn't they? – if they knew he was destitute and homeless (well, nearly homeless, certainly homeless if he didn't find some money quick-sharp) wandering the streets. If they could see him bruised and beleaguered, misunderstood. It would be the last thing they'd want: their only child, their first-born, hungry and out on his ear! Christ! It was nearly two o'clock and all he'd had to eat today was his thumbnail!

It had to be a mistake on the part of the bank. He had heard of such things happening before: when he was at school a boy had found his allowance mysteriously stopped and had to rely on writing post-dated cheques to his friends for cash. It eventually transpired that his father had mixed up his direct debits and accidentally cancelled the one to his son instead of the one to his tailor. This had to be something similar. Not that George's father had a tailor, but George was sure there must be other bills that he paid. He watched a woman with a buggy stop and bend down to adjust the seat-belt across her daughter's chest. Perhaps if he went to see his father it would all be sorted out and then George could get himself on an even keel, have space to think, and embark on his extraordinary future.

He nodded to himself. The way was clear: he would go and see his father. Of course, it would rather spoil the grand gesture of walking out and returning a self-made, unconventional success but, after all, you had to be realistic about these things. Rome wasn't built in a day. And he wasn't one to spoil the ship for a ha'p'orth of tar. Oh no, let it never be said that George French was too proud to ask for help!

He set off along the street, weaving his way between pensioners and truanting teenagers defiantly sucking on menthol cigarettes, trying to look cool. He smiled. Really, it would be rather big of him to put in an appearance; to face up to his failings and admit he couldn't do it all on his own. More than that, it would be a kindness: letting his parents see that he still needed them, that he accepted them for all their foibles and faults, their nagging fits and affairs. When he thought about the scene in the kitchen now, the hand on the arm, the whole thing seemed overwhelmingly drab: two faded, middle-aged people seeking for a bit of excitement and the odd fumbling caress amidst the grey grind of their lives; an undignified weakness that others were best to ignore, like someone picking away at the leftovers in the kitchen after a family lunch. And so what if his father knew? Probably he did, but didn't mind. Probably that sort of thing was neither here nor there once you reached a certain age. Well, George would let him see that it didn't matter to him either, that none of it mattered: he was big enough to look beyond it all. He congratulated himself as he pressed the button at a pelican crossing for his generous-spirited, liberal mind.

Actually, he thought as the lights changed and he began to walk, he supposed they might be rather worried about him. After all, he had walked out with no word of where he was going; had left them without their only child, bereft. They must have been searching. They'd probably reported his absence to the police. For all he knew, they might have appeared, tearful and drawn, on the national news, appealing for any information. He could be a minor celebrity by now without knowing it. He looked quickly around, but there was no flicker of recognition on the grim faces of the people trudging by. Still, they'd be beside themselves, wouldn't they, his parents? Distraught? Asking themselves over and over where on earth they went wrong? Good Lord, the poor things were probably half-mad with grief. Well, he would come to the rescue. He would pay his father a visit in his office and gladden his poor, sorrowing heart. Really it was the least he could do.

9

The walk across town took less time than expected. Funny how quickly the streets flew by when he knew where he was heading. In no time, Old Street station was behind him and he was weaving his way through the back streets beyond, navigating easily by the landmarks learnt as a boy: the crumbling Victorian fire station at the crossroads; the general store with the hand-written sign "Please wipe your feets" still hanging in the window; the battered iron sculpture of a dog that he used to imagine came alive at night; the red phone box on the corner with its peppering of call-girl cards. Little had changed, though it had all somehow shrunk and faded as though it had been run through a photocopier and reduced to three quarters of its size.

Before he knew it, he was in the little cobbled mews, standing in front of the light blue door in the dumpy building that, as a boy, he had been convinced must harbour a nest of international spies. He rang the bell and listened. There was silence, then the sound of clicking heels. It would be Carole, George remembered, his dad's frizzy-haired secretary. The last time he had seen her was when he did two weeks' filing work at the office in the summer after his GCSEs. He had sat in her small beige-tinged office with its carpeted walls and window looking out onto a blind, brick wall, and sorted papers into alphabetical piles whilst she leafed through magazines, typed up his dad's letters and asked him now and then whether he had got a girlfriend. Two weeks had been enough. Having exhausted the novelty of earning his own money, George returned to his customary position on his parents' sofa and resorted to asking his mother for 'loans' whenever he wanted to go out.

Now, hearing Carole approach, he straightened his posture and fixed his "parents' friends" smile on his face, a cross between his new boy's beam and his prefect's simper, guaranteed to please. He held it as the door opened and the secretary's face appeared, framed on either side by an unruly mass of permed hair. Six years had passed but you wouldn't have known it to look at her: she still had bright orange lipstick round her mouth and on her teeth and a large, improbable bow clipped to the side of her head. For Carole, life was a scratched record, stuck perpetually on the same phrase, at a school disco back in 1985.

'Yes?' she said, taking in George's dirty clothes, the bruises and unkempt bristles on his face.

George adjusted himself and simper-beamed again.

'Did you want to see someone?' said Carole in a pinched, nasal voice.

'George French,' said George, holding out his hand.

Carole backed away from it.

'No-one of that name here,' she said uneasily, glancing behind her as though planning her escape.

'No,' said George, 'I'm…' He stopped. Better perhaps to save the moment of recognition for his father. It would be a shame to have to go through all that joy and disbelief twice.

'I mean Geoff French,' he said. 'Geoffrey French. I'm here to see Geoffrey French.'

Carole looked at him.

'Are you sure?' she said.

George looked around. 'Er, yes,' he said.

'Wait there.'

She shut the door and trotted up the hall. George heard her footsteps on the stairs and the sound of a banging door. He stepped back from the doorway and gazed up at the building's tattered face. After a moment, he was disconcerted to find his eyes met by his father's staring down from the window above. Geoff French looked at him for a moment or two, and then turned away into the room. George blinked. It was hardly the moment of joyful return he had expected. Still, shock affected people in funny ways. And it must have been an emotional rollercoaster of a week for the man. Or perhaps his father didn't recognise him either? It was entirely possible: he'd barely recognised himself on a couple of occasions when he caught sight of his scruffy figure reflected in the windows of shops and buses he walked past.

The door opened again.

'George!' joshed Carole with a giggle in her voice. 'Why didn't you say? I didn't recognise you!'

'Er, well –' said George taking a step towards the door.

'The fashions these days are… distracting, aren't they?' she said, glancing again at his clothes. 'Anyway, come in. He's waiting for you. I think he'll behave. But if he's naughty you tell him Carole says he has to be nice. After all, you're only young once.'

George followed her into the hallway and shut the door. The smell of the place – musty, stale and tinged with new carpets – engulfed him, drawing him unsettlingly back to the memory of those two weeks spent shuffling papers and listening to Carole's voice. As he followed her climbing the stairs at the end of the corridor after she had cracked her old 'The only way is up' gag, he had to remind himself that he was twenty-two now – a man – and not simply about to slip back into that bleak routine of staring out of the window and slipping off to masturbate in the loo. Those days were gone.

Carole opened the door to his father's office and stepped back to let him through. It closed behind him with a click.

Geoff French was sitting at his desk, staring intently at his steepled hands. Around him, the room was just as George remembered: shabby, airless and untidy. There were the old filing cabinets with papers piled on top; there, the chipped and mug-ringed desk with its solitary photo of George and his mum; there, the dusty yucca plant, and, behind it, the window with its view out over semi-derelict warehouses to the forest of tower blocks beyond.

'It's me,' said George after a pause, staring at the dents in the carpet made by the chair that had been on his side of the desk. Someone had moved it recently to the far corner of the room.

'Yes?' said his father, still staring at his hands. A muscle flickered on his jaw.

'I've come,' said George, 'To say that I'm alright. And to say that there's been a mistake.'

His father glanced up.

'A mistake?' he said.

George looked away, suddenly awkward. Things were not going according to plan. Surely this was one of those prodigal son moments where his father should be gathering him in his arms? Surely, seeing the state of George's clothes, his wallet should already be out, proffering cash? Hell! He'd been away for nearly a week! He'd been without his mobile phone! Was he really going to have to lay out the whole boring business of the cash machine before his father would offer him any help?

'With my allowance,' he said and winced.

God, it was a messy business, this issue of money. Talking about it was the worst. There was something sordid about saying that this was the way you lived, that this was what you needed to survive. It was like opening your mouth when you chewed, showing the workings of your teeth with the food: something better kept out of sight.

'What about it?' said his father, returning his gaze to his hands.

'Well,' said George, 'It hasn't gone in. There's no money in my account.'

'Mmmn,' said his father.

George frowned and tried again. 'There's no money in my account. And, you see, that leaves me in a bit of a hole.'

'Yes,' said his father, folding his arms in front of him. 'I suppose it does.'

'So –' said George and stopped. He met his father's steely glare. 'Look, aren't you even a bit pleased to see me?'

'Why should I be pleased to see you!' stormed his father suddenly. 'Give me one good reason why, in God's name, I should be at all pleased to see you!'

George stepped back, disconcerted that such a large voice could come out of his small, combed over father.

There was a knock and the door opened.

'Tea?' said Carole, nosing through. She held out a tray bearing two mugs and a plate of Custard Creams.

'Thank you,' said George's father, gesturing towards the cabinets on the far side of the room.

They waited whilst she bustled over, behind wiggling, and deposited the tray. At the sight of the biscuits, George's stomach growled.

'Look, the thing is –' he said, after Carole had shuffled out, bobbing and shutting the door.

'No, George,' said his father, 'This is the thing: you behave appallingly badly, you drag the family name through the mud, and now you come here expecting a hero's welcome, demanding money of all things! It beggars belief.'

George blinked. Dragging the family name through the mud? What was this? One of those appalling costume dramas full of significant looks and genteel intrigue that Jennifer used to be obsessed with? Surely no-one talked like that anymore? And besides, what had he really done? Broken a wine glass and gone AWOL for a few days? Hardly anything to write home about! In fact, surely Emily had upstaged him in the shock-stakes? Standing in the hallway with her bazookas on display? Why wasn't his father angry about that?

'Look,' he said uneasily, 'If this is about the party –'

'Oh the party,' said his father, waving the words impatiently away, 'I couldn't care less about the party!'

George frowned and fiddled with the grubby hem of his shirt. On the edge of his field of vision, the plate of Custard Creams hovered, basking in a golden, biscuity glow. Perhaps it was time to try a different tack?

'Look,' he said, his voice quavering suddenly, 'I came because I thought you'd be worried. I thought you'd be out of your minds! Your only son disappearing! I came here to put your minds at rest.'

He nodded, it was true. The money had nothing – well, very little – to do with it: he had come here to lift the burden of sorrow from his poor father's frail old shoulders. Out of the corner of his eye, he saw the biscuits loom closer. God, he could almost taste them: the yielding crunch of them; the sweet, creamy filling smooth on his tongue.

'How thoughtful of you,' said Geoff French with a dryness George had never heard from him before.

George blinked again. Was this really his timid father, then? The man with a liking for county cricket and kedgeree? The man who thought driving round the Hanger Lane gyratory system was an adventure?

'Well, yes,' said George uncertainly. 'Because, you see, you haven't known where I've been, what I've been doing –'

'On the contrary,' said his father. 'I know exactly what you've been doing.'

'You do?' said George, glancing uneasily around him. For the second time that day, he had the unsettling feeling that this might all be some great, grand televisual hoax and that any minute an orange-tinted host might pop out of one of the filing cabinets, brandishing a microphone.

'Yes,' said his father, opening a drawer and pulling out a newspaper folded open at the centre page. He chucked it towards George. 'You've been lounging around West London, spouting nonsense to journalists about being artistic and misunderstood.'

George bent down and picked up the paper at his feet. It was *The Times*. The headline glared at him: "**Art for art's sake? Ben Miller meets one of the many arts graduates struggling to get on the career ladder post university.**" Above it was a half-page picture of George smiling blearily at a pub table, a pint glass tilting crazily in his hand. He couldn't even remember it being taken. Bewildered, he stared at the headline again. Ben Miller, Ben Miller. Hold on, wasn't Ben Miller the guy from Emily's party? The one he'd met in the internet café? The one who'd taken him to the pub? And all the while he'd been writing for *The Times*? Well.

'I thought it was for something else,' he said blankly. 'I thought it was a piece on internet cafes for the local paper.'

'Evidently,' said his father.

George stared back at the page. Phrases leapt out at him like written reproaches: "Despite a good degree from one of London's top universities, George French's ambitions seem to consist of nothing more than a yearning in the general direction of art, a yearning which he is reluctant to define. 'A fish doesn't become any more fish-like because you tell it it's a fish,' he mumbles into his pint"; "French smiles and fumbles for a parallel between himself and his erstwhile literary hero, Evelyn Waugh. 'We're very alike, Waugh and I,' beams French, 'So much so, that I sometimes wonder whether there might be something in reincarnation after all.'" George winced. God, he hadn't really said that, had he? What else? His eyes scanned the page but already his mind was furnishing him with a wealth of excruciating statements all circling around his paternal desire to protect Ben from the hard realities of the world. Hadn't he made some appalling speech about how well Ben was doing, about not undervaluing himself and sticking to his guns? And all the while Ben had probably been thinking of his next sumptuous journalistic lunch, his next interview with one of the great and the good. God, he must have sounded like a berk. The word 'poncey' came dancing unbidden into view and he pushed it hurriedly away.

He glanced up with a nervous laugh.

'Makes me sound like a bit of a twit, doesn't it?' he said.

His father picked up a pen and turned it awkwardly in his fingers.

'You've also,' he said, with a quick glance up at his son's face, 'Been going around telling people your mother's having an affair.'

George stared back down at the page. He hadn't blurted that out as well, had he?

'Not there,' said his father. 'That Emily girl told your mother you'd mentioned it to a friend. She thought it might be the reason you hadn't been home.'

George thought: Jennifer. Of course. He should have known: the network, women talking. Still it was true, wasn't it? There was definitely something going on.

'But she is!' he said. 'Sorry, Dad, but it's true. I saw them in the kitchen, her and Robert. They were all over each other.'

Geoff French coughed.

'What exactly did you see?' he said.

'Well, she was crying and he had his hand on her arm and –' He stopped.

'Bob's your uncle,' said his father.

George started, surprised by the flippancy of the phrase. Surely you'd take learning of your wife's infidelity more seriously than that? Still, we all dealt with shock in different ways.

'I know,' he said, shaking his head sadly. 'I mean it just all seemed to fall into place –'

'No,' said his father. 'Bob – Robert – is your uncle. Your mother's half brother. If you want to accuse anyone of anything, try your grandfather.'

'But,' gaped George, 'Why –'

'– didn't we tell you?' completed his father. 'Well, because we didn't know ourselves. No-one did. Not until your grandfather wrote Bob a letter last week, laying it all out. He said he wanted to be sure of everything, be straight in case anything happened to him. He'd had a fall a few days before that shook him up.'

'But why did he keep it secret?' persisted George. 'Why hold it all back until now?'

His father sighed and put a hand to the knot of his tie. 'They were both married to other people at the time. They made sure Bob and your mother knew each other, stayed friends, but things were different in those days: formal. I suppose they thought it was for the best.' He coughed before continuing: 'Funny, really, but it goes some way to explain the affinity he's always felt for you. Helping you on, paying for you at school –'

George started. 'He paid for me? But I got a scholarship, didn't I? An assisted place?'

His father shook his head. 'No, that was what we told you. Actually, Robert paid.'

'But why tell me that? Why lie?'

'Because,' said his father with a snort, 'We didn't want to put any pressure on you. Didn't want to make you feel you owed anyone anything. Unfortunately, it seems to have worked rather too well.'

George stared down at the paper held limply in his hand. The floor seemed to tilt crazily beneath him. Why was everything so complicated? Life seemed a continuous dance in which people were forever changing positions and associations, realigning themselves like colours in the kaleidoscope: look away and the picture was utterly different when your eyes returned. First Jennifer and Edward, then Ben with his job, and now this: his mother and the uncle he never knew he had. And in the midst of it all, himself: the golden child that never quite was; the understudy thrust into the leading role; the boy who never measured up.

'Anyway,' said his father, shifting in his seat. 'That was why you saw… what you thought you saw: your mother crying and all the rest of it. That, and the fact that Bob was offering to pay for you to publish your book himself, to help you along.'

'Oh,' said George, flushing.

His father looked up at him, standing, twitching in the musty room.

'Look, the thing you've got to understand, George-boy,' he said, softening, 'Is that it was all done with your best interests in mind. All done to give you the chances I never had, the choice.'

George rolled his eyes, anticipating the old story of his father's father's illness, Geoff's having to step into the breach at the firm when he was only sixteen years old. Funny how when he talked about his life, his father always made it sound as though he'd never had a choice, as though everything he'd done was because of other people, as though life was something that just happened to him which he was powerless to change. George hoped he'd never be like that. Mind you, he thought as his stomach growled and his eyes crept once more to the biscuits on the side, he probably wouldn't have a chance to be much of anything if someone didn't give him some food soon.

His father was still talking.

'I wanted to be a lawyer, you know,' he was saying, his eyes staring at a spot on the ceiling as, in the sky through the window behind his head, a plane dipped and circled and appeared to vanish into his ear. 'I wanted to –'

'Look, Dad,' he said. 'I didn't get the placement anyway. Farrell & Fortune, Robert's firm, they turned me down.'

'I know,' said his father.

George blinked and glanced down at the paper. Had he told Ben that too?

'I asked Robert not to accept you. He said they would have been happy to but I asked him not to.'

'Oh,' said George, bewildered. 'Why?'

'You seemed so caught up with your book, your other things. I didn't want you to feel you had to accept out of loyalty or duty or anything like that. Perhaps I was wrong.'

'Oh,' said George, his mind whirring to try and order the mass of thoughts and impressions that circled it like bees around a hive. He stared down at the page. 'Did I really call all the guests at Mum's party "cultural dinosaurs"?' he said.

A glimmer passed across his father's face.

'Look,' he said. 'Why don't you just come home? Come home and sort yourself out.'

George thought for a moment: home, hot showers, his bed! The smell of his mother's Spaghetti Bolognese! His stomach growled again and he was no longer able to resist stepping across and helping himself to a Custard Cream. He could hardly help groaning as the biscuit crunched and spilt itself on his tongue. God, he'd needed this!

'You could sign up for another post-grad course,' continued his father, with mounting enthusiasm. 'Go back to working on the book.'

George paused, mid-chew. The prospect of returning home bore down upon him: endless ranks of days spent staring at the walls, lying on his bed, wading his way through daytime TV; watching himself shrink and shrivel back into his schoolboy self; the narrowness of it all. What greatness could be found among his mother's ornaments and the smell of *Kitchen Fresh*? He stared down at the carpet. Its pattern danced before him: squares striped with black lines; prison bars; cricket stumps. He was being sucked back into the game. If he went back now he would be running and diving for the polite applause of the pavilion crowd in no time, wearing the uniform of the city, bowing to the umpire's flailing hands. He sighed. No, if he went back now, it would be the beginning of the end.

He looked squarely at his father, noting how thin his hair looked against the milky light of the sky.

'Look,' he said, 'Are you going to give me any money or not?'

'George, George, George,' sighed his father over steepled hands. 'Didn't they teach you any manners at that school?' He turned his head and regarded his son narrowly out of the corner of one eye. 'You're not on drugs, are you?'

'No,' said George. Clearly, his father had been reading the *Daily Telegraph* again.

'The Christians haven't got you, have they?' mused Geoff.

'What?' said George, horrified. 'No!'

'Hmmn. Is it a girl? You haven't got a girl into trouble?'

'No Dad!' said George. 'Anyway they don't call it 'getting into trouble' anymore.'

'Oh? What do they call it?'

'How should I know? Anyway, the point is, I'm not any of those things. I'm going to be an –' he glanced down again and caught sight of the picture of himself leering over the table in the pub, eyes sodden with the romance of art. Had he really looked that much of a twat? '– A sort of creative celebrity,' he said.

'Like Rolf Harris?' suggested his father.

'No!' said George, his hands clutching the air, clawing for something to say, some pattern of words that would flick the catch of his father's understanding and set him free to roam off and become great.

'And how are you going to afford to do that?' said his father.

'There are grants,' mumbled George sulkily. 'The Arts Council.'

'But,' said his father in the maddening, nit-picking way in which he always corrected spelling mistakes and split infinitives in items on the news, obsessed with small details, 'Surely you need to have done something to get a grant? They don't just hand them out to anyone, you know.'

George rolled his eyes. Didn't his father think he would have thought all this through? Didn't he think he would have got it all worked out? What kind of a fool did he take him for? After all, he was nearly a genius, wasn't he? Hadn't he got a schola– … well, hadn't he got in to a very good school? They were going to have to trust him.

'I'll make it work,' he muttered.

'Mmmn,' said his father. 'Is that why you're standing in my office asking for money?'

There was a silence during which exasperation boomed between them, a noise outside the range of audible sound turned up to screaming pitch.

'Look, George,' said his father, sighing. 'I'm on your side. We all are. Your whole life, we've tried to give you opportunities – tried to shield you from being forced into anything you didn't want to do. That's why we paid for you to go to university, that's why we sent you to a good school. We wanted you to have choices.'

He picked up the pen again and began passing it from hand to hand, the gilt ring around its middle glinting in the light. It was the one George had given him for Christmas, picked hurriedly off the shelf in WH Smith half an hour before the shops shut on Christmas Eve.

'But choices are only as good as what you make of them,' continued his father. 'And now it's time for you to decide. I'm quite happy for you to come home while you sort yourself out – I hope you will – but I'm afraid I won't be subsidizing your enjoyments anymore. I can't keep footing the bill for your swanning around.'

George gritted his teeth. So that was what they thought, was it?

'Enjoyments!' he spat. 'Swanning around! You just don't get it, do you? You haven't been listening to a word I've been saying! This is my choice! This is my life! This is what I'm going to do!'

'What, exactly?' said his father.

'Ugh!' exclaimed George. He picked up another Custard Cream and chewed furiously on it, glancing around the office as he munched. So narrow! It was all so narrow! So horribly precise, this little room lodged above the great yawning warehouse where the paper lay stacked in great, blank piles. You could die here, you really could.

His mouth was dry and sandpapery with crumbs, rubbing his ulcers and irritating his swollen gums. He didn't even have the money for a toothbrush! He reached for a mug of tea and sipped it, but it had gone cold. Even that would not offer him the consolation it should. He banged it down, slopping the liquid onto the tray.

'Look,' he said again, irritated to find a tearful quaver in his voice, 'Are you going to give me any money?'

His father regarded him.

'No,' he said at length. 'Quite frankly, George, your coming here, demanding money after the way you've behaved. After all we've given you. Well, it's rude, it's childish…' he met his son's eye. 'I'm afraid it's just not cricket.'

George's eyes flashed.

'Exactly!' he cried. 'Exactly! Thank God, *thank God*, it's not cricket!'

And with that he turned and stormed from the room, barging past Carole in the cramped corridor, down the stairs and out into the street. He walked quickly until he reached the main street and stood on the corner next to an overflowing bin. How dare he! How dare his father try to blackmail him like that? Offer him food and a bed in return for selling out, for crucifying his artistic soul! Surely this, of all times – the crux of all George had worked towards, the moment at which he spread his wings and unfurled his glorious self – was the point at which they should be doing most to spur him on. They should be standing on the finishing line roaring and waving scarves as he went steaming past. But instead they wanted him to creep home with his tail between his legs, like some naughty teenager caught drinking cider in a park. Well, he'd got them now, hadn't he? Caught them out in all their pedestrian greyness, circumscribed the narrow margins of their lives, their obsession with the rules. The way they'd shaped and moulded the truth, as though he was their toy, their creature to train and direct as they chose! God, it was appalling! He'd rather the affair than that; would rather catch them out in some seedy, suburban love triangle than face this web of superior posturing and truth-sculpting! And now they would not help him. His parents and his so-called uncle, they were going to leave him to go it alone; to manage all this for himself. All the rest of it, the schooling, the funding through university, the post-grad fees, they had simply tumbled into his lap unasked. But this, this one thing he was asking for, this one bit of help, they would not give.

The cold wind barrelled down the street, slapping him with the frigid truth: they were jealous, that was the crux of it. They wanted him to succeed but not too well, not so that he left them grovelling in his dust, trailing far behind. They would help, but only so long as they remained in control. Beyond that, he was on his own.

There was a half-eaten sandwich resting on the bin beside him and he picked it up and bit into it angrily. He was hungry after all and what was dirt? Just some squeamish middle-class invention trotted out by people like his parents to make everyone else afraid to really start to live. He munched fast and stared around the street. Surely this was the moment for the mysterious stranger to appear? The person who'd been following his progress all along and knew what he was really worth, who would whisk him off to some bold and glamorous career? He peered up and down the street. But there was nothing: the brick buildings huddled, cloaked in the filth of two hundred years, beneath the oblivious sky. Only a newspaper flapping fitfully along the pavement suggested that there might once have been another thinking, feeling being in the place. He stepped to the side as it passed and trapped it with his foot. Looking down, he saw the lottery numbers printed at the bottom of the page. His pulse quickened momentarily. Would there be comfort here, a sudden reversal? But no; the numbers were all small, mean single figures when he had chosen an even spread. He sighed, he should have known: this was real life, not *Charlie and the Chocolate Factory*, of course there would be no golden ticket for him. Because that was the way life worked. That was what it did to you: if it couldn't get something out of you, it tried to fuck you up. The world was out to get you, to claim its pound of flesh. In the end, whatever you did, you would only ever lose. Well, fuck it. He didn't care. Fuck them all, quite frankly.

The telephone box on the corner glowed dimly in the evening light. He went to it, hand grubbing in his pocket for that last ten pence. Why not spend it here and now? Spend it and have done! The familiar numbers clicked beneath his fingers and he dropped the coin into the slot when the message cut in.

'Hello,' said the voice, bright, female and with a hint of the estuary about it, 'And thanks for phoning *The Trudy Show*, the daytime entertainment experience that puts you, the audience-member, centre-stage. We're always looking for interesting new people to feature in our guest slots, so if you leave a message with your name and contact details and a brief bit about yourself, we'll be sure to get back to you just as soon as we can. Alternatively, if you are calling about the Bo Jangles Bath Mix promotion, please press the star key now.'

A pause and then the beep.

'George French,' gasped George. 'I'm George French…'

He shrugged and thought for a moment. But there was nothing else to say.

10

The city shimmered in the afternoon sun although it was not hot. Glimmers of the coming spring bounced off the buildings and sent shafts of light ricocheting among them, blazing out to catch his eye from windows and glass walls. Fairies his mother had called them when he was little, fairies. Or was that something else?

He didn't know how long he'd been standing there, staring at the buildings out beyond the curve of the river whilst the crowds bustled behind him, but the buildings seemed to be swaying now, rocking gently with the turning of the earth. He glanced behind him at the grey mass of people hurrying past, heels clicking, briefcases swinging, rushing who knows where. Did any of them see it, he wondered? Or was he alone chosen a witness to the weirdness of the world? Nothing in any of their faces registered recognition of the sight of the Gherkin jiving gently by the dome of St Paul's. Perhaps it was his eyes playing tricks, his faintness – the hunger. But he was not hungry now. He had walked his way through hunger in the purple dark of the city nights the grey half-light of the days, until his stomach ceased protesting and lay slack and empty within him: a tenant in a poorly maintained building, resigned to doing without.

Time. Funny business wasn't it? Funny how it just continued and continued, regardless of anything . He glanced over his shoulder at the be-suited city people, heels clicking along the pavement, briefcases swinging still. All these people rushing to and fro as though they earnestly believed that the world might stop turning if they didn't, as though time itself might cease. Had there been a time when he'd been like that? There'd been something, hadn't there? Something to get him going? Something to quicken his pulse? What had it been?

That was before he learnt the secret, of course: that if you stood and stared up the river and felt the brush of the wind in your face, the day would roll on and the sun would scroll across the sky, bringing on night, unbidden; that the world stood impassively by whilst people scrambled over its face, serving their insistent little needs. He coughed and stared back at the view. Well, perhaps it was for the best that not too many knew what he knew.

And it was strange, this business of needs, these tiny goals that life kept strewing in your way like potato-peelings thrown in the path of a wary pig to tempt it into the abattoir van. For this moment, standing here on the concrete bridge with the air and the sun on his face, he required nothing. Right now he was no worse off than any of these hundreds of people hurrying past him in their suits and skirts and shirts – better off, probably, for they were rushing and he was, well, just here. And if he stood here for another five minutes, for another ten, even for half and hour, he would probably need nothing more. But soon, at some unspecified time in the future, the needs would start to crowd in. He would want something to drink, the hunger would return, his bladder would begin to complain. Then there would be the question of sleep. And basic things like toothpaste, soap and clothes. Funny how you could cut your needs down, right down, to a very few things, how you could do without the music and the videos and the mountainous piles of books, without the rich meals and the nights out and the taxis, tubes, and trains, without the aftershave and the shaving foam and even without shaving at all, and yet at root there was still this fundamental core of needs that could never be quite erased. You could squash yourself down into smaller and smaller boxes but the quick of you always remained, like the pilot light after the gas fire has blown out.

And yet, standing here, gazing out over the river and the jumble of buildings beyond, the bulbous Gherkin, the dome of St Paul's – never quite real, always half-drawn – and the Tower, it was hard to believe that he was really there at all. Surely anyone looking would see only an empty space, a jumble of wisps in the breeze? Surely they would see straight through him to the grey river below, the evil-smelling mass of water masking the depths of London's despair? Memory tugged. That was it: art. That had been the thing. Once, not long ago, he would have urged himself to write that down, stuff it in a pocket and save it, ready for the coming together of all his ideas, that moment of pure creation. But not now. Who would read it after all? Why should anyone care what a middle-class boy from North London thought about the River Thames? A boy who, let's face it, had little to show for himself except for a measly plastic trophy and an essay prize from a minor public school, neither of which had any bearing on his ability to create art. What gave him the right to make people listen? To vomit words onto a page? To waste trees? What authorized him to expect any one of these people bustling by to give up hard-won time poring over his sentences? Besides, what was the point?

He stood still for a while, watching the water flowing beneath. It was bleak water, ugly, moving lugubriously like a huge, living slug. Suicide soup. The sort of water that would suck you in and tug you down, snatching life from you before you'd had a chance for last thoughts and memories, rolling you along to the belly of the sea, and the stinging clutches of the jellyfish. He frowned. Jellyfish. Hadn't that happened once: someone swimming out to sea to try and end it all, but turning back because they ended up getting stung? The cogs of his brain creaked. Evelyn Waugh, that was it, Evelyn Waugh. He twitched a smile. Of course. Even in this he wasn't free of the bastard's clutches.

He stared at the water. So was that it then? Should he pitch himself over the handrail right now? Have done? He watched a crisp packet float lazily out from under the bridge and away towards the east. The idea had much to recommend it: a clean break from this endless chain of heckling needs, a rest, nothing to decide anymore, nothing more to choose. Except that it seemed such a large, desperate gesture on such a nondescript day. It would throw everything out of kilter, like a trumpet blast in the middle of a minuet for strings. To make this day the finale, this moment the last, would grant everything a grand significance that it simply didn't deserve. It was like writing "The End" instead of a conclusion: a childish, wriggling way of getting out of making sense. It was like seizing the role of the tragic hero when he was really nothing but an attendant lord; a puffed up character part in everyone else's lives, an extra. No great, grand destiny for him. No story written in the stars. Only gambolling and clowning and exiting followed by a bear. It wasn't for him to wrench Wednesday out of whack.

He stared at the shifting buildings. Somewhere out there, there were musicians, artists. They had to be out there, those colourful figures that you saw now and then talking lazily on the news. Hundreds of them, living extraordinary, bohemian lives. Hundreds of them, who, having found a route off convention's polluted highway, were free to wander in the woods beyond.

But what were hundreds amid nine million? What was a handful in a mountain of sand? If there were some mystical path away from the daily grind, he had looked for it and failed. The door to Narnia would not open for him. He was the wrong pedigree, the wrong breed. He was too conventional, too staid, too beholden to restrictions and rules. A middle-class boy from North London trying to have a crack at art? What had he been thinking? All he could ever hope for was the back of the wardrobe and an armful of moth-eaten coats.

A train passed along the track behind him, shuddering the footbridge so that the city around him swam. He looked along the river at the mud-flats left raw and naked by the tide below the towering streets. They were out there, his contemporaries, slaving, kow-towing, steadily getting on. Perhaps for them the imaginary crowd still existed, urging and cheering them on. Or perhaps it had never been a factor in their minds. Perhaps they had known the cold truth of things from day one and it was only he, George, who had tripped blithely through the supposed script of his life, like a child with its imaginary friends, like the little boy who believed Evelyn Waugh lived up the road and would one day invite him for tea. They gave trophies to practically everyone at school – why hadn't he realised it before?

At any rate, he doubted they'd know him now, deflated and crushed as he was: a battered, punctured football of a man, dumped to the side of the pitch. He was no good any more. He was finished. He doubted even his own parents would –

'Porge!'

He turned. Emily stood before him, suit flapping in the breeze.

'I thought it was you,' she said. 'As I came up the steps I said to myself, 'I bet that's Porge looking all melancholy over the handrail'. I've been hoping I'd run into you. Ever since Edward told me about seeing you in that café and you looking so glum, I've been thinking 'I hope I bump into Porge today' and now at last I have!'

'Emily,' said George, glancing desperately up and down her portly frame for something to say. 'You look… thin.'

'Nonsense, Porge, I've put on half a stone.'

'Well,' said George, with a helpless shrug. He wondered how long it would be before the questions started. Already, the rusty phrases were lining up inside his head: 'taking a break', 'weighing up options', 'things in the pipeline'. When would it leave him, he wondered, this dreadful urge to play the game?

'Now, *you* do look thin,' said Emily, appraising him with a critical eye. 'What have you been doing to yourself, Porge?'

The wind whipped her hair about her face, dark tentacles thrashing. With a jolt he remembered that the last time he'd seen her she'd been unbuttoning her blouse, prodding forth a breast.

'Oh, you know,' he shrugged again. 'Just walking around.'

'Well, you're very naughty. Everyone's been worried sick. Now come on,' she said, helping herself to his arm, 'You're coming with me.'

She marched him determinedly to the top of the steps. George allowed himself to be walked, numbly wondering who they were, these people who'd been worried sick, as the city skyline slipped from view.

On the tube she said: 'You didn't have to go the whole hog, you know Porge. You didn't have to disappear. Just walking out would have been enough. More than enough, if you ask me.'

George said nothing, swaying with the motion of the carriage. He wasn't entirely sure to which of the various eccentric episodes littering the last few weeks she was referring. It all seemed so far behind him, another life.

'I mean, don't misunderstand me, Porge. I'm the first to admit that emotional stress can make people do extreme things. Just look at me. In the last two weeks before finals I ate nothing but Red Leicester Cheese.'

George frowned. It wasn't quite true. He'd seen her in the canteen, helping herself to the greens.

'But,' Emily continued, 'We have to be measured about these things. And your poor parents. Walking out like that, leaving them with no idea whether you were alive or dead! And spreading all those lies about your mother having an affair! Porge, I know you're hurting, I know you're confused, but I think you've made your point, don't you?'

George gritted his teeth and put his head in his hands. He thought of his father sitting primly at his desk, the blank, city sky behind. He groaned.

'Oh but poor Porge!' said Emily, draping a generous arm across his back. 'We don't have to talk about it yet. We don't have to talk about any of it. Let's just sit here and hold each other and be glad that I came along when I did.'

George groaned again as he felt her arm reach up and press his head into her lemony shoulder and hold it there. He felt cornered, caged; a donkey newly-bridled, about to be led back to plodding petulant children up and down the beach. Surely he should wrest himself away from her and jump off at the next stop? Elbow through the crowds and out into the open air? Break free?

But it was very hard when what he was being led from was the grey wash of the waters, the light glinting off buildings reflecting back the sky, and the tramping of unseen, city feet. And besides, the tube was warm, its motion lulling, and he was very tired. He closed his eyes against the orange light and nestled his head deeper into Emily's substantial shoulder, firm yet yielding as an old, padded couch. Good old Emily. Dependable old Emily. There were certainly worse people to be found by. And it would wait, wouldn't it, all that nothingness? The bridge and the river and the sky? He yawned as the waves of sleep came flooding in. He would ride the tube to Clapham, at least. Maybe have a cup of tea, something to eat. Perhaps even a shower. He wouldn't stay long, not long. Just long enough to get something of himself back. Just long enough to have a little rest. He deserved that, didn't he? A little rest? For he was so tired. So very, very tired. The tube swayed round a corner.

'There,' said Emily, patting his filthy head. 'There, there.'

*   *   *

Outside Emily's front door, he paused, head hung, waiting while she found her key. The wallpaper in the stairwell depressed him. He remembered staring at it, leering at it, his head swimming with wine. Then it had seemed shocking and alive, a writhing mass of living vines, capturing something new and important about the essence and nature of grapes. Now it was flat and faintly vulgar; the sort of print sold with the label "Prestige" in department stores up and down the land.

Inside, the flat was different, too. The hallway, once long and palatial, was narrow and poorly lit. There were cracks in the ceiling he hadn't noticed before and a strange smell of cabbage from the flat downstairs. Even the bathroom, that emporium of pink and beige, was tired and tatty in the cold light of day. Specks of mould peppered the grouting round the bath and several of the tiles were cracked. George noticed spots on the carpet around the toilet and winced.

He took his time washing, mesmerised by the streams of dirty water that ran down his legs and circled the plughole. Emily had given him a yellow towel, a fluffy, feminine affair, and he draped himself in that, surprised at how pungent and synthetic the fabric softener smelt as he wrapped it round. The carpet felt soft beneath his feet after the rub of his battered shoes and he stood for a moment wriggling his toes, before opening the frosted window to let out the steam.

His clothes were unwearable, grown stiff and grey as the city stones, so Emily lent him a dressing gown, voluminous, pink, and liable to gape at the front. He spent a while arranging himself into it, sitting on the single bed in the spare room surrounded by crates and boxes piled against the walls. The silk of the dressing-gown clung loosely to his skin, enfolding him in its watery clutches, making him feel at once exposed and horribly held. He wanted to strip it off and climb beneath the perfumed sheets where sleep was waiting for him. He sat nodding until, brought to by a clatter of pots, he left the room and made his way along the passage to the kitchen, from which emanated a collection of sour smells.

Despite the efforts of the dinner party, Emily was not a good cook. In her day to day life, she relied on three or four staple dishes which she had been taught to cook by her Polish nanny every evening when she came home from school. All of them consisted of frankfurters swilled round in copious quantities of tinned tomatoes.

'Blur-shnink-pa,' she said – at least that was how it sounded – as George looked gingerly into the pot. 'I've been making it since I was twelve.'

'Mmmn,' said George.

Strange, he'd been hungry for days, but now, when it came to the actual business of eating food, his stomach seethed and bubbled and threatened to rebel, as though it, like his mind, had turned from conventional functions in disgust. Or perhaps it was simply Emily's stew with its bloody-mud colouring and pickled smell, not calculated to appeal to anyone other than the most hardened sauerkraut fan. He watched it slop and spread as she ladled it onto the plates.

'I've called Jean,' she said, setting the plates down on the counter and drawing up two stools.

'Jean?' said George bewilderedly, running a hand over his hair. It was strange to feel it free from grit and grease. Where was he again?

'Your mother, Porge,' said Emily, busily climbing onto a stool. 'Jean your mother. She wanted to speak to you, of course. But I told her you were too exhausted. Said you'd give her a call when you were more yourself. She trusts me, you see.'

'Oh,' said George. 'Right.'

Emily patted the stool beside her.

'Come on Porge,' she said. 'Come and eat.'

George glanced futilely over his shoulder at the table through the hatch as he stepped towards the stool. He yearned for the straightforwardness of the table, for the easy frankness of a chair that was planted solidly and squarely on the ground. Sitting on the stool he felt he might suddenly list, fall and sink through the lino of the floor.

'More intimate here,' said Emily, as he climbed on. 'Less formal.'

'Mmn,' said George, looking down at the chunks of frankfurter swimming in red, viscous goo. He reminded himself that there were places in the world where people were starving, that he himself hadn't eaten properly for days.

'Now, Porge,' said Emily, liberally sprinkling her plate with salt. 'Tell me about you.'

She had taken off her jacket and undone another button on her blouse, so that he could see her breasts, trussed up in another enormous bra, bulging within. They reminded him of a pair of balloons twinned up for a stag night or someone's birthday bash: unnatural and strangely surreal.

'Well,' said George, chewing cautiously on a piece of gristle. 'There's not much to tell, really. I... got pissed off at my parents' party, so I went away for a while. And now I'm here.'

'Poor Porge, brave to the last,' said Emily, slipping a hunk of sausage between her lips. 'Misunderstood, alone, carrying all that hurt! Isolated Porge, with no-one to take his side! No wonder things... happened the way they did.'

George looked absently at her. He seemed to be seeing everything through some sort of tunnel, as though he were standing behind his own shoulder, peering through a telescope at the world. He looked down at his hands manoeuvring the cutlery around his plate and had the unsettling feeling that they were nothing to do with him at all.

'Oh,' he said, shrugging, 'It wasn't that b–'

'Because no-one ever listens to you, do they Porge?' continued Emily, tears budding at the corners of her eyes. 'You're always the strong silent type. The uncomplaining one. People talk and talk and you just carry on! Well, Porge,' she said, turning so that her knee brushed his, 'I want you to know that I am here for you!'

He glanced down. Her skirt was riding up her thigh, revealing a hint of something lacy and stringy beneath. He blinked and looked away.

'Thanks Em,' he said to the wall, staring at a tile with a rustic motif of flowers surrounding a basket of fruit, 'That's really… generous, really it is, but –' he laid down his cutlery as his mouth expanded itself into an overpowering yawn, 'Actually I'm really quite t-'

'Oh Porge! You don't have to be brave!' wailed Emily, clutching at his arm. 'Let it go. I can take it! I can take it all!'

George coughed. The extractor fan above the cooker hummed.

'Really, Em,' he mumbled, struggling to find the words that would speed his way to sleep. 'I'm fine. I just thought I might like to be an artist and wanted to have some space to give it a go. That's all.'

He shrugged and smiled muzzily as sleep crackled in his ears. God, he was going to get into a bed! A real bed!

'Oh yes,' said Emily, her expression cooling. 'All that stuff in *The Times*. Ben's piece. Well, anyone could see that was a red herring.'

'Oh,' said George. 'Could they?'

'Oh yes. As soon as I read it, I knew it was nothing but a desperate cry for help.'

George frowned, eyes swimming in and out of focus.

'In what sense?' he said.

'Well,' said Emily, scraping together some slabs of onion on her plate, 'Let's face it, Porge, you were never going to pursue it, now, were you? All that meaningfulness and soul-searching and drinking herbal tea, it's not really you. It's not really any of us.' She loaded her fork and conveyed the dripping mass to her mouth. 'And anyway,' she said, chewing, 'There's no sort of living to be made out of it. How could you ever expect to buy a house or put your children through school?'

George nodded tiredly. She was probably right. What was he really but an overgrown teenager still strumming weakly on a guitar whilst everyone else was getting on with things. He'd thought he would be famous, but, really, who'd want to listen to him?

'It was only ever a dream, wasn't it, Porge?' said Emily softening, sweetening.

George nodded again, his body aching for the feel of cool, clean sheets.

'It was never going to come to anything, was it?' said Emily, shuffling closer and reaching up to stroke his hair.

He shook his head as she pulled him gently down towards her bosom, mumbling. He'd been foolish ever to think of it.

'Because that's not the way things are, is it Porge?' she said, running her hand down his neck. 'That's not how life works.'

He lay against the bulk of her, smelling her lemony scent with its overtones of air freshener and citrus bathroom spray. She wasn't bad, was she, old Em? Jolly old Em. So straightforward, so simple, so black and white. He wished he could be like her, could put some of her no-nonsenseness on, could trot every day to the open-plan office to cross the t's and dot the i's of other people's lives. What did it matter whether you were wrong or right if you could believe so totally in the way you saw the world? What did any of it matter when you laid it all out?

At length, Emily cleared the plates, sweeping his leavings into the bin. George sat limply on the stool while she did so. He supposed he should offer to do the washing up, should play the helpful guest, but he could find no impetus to do so within him. He could only sit as a succession of images flitted through his mind, fragments of things he had thought and seen: London cold and drab before him; his father sitting at his desk; a house and sky; three figures by the cricket pitch.

Once, he said: 'You know, my father wanted to be a lawyer.'

'I know, Porge,' said Emily with a sad little smile. 'I know.'

'But he had to take over the paper firm instead.'

'– Sitting in a grey little office somewhere in the East End. Yes, Porge, I know all this. Well, don't worry. It's not going to happen to you.'

He frowned. Was that what he'd been worrying about? Was that it after all?

She ran him a glass of water and stood over him while he drank it, as though doubtful whether or not to trust him with the glass. The liquid tasted clear and pure after the rusty offerings of public taps.

'Right,' she said as the last drops drained, 'Bedtime.'

'Yes,' said George, gratefully.

She took his hand and led him to the box room at the end of the hall. She'd been in while he'd been picking at his food and tidied his clothes away. There was a fresh mug of water on the box next to the bed and the duvet had been turned down. George nearly cried when he saw it, so much did he want to sleep.

He walked over. He was about to take the dressing gown off and get in when he remembered she was still in the room.

He turned.

'Thank you,' he said.

'That's alright, Porge,' said Emily, softly. 'What are friends for?'

'Night night,' he said.

But she did not go. He sat down on the bed and still she stood in the doorway, fingering a strand of her hair. He coughed and she came and sat next to him, nestling her buttocks into the space between his body and the duvet's folds.

A moment passed. George looked at the boxes stacked against the opposite wall. Here and there he caught glimpses of their contents: the arm of a long-forgotten teddy bear; an Enid Blyton book now fringed with dust. His mind began to drift out and away above the city, so that when she spoke he was shocked to find her there and himself, sitting next to her on the single bed.

'You know, Porge,' she said, her thigh pressing warmly against his own. 'Everyone was very worried about you.'

He nodded.

'Your parents, they ran through all sorts of questions in their minds –'

'My parents knew exactly where I was,' said George. 'They saw it in the paper. You told them Jennifer had seen me –'

'Yes, but before that, Porge,' said Emily. 'The first couple of days and afterwards again.' She sighed. 'They were going out of their minds with worry. Running through all sorts of scenarios. All sorts of possibilities. Porge, they even wondered if you might be… gay. If maybe that was why you ran away, because you were scared to tell them.'

'Oh,' said George. 'Well, I'm not, so –'

'Oh I know you're not, Porge,' said Emily, running her hand lightly along the outside of his thigh. 'I know you're not. I told them. About us. About that night we first kissed years ago. About the way you've looked at me ever since. About that time at my dinner party when you couldn't help yourself and you had to… touch me.'

George started. 'You told my parents that?' he said.

Emily turned towards him so that her hand slid over towards the middle of his thigh and her breasts – full, disturbing – brushed his arm.

'They were pleased to hear it, Porge,' she breathed. 'Glad that you were so… passionate. Impulsive. Urgent.'

He looked down. There was her hand undoing the knot of the dressing-gown, there was her leg sliding up between his own and – oh God – here was his treacherous body rising to meet her.

'Em –' he said quickly.

'Ssh, Porge, ssh,' she said, pushing him down onto the bed. 'You mustn't be embarrassed about what happened last time, about being… shy. It happens to lots of boys – you'd be surprised how many. Just leave it to me. I've read books.'

With one hand on his shoulder, she ridded herself of her undergarments, fingers working deftly beneath her navy skirt. Had she practised this, George wondered? Astride a pillow on her bed?

His mouth flapped feebly as she readied herself above him. He put his hands up to push her away, but she only wriggled into them, making whinnying sounds, nestling so that he was in full possession of her breasts. He thought fast, his mind struggling back through the undergrowth of recent days for something familiar, something of use. Surely there was a way of extricating oneself from these sorts of situations? Some trusted form of words: witty, debonair, yet unquestionably firm? Surely James Bond had found himself in an uninvited clinch once in a while? Surely Humphrey Bogart had had to ask Sam not to play it now and then?

But it was no good: he was not James Bond, nor was meant to be. He was George French, merely. George French, winner of the Piffle Prize and one House award. George French, flushed and gasping in a phone box. George French, in a borrowed dressing gown. George French, sinking now beneath a welter of grasping hands.

Outside the street-lamps flickered. And she was upon him. She had got him. She was King of the Castle. And for now there was only this, and this, and this.

11

The instructions said pull and he'd pulled. They said twist and he'd twisted. They'd advised him to wash his hands and he'd done that, even though he'd had a shower only half an hour before. He'd done everything asked of him. He'd even mimicked the bright smile of the woman in the cartoon diagrams. But it was no good. The carton was staying resolutely closed. He could not open it. In fact he'd had very little effect on it at all other than to shred one of its flaps into a collection of little fibrous pieces now scattered over the kitchen surface and the floor. He plonked it down in disgust. Who bought milk in cartons nowadays anyway? What sort of sado-masochist try-hard shopper actually trundled round the supermarket, stopped, and said 'Oh yes. Milk in a carton! What a good idea'? The answer stared up at him mutely from a picture in a little plastic frame beside the toaster: Emily striding manfully across the Chiltern Hills.

He left the shredded carton and ran himself a glass of water instead. She'd clear it up when she came in. She always did. She didn't mind. In fact, he suspected she rather liked encountering these signs of his ineptitude; proof that he could not cope own his own, that she had indeed rescued him from slow, maddening disintegration. He'd caught her whistling the other day as she cleaned the remnants of his shaving from the tidemark round the sink. At any rate, it was better to leave it for her than make some attempt at rectifying things only to have her tut affectionately over his efforts and then involve him in a long, suffocating kiss. He could cope with her being bossy but grateful? Jesus!

He picked up the plate of lunch she'd left for him – she didn't like him going in the fridge on his own, unless specifically authorized – and fumbled for cutlery in the drawer below. There was a note on the surface where the plate had been, looped in Emily's firm, open hand, but he didn't bother to read it. Something about tonight, no doubt: instructions. Well he'd read it later. Or perhaps pretend not to have noticed it at all. She liked it when he did things like that: made obvious, basic mistakes. No doubt she'd tell them about it later and they'd all laugh, smile, and remember that he was quirky George, George who, bless him, had really thought he might be in with a chance of having a crack at art, George who once went to a tutorial in the middle of the night. Well, what did it matter? He had done that, after all, hadn't he? And, now he came to think about it, it was a bit of a mental thing to have done, even taking his mother's error with the alarm clock into account. After all, it had been dark.

He carried the plate through to the living room to settle down for an afternoon in front of the TV. It was where he spent most of his time these days, slumped on the bulbous sofa, staring at the brightly coloured pictures on the screen. He'd become quite adept at navigating himself through the daytime schedules, weaving between antiques shows and cooking programmes to bring himself safely to the *Neighbours* theme-tune and six o'clock and the click of Emily's key in the door. In the mornings he gave himself over to *David & Trudy* who seemed to have called an uneasy truce involving Trudy managing the studio links whilst David roamed the country sending back on-the-spot reports. The afternoons were more difficult. After the *News* and the first shot of *Neighbours*, a yawning wasteland of birthing programmes and tame murder mysteries tested his endurance to its limit. The highlight of the week was *Think Well with Lucy* on Tuesday afternoons in which the leggy psychologist delicately picked apart the dignity of a range of snivelling delinquents. George particularly enjoyed watching the way she ran her hands absent-mindedly over her thighs as she explained whichever morbidly fascinating disorder was taking centre-stage that week. He could tell she was getting off on it nearly as much as he was, reaching through the screen to titillate him with her eyes. Other than that, it was slow going. The afternoons were punishing and it required all his ingenuity and some pretty nifty work with the remote control to keep the cogs turning and the conveyor belt of time carrying him through. It was draining, but, for the most part, George managed it. Only occasionally would he turn the television off and sit staring at the wall. Only sometimes would he creep out to the hallway to whisper his name age and who and where he was into the phone.

Sometimes he went out for walks, strolling along the paths of the common between the dogwalkers and the mothers and the teenagers bunking school. His new T-shirts, the clothes that Emily had bought him, tugged him under the arms as he moved, but he didn't mind. He was happy enough with the air, the exercise, the gentle pace. In fact, there wasn't much he did mind these days. It all felt very distant and unlikely to impinge, as though he were wandering perpetually through a huge aquarium and life, teeming with sharks and angel fish, was gaping at him from the other side of the glass: a different medium.

From time to time, he thought about applying for jobs, knuckling down in front of Emily's computer and hashing up a CV. But the whole idea seemed very far away and also faintly ridiculous, like expecting a monkey to drive a train. How could he, this flimsy bundle of inconsistencies be trusted with anything so serious as a job? He barely knew what he was going to be like from one day to the next himself! How could anyone else be expected to entrust him with doing a particular thing at a particular time for any number of years! He'd never be able to keep a straight face.

Just thinking back on the things he'd managed thus far left him bewildered and faintly suspicious that he had somehow been swapped into a body that was not his own. Had he really been working towards his finals a year ago? Turning in articles for the student paper, the *Spotlight Review*? And all those parties, ents and raves – and let's face it, there had been several – how had he ever had the energy for those? He must have been on some sort of mad, natural high: young, a student in London. It was the only explanation. And then there was school. God! He couldn't even begin to make sense of that one! Activity from eight in the morning until eight at night, lessons and rehearsals and endless, urgent games. No chance of a lie-in, no chance of a rest. How had he ever managed it? It was extraordinary, a feat. He applauded himself for it. But he couldn't see how he could ever find his way back to that level of activity, that drive, again. It was as though something within him had seized up, something ossified and fused, so that the elastic potential he once had, the feeling that anything was possible and all could be achieved, had shrunk and solidified leaving him trapped within a brittle shell. The course of life had been diverted and he lay, beached, on the sofa, remote control in hand, as days flat and colourless as the dishwater in the sink, unwrapped themselves, stretched, and packed up in the streets outside.

It wasn't a bad life. In fact, as he frequently reminded himself, it was the sort of life a lot of people dreamed of. Free from responsibility, free from strain, all his wants supplied and kept by a woman who couldn't get enough of him when she returned from the office every day. Wasn't it peachy? Wasn't it a breeze? Wasn't it exactly the sort of thing that most men fantasised about, gasping away over their top-shelf magazines? A strong, demanding woman returning home every evening to collect the rent? After all, when it came down to it, sex was at the root of everything, wasn't it? Sex was what made the world go round. Forget money, forget love, forget all those other things. What was the point of chasing after wealth and prestige and an interesting career if you could skip all of that and go straight to the main event? Food, sex, and a place to sleep. What more did a man need? In terms of the game, he'd aced it, hadn't he? Got to the finishing line without even running the race! And wasn't it a comfort to know, as he heard the key click faithfully in the lock each day, that it wasn't his money or his power she was after? Oh no: she wanted him for him.

And God did she want him! Often he was not allowed off the sofa for several hours after she came home. Sometimes he could only get a breather by pleading thirst or saying he needed to go to the loo. He had even toyed with saying he had a headache once or twice, anything to buy a moment's respite from the grasping hands and gobbling mouth.

She had taken to going to various to going to adult shops during her lunch-break and delighted in wriggling her way out of her office clothes to display whatever fringed, ribbed or zipped creation was hugging her bulk beneath. A few days before, she'd even appeared in a pair of edible, strawberry-flavoured knickers and insisted that he eat them off her while she watched the evening news. Sometimes, watching her bouncing away on top of him – this was her favourite position, although she had made him try them all, instructing loudly, so that he often felt it was he who had been the virgin and not Emily at all – he found he had to work hard at remembering what there was about her to like. She did have very large breasts and her hair was surprisingly soft. Also, he was growing used to her cooking, detecting previously unsuspected strains of flavours amidst the blare of tomato and the honk of frankfurter meat. And she had saved him from whatever it was he had been contemplating on the footbridge over the Thames. And sometimes, when she bent down to get a plate from the bottom shelf, he had a faint, yet definite, urge to grab her arse.

Thinking like this, he usually managed to claw his way to the orgasm that she demanded he had before she would make him any food. But it was getting more difficult. Increasingly, as she writhed and twisted above him and the crucial point approached, he found himself reaching for the image of Lucy Thinkwell, svelte and ice-maidenly, sealed in the bright world beyond the flickering screen, to nudge him over the edge.

But there were other times – and these were worse – when she came home with things other than physical closeness on her mind. She'd been reading magazines, trashy, terrifying things which bandied around words like 'commitment' and 'love' and at the weekends she would insist that they lay for hours on the sofa watching ghastly, saccharine films, whilst she cradled his head against her. Once – he had caught her at it – she had tried to mop his brow. She would say things like 'Have you ever seen the film *Jane Eyre*?' and become absorbed in the picture that hung on the far wall: a painting she had done for her GCSE Art class showing a woman draped languorously over a chaise-longue in the shadow of a man.

There had even been a nasty episode when he had been sent through to attack the coffee table with a can of polish. Entering the living room, he had been confronted by a casually placed article on romantic locations to propose. He had tidied it wordlessly away but it had taken several sleepless nights and a lot of vigorous hoovering to drive it fully from his mind.

*　　*　　*

The key clicked in the lock just as the news jingle was thundering to its climax, pounding gravity home. George turned to see Emily bustling in, shopping bags swinging, and depositing her purchases just inside the kitchen door. She wobbled through into the lounge. In spite of the vigorous exercise to which she had been submitting herself, she seemed to be growing in size. Although never slim, she had, since George moved in, ballooned, developing rolls of flesh in unaccustomed places and a shininess to her hair and skin which reminded George of the hide of a prize heifer or show pony. Watching her shudder her way about the flat, forcing groans from floorboards that had never before complained, he had the unnerving feeling that she was somehow feeding off him, fatting herself on his presence.

'So,' she said, shimmying towards him – for all her bulk she could still bust a move – 'How's my boy?'

'Oh,' said George with an absent glance at the TV screen, 'Fine.'

'Miss me?'

'Mmn. Who's coming tonight?' he said quickly as she swooped towards him, moving in for the kill.

She paused, eyes looking off to the side, thinking.

'Jenny and Edward,' she said, counting them off on her fingers, 'Andy and Susan – you don't know them, Andy's a bit of an oddball, a friend of my cousin's, never had a girlfriend until now, apparently she's much older – and, er, you and me. In more ways than one, I hope.'

'Mmn. Is Ben coming?'

'No, he's off interviewing some writer. Quite famous apparently. Name has something to do with fish.'

'Er, Jonathan Bate?' suggested George.

'Salman Rushdie,' said Emily, reaching up to free her hair clip and shaking out her mane.

'Salman Rushdie!' said George. 'But that's extraordinary!'

'Is it?' said Emily, shrugging.

'Come on!' said George. 'Salman Rushdie? Author of *The Satanic Verses*?'

Emily shrugged again.

'I'm not really into horror,' she said. 'Anyway, enough about Ben. We've got business to attend to.' She glanced up at the blonde-wood clock on the wall, fingers tugging at the buttons on her blouse. 'Time for at least two gos before they get here. But you'll have to be quick, Porge. None of this saving yourself tonight.'

George watched, dismayed, as her fingers worked their way down the buttons, pushing the material back to reveal something pink and shiny underneath. He'd banked on the dinner party winning him a reprieve tonight, not forcing him into some sort of Olympic time trial. He could barely stifle a groan.

Emily turned away from watching her reflection undress in the window and looked at him.

'What's the matter, Porge?' she said 'Are you worried about tonight?'

She'd put one leg up on the sofa, blocking his view of the screen, so that in place of the newsreader's head he could see only flesh vanishing into darkness between her thighs. He shuddered and looked away.

'No,' he said. 'It's just –'

'Because it's a big thing, seeing everybody for the first time since your... funny turn. I wouldn't be surprised if you were feeling a bit tense, a bit wound-up. That's why I went to town a bit today with your surprise. I know how you boys like your toys.'

So saying, she undid the last button and shrugged off the blouse to reveal a vast, pink PVC creation, loaded with chains and zips and holes in improbable places, a sort of adult activity centre.

'Go on,' she said, waggling herself in front of him, 'Have a play.'

So George reached up to knead absently at it, all the while staring past her at the screen, hoping for a feature on teenage models or underwear shortages, anything that might help him on his way. There was a half-decent new weather girl on this side and he fought desperately to construct some sort of lurid fantasy with her involving wicked misuse of the stick-on suns.

'Right!' said Emily after a minute or two. 'Let's crack on!'

She wriggled her way out of her skirt and began to tug at the buttons of his fly. They were new and stiff – these were some of the jeans she had bought him – and it took her several moments to get the better of them, grunting as she tugged and pulled. At length, she had done it and she clambered triumphantly aboard him, positioning her legs, clutching the back of the sofa, and –

'Porge?'

She was looking through the hatch into the kitchen.

'Mmn?' said George.

'Did you read my note?'

'Er,' said George weakly. 'No. I didn't know I was meant to.'

'Oh Porge!' cried Emily. 'You were supposed to do the marinade and start preparing the sauce!'

She looked down at him, thunder in her eyes. For a wild, glad moment George thought she might be about to get cross. Then the storm passed and she softened, melting over him. After all, he was her Porge, wasn't he? And it was sweet how much he needed her, how little he could do on his own. Really he was little more than a dear, sweet, sexy baby.

'You know,' she said happily, clambering off and making her way through to the kitchen. 'I really think you might have to marry me, Porge. I can't see how you're ever going to manage by yourself.'

She began to clatter pots and pans, the chains on her basque rattling as she moved. George lay, wide-eyed and staring, watching a fly crawl up the wall, barely daring to move.

At length she called him.

'Mmn?' he replied.

'Could you come in here?'

So he went through, squinting against the bright, yellow light. She was standing, tilted awkwardly at the cooker, stirring a sauce, with her feet planted squarely on the floor. She looked at him.

'We couldn't have a go while I do this, could we?' she said, jutting her rear end towards him. 'It might make it a bit more interesting, add a bit of spice.'

'Oh I don't know, Em,' he said quickly. 'The angle... it might, you know... the sauce.'

She was forced to admit he had a point. In the end she had to content herself with pouting moodily at him and shimmying the chains into a frenzy every time she reached for some salt or herbs.

She had committed the pot to the oven and was advancing on him with the spatula, her tongue lolling rakishly from her mouth, when the phone rang.

'Better answer it,' blurted George.

'Oh,' Emily whined. 'Let them wait.'

'Better answer it,' he said again, watching a drip of sauce run down the spatula towards Emily's grasping hand.

Pouting, she turned and reached for the handset, which lay on the counter, shuddering towards the edge.

'Emily Goodchild,' she said in her business voice.

The extractor fan hummed.

'Er –' she said, glancing at George. 'How did you get this number?'

George looked down at himself. He was sweating, he realised, through the fabric of the grey T-shirt she had said would bring out his eyes.

'I see,' continued Emily. 'Well, I'm afraid he's not actually… very well at the moment… Mmmn… I'm sure he'd be more than happy another time, but –'

George looked up questioningly at Emily but she turned and stared out of the window, clutching the phone to her ear.

'Mmmn. Mmn. Well, I'm sorry about that… Yes, I'll certainly let him know… Alright, then. Bu-bye''

She turned and slid the handset into its cradle on the wall.

'There,' she said.

'Anyone important?' said George.

She looked at him, chains glinting under the kitchen spots.

'Oh, no-one, Porge,' she said. 'Telemarketing.'

'But they were asking for me?'

'Yes.' She checked herself. 'Well, no, no they weren't. Actually, they were just asking to speak to the man of the house.'

She looked at him steadily.

'But –'

'Really, Porge,' said Emily, slipping back into her bedroom drawl. 'I'm surprised you're going on about a silly thing like that when you've got a half-naked woman standing in front of you ready to do… anything.'

A faint spark of interest ignited within George.

'Anything?' he said.

'Well,' said Emily, blinking. 'A lot. But,' her eyes glanced up to the clock, 'We better be quick about it. Otherwise they'll find us, Porge. They'll come in and find us. They'll see us… in full flight. See how rampant we are. How… unrestrained!'

She was gasping now, wobbling towards him, hands running up and down her festooned bulk. George gritted his teeth. God, he was lucky, wasn't he? God, he had landed on his feet. God, wouldn't lots of men –

The sound of the buzzer jabbed sharply through his thoughts. Emily froze and both of them looked towards the door. Emily went to the intercom.

'Hello, it's us,' crackled a male voice.

'Great!' cried Emily. 'Come on up!'

She pressed the release button to open the outside door.

'Oh,' she pouted. 'They're early. Not fair.'

She went out into the hallway and stepped towards the door.

'Emily!' called George.

She paused. Her nodded at her body. She glanced down.

'Oops!' she said. 'Nearly forgot! That would have been a clanger, wouldn't it! Mind you,' she glanced sidelong at the door, 'Three or four might be rather fun…'

'No!' blurted George, panicked by the thought of Jennifer and Edward waiting in the stairwell, clutching matching bottles of Sauvignon Blanc. The idea was too horrible to contemplate.

'Just joking, Porge,' said Emily with a triumphant smile. 'Besides, I want to keep you all for myself, too. You let them in. I'll go and throw on some clothes.'

So saying, she stumped up the hall, into her bedroom and shut the door. George took a deep breath and stepped out into the corridor. The door confronted him at the end, beyond the table and the hooks for coats. The reality of the situation hit him for the first time: outside in the stairwell were people, friends of Emily's, possibly of his, maybe even his ex-girlfriend, and here he was, welcoming them to Emily's flat, presenting himself as Emily's, what, boyfriend? Was that what this was called?

He stood stock still. What if he just stayed here, whispered a voice inside his head? What if time stopped and he just stood here forever, staring at the door? That wouldn't be so bad, would it? Just standing here?

Someone rapped the knocker and the sound of it echoed through the flat.

'George!' called Emily.

'Yes,' he replied. 'Coming!'

He stepped up and opened the door. The lights of the stairwell flooded in. On the landing outside stood a woman in her thirties with a sharp, heavily-coloured bob, and a younger, pudding-faced man with glasses, a hefty leather jacket and hair hedge-hogged with gel.

'Sorry to keep you waiting,' said George, gesturing vaguely towards the kitchen. 'We were just –'

'George!' exclaimed the woman. 'Who'd have thought!'

George peered at her.

'Sue?' he said, hesitantly.

'It is indeed,' said Sue proudly, turning herself from side to side. 'Look a bit different now, don't I? Amazing what the attentions of a younger man will do.' She giggled. 'This is Andy –'

'We've already met,' said the man. 'At your parent's party. I was there with Mum and Dad.'

George frowned, a memory from the early part of the party dropped into place: a geeky character with buck-teeth talking about astrophysics.

'Of course you did!' gasped Sue. 'How silly of me! That was the night we met, the night we first –' Her face fell suddenly. 'Listen, George, you won't mention this to Mum will you? Not just yet. Only I'm not sure she'd understand. And we're trying to keep it… you know.'

'Don't worry,' said George. 'I haven't spoken to my parents in nearly a month, so –'

'Oh good,' said Sue, pushing back her hair. 'How are you, anyway? You look well.'

George glanced sideways and caught a glimpse of himself in the mirror by the door. His hair was standing on end from Emily's tuggings and there was a drained, vacant look about his eyes. For a ghastly moment, he reminded himself of Jack Nicholson's character in *One Flew over the Cuckoos Nest* after the electric shock treatment has found its mark.

'And it's a nice place you and Emily have got here,' said Sue, nosing into the flat. 'Very modern.'

'Well it's not really my –' said George.

'We're still looking, aren't we Andy,' said Sue.

'We are still looking, yes.'

'Thought we'd get a nice place of our own. Make a fresh start. Now that there's nothing to tie me to that old house any more. Silly, really, I should have done it years ago. Even the cat got out before I did. It's time to move on.'

'It'll be good for both of us, psychologically,' said Andrew.

'I mean,' continued Sue. 'Don't think I wasn't sad when Toffee went missing. I wept for days, didn't I, Andy?'

'Days.'

'I put up posters everywhere. I thought it was some sort of judgement, a punishment.'

'A sexual punishment,' added Andrew. 'For the two of us, having sex.'

'I had all sorts of hang ups, didn't I, Andy?'

'All sorts of hang-ups.'

'But after a while, when she didn't come back, I realised that, lovely though she was, Toffee had been holding me back. I lived for that cat. After Jim left, I made her the centre of my world. And it wasn't healthy. It wasn't good for her and it wasn't good for me. You saw how fat she was getting. And I began to think maybe she'd gone to make things easier. Maybe she'd left to set me free. Because they do that, don't they, animals? They know. She saw me with Andy and she knew: my gap was filled.'

'Mmn,' said George. 'And, er, how's the science going, Andrew, er, Andy?'

'Actually, I'm not doing it anymore,' said Andrew, running a hand over his rigid hair. 'It was very limiting, very cold. No. I'm thinking of training to be a psychotherapist instead.'

'Well,' said George. 'That's –'

'Isn't it?' said Sue, beaming at Andrew with moist eyes.

'Porge!' cried Emily, bustling down the hall in a figure-hugging black dress with a slit up the side. 'Where are your manners? Are you going to leave our guests standing on the landing all night? Honestly!'

She snatched the door from his grasp, flung it wide, and beckoned Sue and Andrew in.

'Susan!' she exclaimed.

'Call me Sue,' said Sue.

'And who's this you've brought with you? Harrison Ford? My word, Dandy! What a hunk and a half!'

Andrew flushed and snorted, whilst allowing himself a fulsome stare at Emily's cleavage.

'Do excuse Porge,' said Emily, bustling them up the hall and thrusting a bottle of wine into George's hands as she passed, 'He's still' – she whispered this, mouth contorting dramatically – 'Re-cov-er-ring.'

They nodded and smiled wanly back down the corridor before disappearing into the living room where the table had been pulled out and set, ready for the meal. Blinking, George wandered into the kitchen and began torturing the neck of the wine bottle with a corkscrew shaped like a fish. So he was recovering, was he? Was that it? He stripped off the plastic wrapping and began jabbing the corkscrew into the neck. Was that what they said about him when he wasn't there? That he was abnormal in some way? Off the rails? Rich, really, coming from those three!

He began pumping at the corkscrew. It was one of those fancy novelty ones, supposed to make opening bottles easy, fun. But if there was a trick to it, he couldn't see it. He cranked at the fluted tail, jerking the bottle crazily around the surface top.

'Porge,' said Emily, standing in the doorway, watching him.

He turned, flushed, eyes flashing.

'It's a screw-top.'

He looked down at the lid of the bottle, through which he had rammed the corkscrew's steely point.

'Ah,' he said.

'Dear Porge,' said Emily, sallying forward to take it from his hands. 'Where would you be without me?'

He watched as she dealt with it, working the corkscrew free, wrenching off the top, leaning across to goose him as she fetched the glasses down. She had told him once that one of her relatives, a great great grandmother or something similar, had been a nurse with Florence Nightingale in Scutari. Seeing her now he could easily believe it: there was a mixture of strength and busy self-importance about her that would look well on any battlefield.

'There,' she said, stretching up to lick his neck, before pushing the tray of brimming glasses to the edge of the hatch and trotting through to the other room.

George reached up to wipe her saliva away, and followed her out into the hall. He could hear the three of them in the other room, discussing Emily's painting. There was nothing she liked better than pointing it out to guests. He hesitated by the coat hooks in the corridor, absently fingering the corner of Sue's wrap. It was soft and furry and reminded him of a blanket he had used to carry about with him as a small boy. What had happened to it, he wondered? Had his mother thrown it away?

After a moment or two, Emily swaggered back into the hall, cheeks flushed, eyes shining.

'Forgot the mixed nuts,' she explained, before hurrying into the kitchen, snatching up the nibbles and pouring herself another generous glass of wine.

She turned to stare at him, breasts quivering.

'What are you doing out here?'

'Oh –' said George with a shrug.

'Hanging around in the hallway, all by yourself?' A smile spread itself across her face. 'Oh Porge, you naughty thing!'

'No,' said George, waving a hand weakly. 'I was just –'

'But Porge,' she breathed, advancing towards him. 'It's so rude! What if someone sees us? What if Andy and Sue come out? Bad, naughty Porge!'

George twitched and clutched involuntarily at the coats.

'Er –' he said.

'We'll have to be very quick and very quiet,' she said, pressing herself against him and starting to wrench at his belt. 'Rampant,' she breathed in his ear.

'But –' he protested as her mouth closed on his.

He winced as she found her way past the buckle on his belt and began an assault on his jeans. Surely they couldn't be about to do it here? Against the coats? With Andrew and Sue-down-the-road in the other room? Surely –

The fart of the buzzer cut through Emily's grunts. She stepped back and regarded him, the skin around her mouth flushed, her hair in disarray.

'Better get that,' he said.

'Couldn't we just –'

'Better get that,' he said again. 'They might go.'

So Emily flounced to the kitchen to press the release button and George stepped to the door, hastily fastening his belt and tucking it back into the hooks of his jeans.

'Hallo,' said Edward, as George swung the door open. 'Been watering the roses again have you?'

George glanced down and saw that he had neglected to do up the buttons on his fly. He flushed.

'Oh,' he said, scrambling to right them. 'I was just –'

'Don't worry, mate,' said Edward patting him bearishly on the arm. 'It happens to the best of us. Even me.' He strode through into the hallway and divested himself of his coat. 'Seen Emily anywhere?'

'Teddy!' came the cry from the kitchen.

'Ems!' bellowed Edward, striding through. 'How are you? Looking ravishing as ever!'

George turned back to the doorway.

'Hello George,' said Jennifer, leaning in to peck shyly at his cheek. A diamond flashed on the hand that held a bunch of tiger lilies, wrapped in white crepe paper.

'Hello,' said George. 'I hear congratulations are in –'

'Yes,' said Jenny. 'Thanks. And how are you?'

'Oh, you know,' said George, 'Fine. Emily's been –' he looked through to where Emily was showing the punctured

bottle top to Edward, vigorously miming his battle with it –
'Great, really. I can't complain.'

'Are you really fine, though George?' said Jennifer, scanning his face. 'Really? I've been so worried about you.'

George opened his mouth to speak.

'There she is!' exclaimed Emily, elbowing her way past him. 'The blushing bride-to-be! Come here, beautiful! Let me kiss you! Are those for me? How wonderful! Here,' she thrust the flowers into George's hands and propelled Jennifer away up the hall. 'In you come. I so want you to meet Dandy and Sue. I just know you'll get on famously.'

She shoved Jenny into the lounge and came bustling back down the hall, hips swinging.

'Excuse us,' she said to Edward who had re-emerged and was studying a map of South Dorset on the wall by the loo. 'I need Porge's masterful assistance in the kitchen.'

So saying, she trotted George through to the kitchen and set him to work buttering bread for the smoked salmon starter, whilst she stalked proprietorially round him, now and then laughing extravagantly and bending to peer through the hatch and check that everyone was looking their way.

The guests were already seated at the table, by the time George carried the starter through. He distributed the plates and sat down with the uneasy feeling of a candidate facing the panel.

'So,' said Jennifer as Emily sat down next to George, helped herself to his hand and plonked it purposefully in her lap. 'George. What are you up to the moment? What have you got planned?'

George stared at her. What was it Ben had said again? That she looked like a goose? Funny, he'd never seen it before, but there was definitely something duck-like about the way she pouted her lips together and tilted her head to one side. He glanced at Edward, gazing complacently at her from the halo of his hair as it glinted in the muted light. That was it! That was what she was: the goose that laid the golden egg!

'Well –' he said.

'Porge is taking a bit of a break from things at the moment,' said Emily. 'It's been a stressful few months and he needs some time to regroup. But after that, well, he might look at doing a teaching qualification. You know, something interesting and engaging and not too heavy on the hours.'

George glanced at her. At her mouth talking, dishing out words.

'I see,' said Jennifer, pecking at a tiny square of smoked salmon on her fork. 'And what about your parents George? How are they?'

'Porge isn't speaking to his parents at the moment,' said Emily. 'We thought it was best just while he got himself sorted out. A lot of the pressures and problems Porge has been struggling with are partly to do with them.'

'Oedipus complex?' suggested Andrew.

'Among others,' nodded Emily.

'Er –' said George.

'I see,' said Jennifer, again. 'And when did you two –?'

'Become entangled?' said Emily, wriggling herself closer to George's fingers, which were fiddling absently with a loose thread on the fabric of her skirt.

'Well,' said Jennifer, ruffled, 'Yes.'

'Well,' said Emily, with a saucy giggle and sidelong glance at George, 'We didn't mean for it to happen. I was just giving Porge a place to stay, but, you know, one thing led to another and, well, Nature took over, I suppose. I'm sure you know how it is.'

'Passion,' said Andrew, licking a fragment of smoked salmon into his mouth.

'Exactly,' said Emily, tugging the slit of her skirt round to bring George's fingers into contact with her thigh beneath.

'You know,' said Sue, swilling her wine round in her glass, 'I'm so pleased you've found a nice girl at last, George. I mean, let's face it, you've never had much luck with girls in the past, have you? A bit of a late starter. And then that awful, neurotic one you spent time with at university. Enough to put anyone off if you ask me.'

'Oh really?' said Jenny, flushing. 'Who was that?'

'More wine, anyone?' said Emily, brandishing a bottle.

Her glass, George noticed, was empty again, whilst his was still full. He glanced anxiously at her, noting the flush around her cheek bones, the hectic look in her eyes. There was a haggard, unfinished quality to her face, as though her young skin were somehow a mask and he could see her future, older features looming through, cleaving to her bones.

'I'll go and get on with the main course,' he mumbled, standing up.

She turned to him with a triumphant beam, her pride in showing him off for once outweighing her desire to get him on his own.

'Porge, what an excellent idea!' she exclaimed, leaning back extravagantly in her groaning chair.

So he went through to the kitchen and set about taming the Bolognese sauce, which was lumpier and thinner than he'd been used to at home. The mushrooms, tomatoes and lumps of meat swirled before his eyes and for one ghastly moment, he saw his own face reflected among them, as though he were stirring it in.

A shadow appeared on the edge of his vision and he flinched, bracing himself for grasping, drunken hands.

'Can I have a word?' said Edward, coming into the room.

'By all means,' said George, suddenly absorbed in trying to scrape a piece of burnt mushroom from the side of the pot.

'Look,' said Edward, settling himself against the counter with a sigh, 'It's not really on, is it?'

'What's not on?' said George, reaching for the metal spatula.

'All this,' said Edward, spreading his arms. 'The way you're carrying on. Taking advantage of things the way you are? Living here rent free? It's a bit much, isn't it?' He coughed. 'By the way, you'll mark the pot if you try and use that, it's non-stick.'

'Is it?' said George, staring at the spatula.

'And flaunting it the way you do. I saw what you were getting up to under the table just now – we all did – and it wasn't a pretty sight. Leaving aside your… dalliance with Jen, it's a bit rich to ask people round for dinner and then put on a display of that sort, don't you think?'

'Well, it would be –' said George, digging at the mushroom with the wooden spoon.

'After all,' said Edward, gravely, 'Bedrooms have walls for a reason.'

'Mmn,' said George. He could certainly testify to that: after one night of Emily's thunderous snores, he had slunk back to the box room in relief. 'But –'

'Alright then,' said Edward, patting him on the back with a laugh. 'Think about what I've said. No-one's saying things haven't been hard for you, but we've got to look out for Em, too. She likes to put across this bolshy, confident image of herself, but underneath it all she's as soft and innocent as they come.'

'Ha!' said George, wondering what Edward would do if he lifted his T-shirt and showed him the nail-marks on his back. He opened his mouth to speak again.

'Glad we understand each other,' said Edward, striding to the door. 'You know, you're really not as bad as I thought.'

'Shame the feeling's not mutual,' muttered George to himself as he picked up a fork to test the pasta.

Edward paused, turned and looked back.

'I'm sorry?' he said.

George flushed.

'Oh nothing,' he said, hurriedly. 'Just talking to myself – you know how it is.'

But Edward was not letting it go. He took a step towards George, his huge shoulders seeming to broaden by the second, as though any moment they would burst from his designer shirt and block out the light.

'Only I thought I heard you say something about me. Something rather uncomplimentary.'

'Oh no,' said George waggling the fork. 'It was… the pasta.'

'Because I hope you realise,' hissed Edward, continuing to advance, 'That you're the last person who should be hurling abuse at me. Particularly under the circumstances.'

'Er –' said George with a bewildered glance at the hatch, 'I'm afraid I've no idea what you're talking about.'

Edward followed his gaze.

'Come on,' he said, taking hold of George's arm. 'Let's talk about this outside.'

So saying, he marched George from the room and out into the hall.

'Porge?' called Emily as the catch on the front door clicked open.

'It's alright, Em,' called George, 'We're just –'

'Straining the pasta,' finished Edward as he stepped over the threshold. There was a nasty look about him, a sort of wild glint in his eye. Were they going to have a fight, George wondered? He had no idea of the form for this sort of thing.

'What on earth –?' began George.

'Oh, don't give me that!' spat Edward, his blonde hair shimmering in the light. 'I can see what you're up to! I know what you're about with your helpless act and arty wank. You're after her again, aren't you? You're trying to win her back. Well, I've got news for you, mate: you're messing with the wrong guy!'

George frowned.

'Is this about Emily?' he said.

'Oh Emily,' said Edward, batting the air and narrowly missing an aspidistra on a plinth positioned against the banister rail. 'Emily's just a smoke screen!'

George blinked. Anything less like a smoke screen than Emily's portly frame would be hard to call to mind.

'It's Jen, you're after,' continued Edward, beginning to pace up and down the landing. 'Sweet, good-hearted, Jen. Trying to claw your way back into her… good graces so that you can ruin her all over again!'

'Ruin her?' said George.

'Oh yes, she's told me all about your little proclivities. The magazine with the horsewhip. The time you tried to get her to… submit to you outside.' He stopped pacing and fixed George's gaze. 'I mean, don't get me wrong, we all have our extra-curricular interests… but girls like Jen, they need to believe that things are good and pure. They need to be looked after. You can't just leap on them and expect them to like it. Subtlety, that's what girls like. Patience.'

George opened his mouth to protest. But Edward wasn't finished.

'But then that's you all over, isn't it?' he was saying, pacing again, warming to his theme. 'You've always been a bit odd, a bit strange. I mean, all that stuff with Evelyn Waugh. That's not normal is it? That's a little bizarre.' He was bunching his fists now, muttering to himself as though he'd almost forgotten anyone else was there. George had the unsettling feeling that these words weren't being spoken for the first time; that they had been hissed in bathrooms and whispered on late-night walks back from the pub. 'And that business of turning up to a tutorial in the middle of the night. I mean, you're not trying to tell me that's sane behaviour, are you? You're not trying to tell me that's normal!' He shook his head, his face flushed. 'It's downright abnormal, that's what it is. Frankly, it's special needs. Probably done for effect, that's the truth of it. Done to make some bizarre, ridiculous point. Or win favour with the girls because he can't do it any other way. Because he's deficient.' He turned sharply on his heel, shuddering the plant-stand. 'There's an explanation, he says. Well there's always an explanation with people like that. It's always someone else's fault. Bloody communists. Frankly, it makes me sick –'

Edward stopped and looked up suddenly to find George standing in the doorway, holding the pasta fork. He gave an awkward laugh.

'Sorry about that, mate,' he said. 'Seem to have –' He took a step towards George and put a hand on his arm. 'Let's just call it quits, shall we? Wipe the slate clean.' He patted George, as one pets an unpredictable dog. 'You know, mate, you're really not as bad as –'

But George would not be mated. He would not be patted and walked over and sent back to the table like a good boy. Not after the week he'd had. Not after frankfurters and floral tiles and fucking *Citrus Fresh*. He shrugged off Edward's hand and, in one smooth, instinctive movement, lashed out and jabbed the pasta fork deep into the blonde's hefty shoulder.

A silence followed. Edward stood staring at George with an astonished look upon his face, the fork sticking out of his shirt at a jaunty angle. He staggered back a step and knocked the plinth, sending the aspidistra sliding to the floor. A moment passed; more stares. Then, calmly, George stepped back into the hallway of the flat and shut the door.

He went to the kitchen and set about draining the pasta and serving the food up onto plates. It was a little overdone but it would do. They could always leave it if it wasn't to their taste.

Emily was already working her way towards the bottom of another glass of wine when he came through. She looked up and gestured gaily at him like a character in a play as he walked in and began unloading the plates from the hatch, setting them down in front of the guests. He put one in front of Edward's chair.

'See,' said Emily. 'See how sweet he is? I hardly have to do anything any more. I just give him instructions and he's away. So caring, so thoughtful. And he's terribly well trained: hardly ever leaves the seat up and never forgets to flush.' She leaned back in her chair, stretching out her arms so that her breasts blobbed to each side. 'And he's terribly tender, aren't you, Porge? Terribly attentive to my needs.'

'Sue likes me to pretend to be a policeman when we have sex,' said Andrew and began shovelling pasta into his mouth.

'You know, I sometimes look at him,' continued Emily, watching George move about the room, 'And I think: surely it's illegal to be this happy? Surely there must be some law against wanting someone, against needing someone so much; against being so incredibly satisfied. But every day I come home and he's here, dear, sweet, dependable Porge. Things have been hard for him, life hasn't worked out quite the way he planned, but he doesn't let it spoil things. He's not threatened by my financial success, by my brains. He's happy just to be here with me. Wonderful Porge!'

Tears welling in her eyes, she stood up and wedged her bulk onto George's lap as he sat down in the seat next to her.

'Em,' said George, in faint protest, his voice sounding far away.

'It's alright, Porge,' said Emily, putting a finger to his lips, 'They're friends. They like to see it. They like to see us here… loving each other.'

An anchor of dread sank down through George and lodged itself icily in his groin as Emily nestled into him and clamped her mouth to his. Her face up-close, kissing, was monstrous: a Cyclops eating in its sleep. Beyond it he saw them all, eating, staring, trying to be pleased, and panic, like a distant drum, began to beat.

At length, she drew away and stared woozily down at him, a faint smile playing on her lips.

'Loving each other,' she murmured again.

The words hung heavy in the air, like toilet freshener sprayed by someone too anxious to be clean. Through it came the sound of Andrew munching, scraping the plate with his fork. George looked round at them, at their mouths, eating.

'Where's Edward?' said Jennifer after a moment or two.

'Oh,' said George, vaguely. 'He popped out for a –'
They nodded.

'You know, Porge,' said Emily, reaching up to run her fingers round his ear, 'If you asked me to marry you right now, I'd say yes.' She shifted, her weight pressing down on his thigh, sending it to sleep. 'Because,' she continued, 'I can't see how it could be any more perfect than this. Any more ideal.'

George stared up at her and swallowed. Was he going to have to propose to her just to get the blood back to his leg? He sighed. Well, what would it matter, after all? It all felt very far away. All rather unreal. Perhaps it was as good a reason as any.

An image of Edward staggering with the fork swam to the surface of his mind and he plunged himself into a kiss to make it go. They kissed for a moment or two, wetly, regardless of their guests. At length, the ringing of the telephone made them draw apart.

'Get that, will you Porge?' said Emily breathlessly. 'I just don't think I can.'

He went through to the kitchen and picked up the handset shuddering on the side.

'Hello?' he said.

'George French?' said a voice.

'Yes,' he said, blankly.

'Oh good, I've caught you.'

George said nothing.

'Look, I know it's late notice,' continued the voice, 'But we were wondering if you might be free to come on the show tomorrow?'

Nothing again. It didn't matter: the voice needed no encouragement.

'The *David & Trudy Show*,' it said, 'Only the Belgian dancers have pulled out all of a sudden and we've got ten minutes to fill.'

'Oh,' George heard his voice say. 'Ok.'

'You will? Great! Where shall I send the car?'

So he gave the address of the flat, all the while staring at the floral motif on one of the kitchen tiles. The pattern was symmetrical, he'd never noticed that before.

'Lovely,' said the person on the other end, scribbling it all down. 'Well, we'll see you tomorrow morning, then.'

'Yes,' said George.

'Goodbye now.'

'Yes,' said George again. 'Goodbye.'

He put the receiver down and wandered through to the other room. They were all still sitting at the table, behind their empty plates. The glasses glinted in the candlelight.

'Turns out I'm going to be on television,' he said with a laugh.

They all looked at him and suddenly he felt very tired and a bit as though he might faint. Without another word, he turned and walked out of the room and away down the hall, past the map of Dorset, and into the box room at the end. He shut the door.

12

He awoke sweating with a heavy feeling round his heart. There was something not right; something he had done; some terrible thing. He groped around in the half-light of his sleep-fogged brain. Touching Emily's breast? Giving up the course? Telling a journalist his mother was having an affair? They were none of them right. What else?

The clouds of his slumber began to disperse. As they parted, a grotesque image flashed upon his brain: the blonde, Edward, wide-eyed and staring, with a stainless steel fork jammed into his upper arm, a fork that had been in George's hand.

He contemplated the image for a moment, waiting for the familiar wash of relief that would signal that the whole macabre incident was nothing but a dream. It did not come. It did not come – he kicked out a leg – because, yes, here he was in the single bed in Emily's box room. Because – knowledge came now in an icy rush – that had actually happened last night! Christ! He drew the foot back in quickly under the duvet and pulled the covers over him. The image of Edward blazed in the darkness: horrified, scandalized, bathed in a blonde, beatific glow.

But what had happened next? Why was he still here? Why hadn't they come to take him away? He thought quickly, setting sail once more on the turbulent waters of the previous evening, trawling his memory for facts. He remembered coming in here and the sound, not long after, of the remaining guests donning their coats for the journey home. They'd been hushed, not wanting to disturb. Emily had whispered busily about his not being quite himself yet; still needing time to adjust. The door had whined and tutted shut. After that: nothing. He must have fallen asleep. Presumably they hadn't found Edward slumped on the landing or – Christ, no! – crumpled at the bottom of the stairs? They'd have come back, wouldn't they? They'd have raised merry hell!

What then?

A nasty thought began to form at the back of his mind: what if Edward had staggered off and was now lying somewhere, dead? That would make George French a murderer, wouldn't it? That would make him a Class A crim! He shook himself violently, shuddering the little bed. No: ridiculous! People didn't die from forks being jabbed into their upper arms, did they? He probed his own shoulder, feeling for weak spots. No, it all felt decidedly stout. And anyway, it wasn't as though he'd intended Edward any serious harm. It had all been a bit of a lark really, hadn't it? A bit of misjudged fun. After all, who'd ever heard of someone seriously attacking a person with a fork? Clearly, it had to have been a joke.

Still, he thought as he gnawed a hang-nail, it wouldn't look good in court, would it? Murder for comedy value? Put like that, it could seem quite sick.

He waited until he was sure Emily had gone before attempting to get up. He couldn't face any of it this morning: not the cooing, nor the kissing, nor the coming at him with a comb. Besides, what if she'd guessed the truth?

At last he heard her emerge into the hallway and wedge on her shoes. He waited, tensed, to see if she would approach the door, try to get inside. But there was none of that: the keys rattled, the door shut, and the sound of footsteps receded down the stairs. Shunting the boxes out of the way, George nosed his way gingerly out into the hall. It was neat and silent, just as he remembered it, with motes of dust shifting gently in the light coming through the kitchen door. No sign of any murderous activity here. Perhaps he was misremembering? Perhaps if he picked up the phone and called Jennifer now, he'd find that it was all alright, all fine: something to laugh about in the pub six months down the line. It wasn't impossible. Perhaps he should call Jennifer and put his mind at rest. But what to say? 'I think I stabbed your fiancé last night – just phoning to check he's alright?' No thanks. Not likely.

He went through to the kitchen to make some toast just as the outdoor buzzer went. He froze. Was this it, then? The police come to take him away? 'We'd just like to ask a few questions down the station, sir' and then bang! Goodbye to daylight for twenty-five years.

Perhaps he shouldn't answer it, pretend no-one was home. But no, hang on, if it really was the police, shouldn't he be helpful and co-operative from the start? Wouldn't that be more likely to work in his favour, get him a shorter stint? Things would be a lot easier if he just came quietly and left it at that. Besides, if it really was the police, they'd probably just break down the door.

He stepped towards the intercom just as the buzzer sounded again.

'Hello?' he whimpered into the microphone.

'Car for George French.'

He frowned. 'But I didn't order a –'

'From the television studio. The *David & Trudy Show*.'

The truth of it broke upon him like the sun bursting through clouds. He beamed.

'Of course!' he said. 'Silly me! I'll be right down.'

Running to his room, he scrambled into the first pair of jeans that came to hand – the grubby pair he'd left home in all those weeks ago – threw on a T-shirt, and hurried from the flat. He hadn't washed, but it didn't matter because they were not the police! Galloping out onto the landing and down the stairs, he was delighted to note the absence of bloody hand-prints on the wallpaper, the orderliness of everything. Even the ruined aspidistra had been tidied discreetly away. Clearly, it was all going to be fine.

But in the car, driving through the grey, rain-smeared streets, panic began to bite. Why had they asked him to come on this show anyway? Was it because of his messages or something else? That awful article in *The Times*, for example. And what if by now they had heard of his exploits with the fork? What if Edward, staggering from the party had gone to a phone box and sold his story to *The Sun*? It was the sort of thing he might do to stick the knife in. He gulped. What if he was already notorious? The South London Sticker? The Putney Prodder? He'd never even been to Putney, but that wouldn't matter to them: anything for a good story; a catchy slogan on the bottom of the screen. He glanced at the driver's eyes in the rear-view mirror: steely, staring straight ahead. There was nothing to tell there. The man had been non-committal, brisk, a consummate professional. Perhaps he picked up would-be murderers all the time.

He stared glumly out at the passing streets, the be-suited people hurrying to work. Christ, what he'd give to be one of them now! To have the day full of little, useful tasks! He watched a woman loaded down with bags, hobbling frantically on four-inch heels. Oh, to be running for a bus! To be late for a meeting! To be up against a deadline at the office! It would be heaven, wouldn't it? Sweet ambrosia from the Gods! But no, such simple pleasures were not for him. He had put himself beyond the reach of water-coolers and shredders and sachets of flavoured coffee that you plugged into over-sized drinks machines.

The car deposited him outside a dingy, rust-stained building somewhere in the back streets towards the east. George looked around him doubtfully as he got out. This couldn't be it surely? This shabby seventies cube wedged in amongst the soot-stained warehouses built to service another age? This pile of withered plastic slowly cracking with the years? But it was: a once-bright sign, now missing a couple of its letters announced that this was indeed the home of *Thamesrive' Television: where cr'ativity flows.* He hesitated on the pavement, seized with an urge to run off up the street. If he made a break for it now, perhaps he could escape up the country on foot and start a new life as a shoe-maker in Aberdeen? But no: too late. A woman with a clipboard had spotted him and was coming this way.

'George French?' she said with steely brightness. 'Great, come this way.'

She led him into the lobby, through a set of double doors, and along a grey, carpet-lined corridor towards a reception desk at the end.

'George French,' she said, rolling her eyes at the girl there, a thin, brightly-dressed creature with hair swept up into a feathery, chaotic arrangement. Job done, the woman turned and was gone.

'I'm –' began George.

On the walls were pictures of David & Trudy in a variety of glamorous and daring situations: riding an elephant; beaming on the red carpet; stepping aboard a yacht on the set of the latest Bond film.

'Yes!' said the girl, flashing a toothpaste advert smile as she glanced at his stained jeans, his greasy hair. 'Of course you are!'

She picked up a receiver and started speaking into it.

'Gerry? You're not going to like this,' she glanced at George and grinned, 'There's someone I think you should – …No, well, I know, neither did I… It's, er, one of the –'

'George French,' said George hastily.

The girl grinned again.

'Yes, I know they're supposed to!' she hissed into the phone. 'But he hasn't!... I don't know!... Look, don't get arsy with me, Gerry. It's not my fault. Just get out here and do something about it.'

She put the phone down and beamed at George.

'Our wardrobe manager should be with you in a moment,' she said and turned back to her screen.

George nodded and stood back to wait. After all, he had better do as he was told, hadn't he? This wasn't the time to rock the boat.

He stared around the reception area, watching the people hurrying to and fro. So these were the hallowed halls of celebrity, the secret haunts of fame? Funny, he hadn't expected it all to be so dingy, so thoroughly worn, like the corridors and classrooms he remembered from his primary school: scuffed and grubby with, here and there, an optimistic stab of colour looming through the grime. Even where they had tried to make an effort – with the desk and the potted ferns – everything looked a little rubbed around the edges: the leaves dusty, the soil dry, the bottom panel of the desk scarred with the scrape of passing shoes. It made him sort of sad.

He stepped over to investigate a picture of Trudy shaking hands with the President of Pakistan and –

'Cheesecloth!' screamed a voice.

George turned. A small spikey-haired man was standing just up the corridor from him, appearing to be undergoing a mild form of seizure. George eyed him anxiously, waiting for someone to step forward and usher him gently to a chair, but no-one seemed to have heard.

'Cheesecloth!' shrieked the man again, running forward to take hold of George's arm. 'Didn't they tell you on the phone? The bachelors always wear cheesecloth! It's what people expect!'

'Oh,' said George, taken aback. 'Sorry. I don't think I have any cheesecloth.' He frowned. 'Bachelors?' he said.

'Hmmn,' said the man, taking George by the shoulder and turning him round. 'Dirty these up yourself did you? Very *My Beautiful Laundrette*. Looks almost real. Still, it's all wrong, of course. All a complete disaster. All going to have to be changed.' He fanned himself with his free hand. 'They simply don't pay me enough,' he said.

'Well,' said George, shrugging – after all, he might as well be hanged for a sheep as for a lamb – 'If it helps at all, you don't have to worry too much about me. I don't really care how I loo–'

'Yes, well anyone can see that, darling,' groaned Gerry. 'The trouble is that, at the moment, in television terms what you're saying is… well, it's like a huge burp. Frankly, sweetcheeks, you look as though you've come to service the tampon machines.' He reached up and turned George's head briskly from side to side. 'When did you last moisturise?'

'Er –'

'No! Don't tell me! I don't think I could bear it!' He sighed and fanned himself vigorously again, looking around to check who was watching. Then seizing George's hand, he dragged him off in the direction of a small broom-cupboard of a room halfway up the corridor, drew him inside and shut the door.

Twenty minutes later, George emerged, blinking, into the light. He'd been plucked and primped and preened. He'd been zipped and zjujed and zizzed. He'd been thrust into trousers and tucked into shirts, twirled, clapped, and made to remove them again. He'd had moisturiser and make-up smeared liberally over his face and a girl with an ominous pair of scissors sweeping his hair repeatedly over one eye. And they'd decided that he should wear specs.

'Sophisticated, darling!' Gerry had gushed, thrusting a pair of NHS frames onto his face, 'Mysterious! Every housewife's dream!' before rushing off to dishevel a couple of make-over victims who had arrived for the show looking too pristine.

Standing in the corridor now, squinting at his reflection in the glass of a picture showing David sprawled on a bed with Paula Yates, George was somewhat bewildered by what he saw. Far from a dangerous criminal, he looked more akin to someone escaped from the local infirmary or, possibly, a member of a declining boy band. If someone had told him that the face that now stared back at him from the glass belonged to Gary Barlow, he wouldn't have been surprised. The make-up felt hot and heavy on his face and neck; already the cheesecloth was starting to chafe his tenderest parts. The one comfort in this, he supposed, was that at least it made him less recognisable. There was a slim chance that some of his lesser acquaintances might not realise it was him. Small consolation, perhaps, but still, in the darkness of his prison cell, it might offer him a shred of satisfaction to think that Jeremy from the third row back in his Classical Civilizations class probably believed he was out there somewhere making a modest success of himself in the world: wearing a shirt and tie and getting home every evening in time for the news at ten. He took a step forward and – 'Ah!' – collided with a small woman dressed all in black, with a clipboard and a mass of chaotically-pinned hair.

'Don't tell me, don't tell me!' she cried, holding up a hand before flicking furiously through the sheaf of papers, 'You're 'When good holidays go bad'!'

'No,' said George.

'Huh,' said the woman and looked again at her list. '"My make-over ruined my relationship'?'

George shook his head.

'What about –' she tapped the page in triumph '– 'Life after liver-spots'?'

'No,' said George. 'I'm George French.'

'George French,' said the woman, skimming her finger down the page. 'George French, George French. No, can't see it. What are you, a dancer?'

'I'm –' said George. 'I think I'm here for an interview.'

'An interview?' said the woman with a frown. 'George French... Ah! Here we are! Eligible bachelors, George French. Of course! You'll be doing the Housework Challenge.'

'Housework Challenge?' said George, bewildered. 'I thought I was going to have an interview.'

'Mmn,' said the woman, tapping a pen against her teeth. 'The thing about interviews is you kind of have to be famous to do them. Otherwise people don't know who you are.'

A glad realisation began to seep into George's mind: so it was the phone calls that had got him here after all. Nothing to do with the article. And they clearly had no idea about the fork.

'Look,' the woman was saying. 'My advice is, give it your best shot. It can't hurt, can it? You might win a Hoover. And there's a breakfast buffet through those double doors, so you'll get a good meal out of it either way. If you go in there and hang around, someone will come and find you when it's time.'

George walked slowly in the direction she was pointing, oblivious to the people he passed. A light feeling was rising up inside him and he had to fight the urge to laugh. They didn't know! No-one knew. Someone near him said 'Oh look, Angela Rippon!' as he passed, but he didn't bother turning and trying to see. He felt distant, removed from it all, as though he were swimming under water or walking in a dream. He had stabbed someone with a fork last night and now they were going to set him the Housework Challenge; thrust a vacuum cleaner in his hand and make him clean a room; laugh and drop innuendos about his suction power, the size of his nozzle; have people vote for him while they drank their morning tea. Christ it was ludicrous, wasn't it? The punch-line to some great, farcical joke.

He pushed through the double doors into the buffet room. They had made more of an effort in here, painting the walls in vibrant colours, arranging stands of exotic flowers at strategic points along the walls. There was a long table in the centre of the room laden with a vast array of breakfast treats, from rubbery continental cheeses to oozing chocolate bites, but George felt too chaotic for anything so structured as handling cups and plates. Let alone cutlery: knives and – ha! – forks. He went to stand beside a riot of tiger lilies, staring vaguely at the figures swarming around the coffee pot like so many brightly-coloured bees. He had to keep a grip on things, he whispered to his whirling brain, keep a level-head. It would be silly to go off the rails and give himself away now. He must concentrate on –

'James Finch! As I live and breathe!'

George looked round. A strangely familiar face, framed with tufts of grey hair and sporting an outlandish monocle, greeted him. It was luridly orange and appeared to be floating above a fuchsia-pink cravat, flaked with croissant crumbs.

'Er, it's George,' said George. 'My name's George.'

'That's right, that's right!' said the face, blinking the correction away. 'How's the Crimean War?'

George stared for a moment as the features of his former tutor, John Worthy, fell into place. He sighed.

'Great,' he said blankly. 'Absolutely fascinating.'

'Good, good,' said the tutor, pausing to crush another handful of croissant into his mouth. 'And what are you doing here?' He mumbled through the crumbs, 'I must say, I didn't have you down as a TV bod.'

'Oh, I'm not,' said George. 'Actually I'm down to do the Housework Challenge.'

'Are you?' said John Worthy, stepping back and taking out the monocle to stare at George, revealing a large, red mark encircling one eye. 'Whatever for?'

George shrugged.

'Apparently you can win a Hoover,' he said.

John Worthy nodded thoughtfully.

'Better than a slap in the face.'

'Mmn,' said George. At the back of his mind, a voice was laughing hysterically to the accompaniment of *Wild Thing* by The Troggs. 'Er…What about you? What brings you here?'

'Oh me? I'm one of the regulars: 'The Professor'.' He stepped back to regard the effect of this on George before continuing: 'I do a sort of mid-morning thought slot, a kind of poor man's thought for the day. It's supposed to make the students feel less guilty about skiving off their lectures to watch the show. All nonsense, of course.'

'Oh,' said George. He wondered what John Worthy would do if he pulled his shirt over his head and ran screaming from the room. 'But that's… How did you -?'

'Bit of a funny story, actually,' said the professor, selecting an apple from a platter on the table and rubbing it vigorously on the lapel of his jacket. 'A while ago I was down on my luck – I got fired from that terrible university, you know: drink, they could never prove it – working in some god awful Community Advertising place –'

'Citizen's Advice Bureau?' said George.

'That's the one,' continued the professor. 'Or was it a Job Centre? Oh well, same thing. Ever been in one? Real dives, aren't they? Anyway, I was working there and one of my former students came in. Funny sort of fellow: one of those wistful, public school sorts. You know the type: terribly conventional and middle-class, yet convinced he was going to an artist and that he had something terribly new and arresting to say to the world. Talked a lot of twaddle. But one thing he did say which stuck with me – even after they caught me having a discussion with the cleaner in the broom cupboard – was that daytime television might be the answer to it all.' John Worthy bit deeply into the apple, sending a jet of juice straight into George's face before continuing: 'I'd never thought of it before but, after they kicked me out, I began to see that he might have a point. So – you'll laugh – I started hanging around Trafalgar Square, seeing if I couldn't get myself included in one of those vox-pops they're always doing, get my face known, and, well, long-story-short, I got spotted. And here I am.'

'Well –' said George. 'That's –'

'George French!' called a voice.

George looked. Over the other side of the room, a small woman in black, sporting a headset was beckoning. She took his hand and led him through another set of doors, and out into a corridor beyond. There was a dank, stale smell about it, reminiscent of the passage outside the locker rooms at school. There was a door at the far end of the corridor above which a red light blazed the legend "On Air". Nudging it open with her shoulder, the woman motioned for George to be quiet and brought him through into the studio beyond.

The place was vast and shadowy, less a room than a warehouse. Piled with pieces of set and equipment, it was cordoned off in places to form separate miniature worlds. As his eyes adjusted to the gloom, George made out the sharp, clean lines of the studio kitchen and the dark, ferny recesses of the studio greenhouse, where someone was setting out a series of seedlings ready for the next featurette. The lights were up on the living room area with its mammoth sofas arranged in front of the window onto the Thames, and there a woman with a loud Geordie voice was discoursing on a holiday incident in France to the programme's travel guru, who was making a show of being greatly amused. In front of them on the fringes of the darkness, clustered like animals at the edge of a woodland glade, were members of the production team, flanked by screens and lights and three mighty cameras on trolleys which shifted periodically, retreated, or zoomed in.

George watched uneasily from the door. The whole place unnerved him: its spareness, its disjointedness. Funny, he had always imagined the studio as a sort of yuppie apartment on the Thames; the sort of place that David and Trudy might linger after hours, drinking Singapore Slings and watching boats glide past. Seeing it arranged like this – a series of tricked-out cells, a bright, life-size doll's house – it struck him as peculiarly cold and strange. Life as an eight year-old might see it, with one wall cut away.

'This way,' whispered the woman, leading him to a section further along the wall.

They'd been busy here, flinging clothes, books and dirty plates around a small, box room-sized space containing a single bed and a chest of drawers. On the walls were a couple of peeling posters showing cars and a non-descript view of a desert scene.

'Tracy Emmin, it ain't,' whispered the woman. 'But we think it's quite effective.'

There were a number of people dotted around the benighted set, as well as several cameras already rigged up. Earnest-looking runners, most of them young enough to be on work-experience from school, scampered here and there, carrying leads, clipboards and cups of tea.

The woman led George over to a man sitting on the edge of the unmade bed, fiddling with his clip-on microphone.

'David, this is George,' said the woman, 'Today's Eligible Bachelor.'

David looked up blowing a wisp of hair from his face. George was disconcerted to see that he was slighter and more pop-eyed than he had imagined; also that he did not smile.

'Well, what do you want me to do about it?' said David, looking through George to the team milling about on the studio-floor. 'Will somebody give George his marks, please? Or is it down to me to direct the whole fiasco as well?'

George looked around, bemused. Marks? Had they been judging him, then? He wondered uneasily if they had made a secret film of him since he arrived; whether there would be scenes of him wriggling into Gerry's tight-fitting cheesecloth trousers enlivening coffee breaks up and down the land. Off in the darkness beyond the set, the camera lenses glinted like huge, insects' eyes.

'David!' came an aggrieved voice. George felt a hand on his arm. He turned and found himself looking down on a helmet of impeccably-coiffed blonde hair and a pair of padded shoulders. Trudy looked up and smiled mumsily. 'So sorry about him, Jeremy. I don't know why he feels the need to be so rude. Here,' she tottered him off to the side of the set, 'You stand there while we do the intro and then we'll call you into shot for the challenge.' So saying, she slid her hand clumsily down George's back, and over his bottom, all the while staring her husband. 'And stop fiddling with your tie, David,' she added. 'It won't win you any sympathy.'

David shrugged and turned away.

'Honestly, Jeremy,' continued Trudy in a stage whisper directed forcefully across the set, 'You wouldn't believe the way he behaves sometimes: tantrums, hissy-fits, bad language! He even raised his hand to me last week! It's quite shocking.'

'Mmmn,' said George, gazing absently around the set. The flimsiness of it all alarmed him, the boards held up by struts of wood. All of it arranged to create an illusion of clutter and busyness and the everyday, when really there was this yawning space, this blackness.

'You'd never do that, would you Jeremy?' Trudy went on. 'You'd never raise your hand to an innocent woman? Engage in physical abuse?'

David stood up.

'Right,' he said. 'That's it!'

'Take it easy, David,' said one of the shadowy figures behind the cameras.

'No,' said David. 'No. I don't see why I should have to put up with this day in day out. I don't see why I have to play the villain – constantly – when I only did what – is it seventy percent of men?' he looked around for confirmation.

'Eighty,' belched someone on camera two.

'Eighty? Is it as much as that? Well, there we are. I only did what eighty percent of married men do. And, I might add, I'm sure not many of them have –' he flailed a hand in Trudy's direction '– Such provocation.'

'Be that as it may,' sniffed Trudy, 'But you can hardly expect me to be all sweetness and light after you've made a mockery of our marriage vows on national television!'

'As though that makes it worse!' hissed David. 'Find me a marriage that doesn't end on-screen these days! Anyway, I didn't hear you complaining when you had the whole show to yourself. You certainly didn't hold back from putting your case!'

'Everyone said I was very dignified!' protested Trudy. '*The Sun* said I was like Princess Diana!'

'What? Dead and rotten?'

'And on you in five' came a voice, '– Four –...'

George edged further away from the light and ducked his head as David and Trudy stepped together stepped together in the centre of the set. A monitor facing them flickered on, showing the window looking out on the Thames and the monstrous sofas on which the two women still sat, hooting raucously. A speaker crackled into life.

'And then I caught my breath,' said one of them, fanning herself with what appeared to be a rope of plastic garlic, 'And I realised it was the man from the bike shop after all!'

Canned laughter wafted around the studio as figures scurried back and forth, readying the last bits of bedroom detritus, adjusting wires and flexes and leads.

'You couldn't make it up, could you?' continued the on-screen presenter. 'Just as well, really, because Jenna's book *The First Time I Kissed a Frenchman* will be out next week –'

'In all good bookshops,' added the first woman quickly. 'Priced fourteen ninety-nine.'

'But now,' continued the presenter, turning to another camera. 'From one kissable French man to another. Let's find out who David and Trudy have got in the bedroom today!'

The lights blazed suddenly as David and Trudy began to manufacture loud, enthusiastic laughs.

'What a wonderful story!' said Trudy.

'Yes,' said David, reading from the autocue. 'I'd love to read the book. In fact – how's this for an idea? – why don't we investigate setting up a book club? You know, get people around the country reading books and talking about them?'

'Don't be ridiculous, David,' beamed Trudy. 'No-one reads anymore.'

A muscle twitched in David's cheek, but he stuck to the script.

'In fact, today's Eligible Bachelor could tell us a thing or two about books,' he said, reaching for the bright pink vacuum cleaner that someone had placed beside him. 'We'll meet him in a minute, but first, for those of you who haven't been following the early heats of the Household Challenge – shame on you! – let me just take you through the rules.'

He launched into a long and involved description, mentioning phone voting, a panel of judges and even some sort of aggregate system. As he talked, George stared up into the lights, which beat down upon him as relentlessly as the summer sun on the cricket pitch at school. Oh to be back there now: gawky and resentful; whooped and clapped by the three figures at the pavilion end. Life had been so simple then.

He watched David gesticulating to the camera. Any minute he would stretch out his hand and force George into shot. Even now, he could see the host's arm extending, his fingers starting to unfurl. He tugged frantically at his rigid hair, trying to pull it over his eyes. What was he doing here? How had he ever thought that this was the answer to anything? And, more to the point, what was he doing here now, this morning, when he had – yes he had – assaulted someone last night? Shouldn't he be out looking for Edward, trying to make amends? If only he could some pretext to get out of this, slip away.

David stretched out his hand towards him as somewhere across the studio a door banged open and the sound of rapid footsteps began to echo across the room. Behind the cameras, heads turned and hands gestured vigorously for quiet. David stumbled momentarily in his speech, before recovering and carrying on.

But the footsteps were getting nearer, hard: spiky sounds, clattering meaningfully across the floor. Behind the cameras, the crew members were miming a series of elaborate gestures, many of which appeared to bear some relation to archaic torture techniques.

'Er,' said David, abandoning the scrolling script, 'I must apologise for the noise off-set. There seems to be –'

'There you are!' crowed Lucy Thinkwell triumphantly, striding into the spotlight, brandishing a folded newspaper.

'Lucy!' gasped David.

'Yes!' announced Lucy, shaking back her hair and glaring round the set to check that every eye was on her. 'Oh don't look so surprised, David! You must have known what would happen when I saw this!' Here she unfurled the paper and made a show of reading: '"Daytime showbiz sweethearts David Waverley and Trudy Donovan revealed today that they are re-united after a marital split that left the nation reeling. Said Waverley: 'We're just as much in love as ever. More, if anything. What happened earlier this year was just a meaningless fling.'" What a load of crap!'

'May I remind you,' ventured a voice from behind the cameras, 'It's a daytime show?'

'Oh piss off!' stormed Lucy. 'Or I'll say the f-word too!'

A gasp rippled round the studio and the gofers that had been edging their way gingerly onto the set, seeking hopefully for some means of salvaging the feature and guiding the uninvited guest away, froze.

'The point is David,' continued Lucy, her slender frame heaving magnificently beneath the fabric of her sleeveless, red dress, 'We all know this is b– We all know this is... not true. We all know the real reason you've gone back to the old bag.' She turned to Trudy. 'Did he tell you he went for Parkinson's job?' she said. 'Mmn? Did he mention that? Oh yes, he wanted to forge a solo career, break free. That's what he told me,' she said, turning her face to the cameras to drive the point home. 'Break free. He didn't get it of course – too much of an ego to talk about anything other than himself. But, oh boy, if he had things would have been different. You wouldn't have seen him for dust. We'd have been off living it up in the South of France by now.' She sighed and mock-pouted. 'But then of course he realised it wasn't going to work out for him on his own, that he really was a washed-up, one trick pony, and that was it: he headed back home with his tail between his legs, begging for his old job back. It's obvious, really, when you look at the two of us. And you can repress it all you like, sweetheart, but it won't change a thing. There was only ever one reason why lover-boy could have come crawling back to you: ratings.'

Lucy Thinkwell stopped talking and stood back to regard the effect of her words, savouring the expressions of horror and fascination festooning the faces of the production team dotted around the set. She allowed the silence to lengthen for a moment, before opening her mouth to speak again.

'And another thing –' she began ominously.

But whatever the other thing might have been, it was lost forever to the viewing public, for in that instant, David leaning over, took hold of a strand of Lucy's hair and, with a sweeping motion, whipped the entire mane clean off her head. He dropped the wig and stood back leaving Lucy centre-stage, her pale, bald scalp glinting.

The whole thing happened so quickly that for a moment, no-one did anything; the cameras continued to roll and Lucy stood, a triumphal smile playing on her lips, a poisonous revelation waiting in her eyes, whilst patches of grey, wispy hair fluttered limply against her scalp. Then all hell broke loose: shrieks rang out, someone fell, and cameras nodded as their operators let go of them and fought to regain control. A voice somewhere was burbling about adverts and the show having to go on, a runner scurried forward with a blanket and stopped as though uncertain how to proceed, and then the room fell slowly still as every eye zoned in on Lucy and every ear strained to process the strange, whimpering sound that seemed to be coming from her mouth. There was a deathly hush. Slowly, deliberately, as an actress on a stage, Lucy reached up and touched her bare scalp. She flinched; she flushed; rage flooded up through her face and curdled in her eyes.

'David!' she screamed, and began to stagger off the set, clutching her head. Then, suddenly turning to face the cameras, she said in her psychology update voice: 'Alopecia is a serious medical condition which blights many thousands of lives.' She blinked. A second passed. The runner edged forward again, holding the blanket like a shield. Something snapped. And suddenly, Lucy Thinkwell was running, running across the studio, heels clattering on the floor, running down the passageway and through the double-doors. From a distance came the crackle of an internal radio as a security-guard mistook her for an interloper and informed control that he was giving chase.

'We could go to unusual pets?' suggested a hopeful production assistant who really was on work experience from school.

But no-one did anything. It was as though time itself had somehow stripped and hurtled screeching from the room. Only the blind scrolling of the autocue gave any sense of one second moving to the next. And there was no-one to read its dictates now, for in the centre of the set, yet somehow removed from the world, stood David and Trudy, gazing at each other with far-off smiles, as though seeing each other for the first time, anew.

'David,' said Trudy, at length, 'That was –'

But there was no need for further words, for, as one, the two of them surged together, clutching and kissing as urgently as starving creatures fall upon food. They stood, clinched, for a moment or two, before subsiding to the bed, leaving the pink Hoover subsiding in the middle of the set, like a dying flamingo.

'Cue ads,' called a voice from somewhere behind the cameras and from speakers dotted around the studio, the familiar jingle heralded a break.

'Fucking hell,' said a bearded man stepping through into the bright studio lights. He stood for a moment, wiping his nose meditatively on his sleeve. 'Still, I think we can turn this to our advantage. Marriage triumphs over muck; the other woman sent packing. Very daytime, very new millennium.' A smile spread across his face, cracking the beard open like a piece of rotten fruit. 'In fact,' he continued, 'Play this one right and we'll have them eating out of the palms of our hands – ratings figures back up to at least the levels of the early nineties, advertising revenue, oh, sky-high. Fuck, it's a gift, now I come to think about it! A solid gold, license to print money. Well-played, David, that's all I can say! Well-fucking-played mate!' He clapped his hands and hurried back behind the cameras. 'Right!' he yelled. 'Places everyone, we're going to re-set to go again after the break. John, or Richard, or whatever your name is,' he continued, waving a hand in George's direction, 'Get in the centre with that vacuum cleaner, ready to bust a gut with it. Go for your life. Mate, I can tell you, this is your lucky day – you're always going to be remembered for this.'

But George was nowhere to be seen, for, in the midst of the chaos, seizing his chance, he had slipped quietly off the set, away to the dressing room and out through the lobby to the street.

Outside, the street was glistening. The clouds overhead were thinning and spreading, leaving the sky an even, translucent white. Cars sizzled past the end of the road and weak glimmers of sun picked out the lines and edges of the office blocks towering above.

George breathed deeply, savouring the cool moisture of the city air after the arid fug inside, the familiar feel of his clothes. He was about to set off along the pavement, when a black cab hurtled along the road, swerved in to the curb and skidded to a halt. The door opened and a familiar, angular figure leapt out, leaving the cab to idle in its wake: Jennifer.

'George!' she cried.

'Jennifer,' said George, glancing anxiously behind her. She seemed to be alone.

She hurried forward, hands out-stretched and then halted suddenly, as though uncertain how to proceed. She had got ready in a hurry, that much was clear: her hair flapped wispily round her face and the circles under her eyes – usually artfully concealed – were heavy and dark, cruel scrawlings worthy of a caricature.

'I had to come,' she said, eyes searching his face. 'I haven't slept since I saw you. So much going round my mind! And then Edward didn't come home – '

'Oh God,' said George, an anchor of dread sinking through him. 'Jennifer, I'm so sorry, I –'

'Not 'til this morning and when he did he was in a foul mood, as though it was me who had run out of the party and left, not the other way round.'

'Oh,' said George. 'Was he... alright?'

'Oh he was fine,' said Jennifer waving his words away. 'Said the two of you had had some sort of fight and that was why he took off.'

'But he wasn't –' George looked at her, seeking the appropriate word – 'Hurt.'

'Oh no. He said it would take more than a pipsqueak like you to damage him,' she checked herself. 'Sorry, he can be very unpleasant. And, in fact, really, that's why I came. Because seeing you again...' She looked up to the clearing sky, a heroine writhing on emotion's rack as the camera zoomed in. 'Seeing you, trapped by that horrible woman, that she-ogre – it brought it all back. All the old feelings. It made me realise, George, that I should never have let you go.'

She looked at him fully now, brown eyes lit with an imploring light, lips parted. George looked at her.

'Gosh Jen –' he ventured as the moment stretched.

'And I was wondering,' she continued, her hand clutching at his arm, the engagement ring flashing. 'If you might come with me. Give it another go. I wouldn't tie you down, you see. I'd let you just be you. I earn enough money for the both of us as it is. It could easily work.'

She was crying now. Big tears rolling down her face.

'And by the way, you were right about Edward,' she continued, talking quickly into the silence. 'It's not just –'

'Jen,' said George, cutting through the weave of her words. He looked down at her: the soft, unblemished skin, the trembling duck-like mouth. It would be so easy to go with her now; so easy to sink into her promises and make of them a life; so easy and yet so ultimately flawed. 'You know I can't come with you, don't you?'

She flinched. A cloud of indignation scudded across her face.

'Why?' she said. 'Why can't you. What on earth is there in the way?' She looked around as though expecting to find the answer sitting in the street. 'If it's that Emily –'

'Because,' said George, the truth arriving fully formed, a package in the mail, 'It's time I sorted myself out.'

'Oh,' said Jennifer. The silence bloomed between them: a drop of dye spreading in the chemist's jar. 'But –'

'No, Jen,' said George, shaking his head. 'I mean look at me. I'm a mess. I can't even look after myself. You don't want to be lumbered with that. I don't want to be lumbered with that, not anymore.' He reached out to touch her lightly on the arm. 'And you, you need someone who can put you first, give you what you deserve. And Edward, well, I might not like him much, but he will do all that for you. He won't let you down.'

She nodded, mouth twitching, eyes staring at something down the street.

'So what are you going to do?' she said at length.

'Oh, I don't know,' said George. He shifted and became suddenly aware of something lodged in the pocket of his jeans, pressing against his leg; a square of paper stuffed in there angrily some weeks before; the letter. He sighed. What was it his father had said again? That they would have happily taken him on? Well, perhaps he would do that, perhaps he would do that after all. If he had to play the game, he might as well play to win. Let's face it: there were worse things. He looked back at Jennifer. 'Basically,' he said, 'It's time I started playing ball.'

'Well –' she said, but there was nothing more to say. After a moment, she turned and walked towards the waiting taxi, her slender form fragile against its beetle-bulk. At the door, she glanced back, the city light glinting on the fluttering wisps of her hair.

'You won't tell Edward, will you?' she said.

He shook his head and watched her go, the taxi bearing her along the side-street to the junction at the end, gathering speed. He turned away.

*   *   *

Geoff French was writing when George was shown in by Carole, who bobbed and winked and clamped her finger over her mouth while she asked him if he'd like a cup of tea. He declined and stood watching his father, waiting for him to look up. A minute or so passed. So this was his father working, he thought, watching the bowed head bent over the page on the desk, patiently following the movements of the pen. This was what he did for all those hours between the front door clicking closed at half-past eight in the morning and the sound of footsteps up the path some time after six. He looked around at the filing cabinets and wall-charts, at the battered computer sitting in the corner on its make-shift stand. So this was work: this filling of the time with small, useful deeds. And in this office, clerks had entered numbers in ledgers and calculated returns for well over a hundred years. That was something, wasn't it? Perhaps that was something after all.

'Dad?' he said at length.

His father looked up, thinning hair glinting in the brightness from the window.

'Yes?' he said.

A blanket of dread descended over George's heart, like a dust-sheet thrown over a parrot's cage. What if he wouldn't listen? What if he sent him back out onto the street? Cast him from him because of the way he'd behaved, the stupid things he'd said? The sluggish, grey water of the Thames oozed coldly through his thoughts, dragging away the great, bright words he'd had ready to say, the proud imaginings, until he was left, a little boy hovering at his father's study door, waiting to tell him Evelyn Waugh was dead.

'What is it, George-boy?' said his father, rising slowly from his chair.

And with that, something within him broke and sobs, full and blubbery, rose, shivering, through his frame.

'I'm sorry!' he burbled messily through the tears. 'I'm sorry. I've been… I've been a fool. I've –'

But the rest was lost as his father stepped towards him and clamped him in his arms.

'God, you reek,' he said, holding his son tighter, burying his face in George's chest. 'Didn't they teach you to wash at that school?'

'I –' began George.

'Come on,' said his father. 'Let's get you home.'

The sun was already starting to sink in the sky by the time the cab pulled its way up through Hampstead, past the old horse pond, and skirted the fringes of the heath. George looked out on the budding trees, the undergrowth ripe with the early promise of spring. Below the hill, the city glimmered: a silvered beauty; an aging hostess sparkling at a party for a birthday she refused to name. It was his to claim or barter as he chose; his to paint in colours it made no promise to wear. His and his father's and theirs, the couple walking past now with the dog, turning their eyes, like him, to the view. The city was everybody's and nobody's; a great, grand trunk in left luggage, full of lavish gifts and dirty tricks. Perhaps one day he would step out and conquer it once and for all. Perhaps one day something great would –

The driver slammed on the brakes. The tyres screeched and the cab stalled to a halt, swaying.

'Get out of it!' yelled the cabbie. 'Go on!'

Peering through the windscreen, George made out a small, dappled form: a cat, frozen in the midst of running across the road from one part of the heath to another. Its long fur was matted and streaked with mud, and, as it turned its head towards them, he could see a small rodent wriggling in its mouth above the shreds of the collar still clinging round its neck. For a second the cat stared in through the windscreen, its eyes, bright and fiercely alive, seeming to lock with his. Then it turned away and was gone, skittering into the undergrowth on the far side of the road, disappearing between the trees.

'Wasn't that –?' said George's father as the engine started again.

'No,' said George firmly, settling back into his seat. 'I really don't think it was.'

The taxi came over the brow of the hill and the streets fell away before them down to the station at Golders Green. It was Friday afternoon and already the figures in black raincoats and hats were hurrying to the prayer houses and synagogues to see the Sabbath in. As they came down alongside the park, George turned and looked for the familiar building, presenting its blank, boxy face to the world: the place that had figured so much in his childhood imaginings and the dreams of his later years; the house of Evelyn Waugh. He stared up at it as they passed the gate, its windows winking in the afternoon sun, its blue plaque vivid against its painted walls. The front door was open and inside he could see a hallway heaped with household things and beyond that a room cast in darkness with a window at the far end. Through this, was the sky: bright with the fading glimmers of the day; white as the score card at the start of a match; blank as the unwritten page.

Printed in the United States
209434BV00005B/151-153/P

9 781849 231060